HIGHLAND AVENGER

"I was afraid they had found me," she said against his chest, her small hands clutching at the back of his shirt. "Too long sitting here whilst the night crept in, I am thinking."

Brian stroked her back until her trembling eased. She was a tempting armful. Even as a voice in his head warned him it was not a good idea, he placed his hand under her chin and turned her face up to his. Stealing one kiss would not hurt, he told that voice, as he lowered his mouth to hers.

Arianna watched his mouth come closer to hers and knew she should pull away. She knew it would not be a good idea if only because they still had a lot of miles left to travel together. The temptation to be kissed by this man was too strong to resist, however. She may have been married for five years but, even counting the few stolen by young men before she was betrothed, she had experienced a scarcity of kisses. And none of the ones who had kissed her had been as handsome as Sir Brian MacFingal. Not one of those kisses had made any grand impression upon her, either. She was curious to see if the man whom she found so intriguing, so fine to look at, would change her mind about the worthlessness of kisses.

The moment his lips touched her, Arianna knew this kiss would be different from any that had come before . . .

Books by Hannah Howell

ONLY FOR YOU * MY VALIANT KNIGHT * UNCONQUERED * WILD ROSES * A TASTE OF FIRE * HIGHLAND DESTINY * HIGHLAND HONOR * HIGHLAND PROMISE * A STOCKINGFUL OF JOY * HIGHLAND VOW * HIGHLAND KNIGHT * HIGHLAND HEARTS * HIGHLAND BRIDE * HIGHLAND ANGEL * HIGHLAND GROOM * HIGHLAND WARRIOR * RECKLESS * HIGHLAND CONQUEROR * HIGHLAND CHAMPION * HIGHLAND LOVER * HIGHLAND VAMPIRE * THE ETERNAL HIGHLANDER * MY IMMORTAL HIGHLANDER * CONQUEROR'S KISS * HIGHLAND BARBARIAN * BEAUTY AND THE BEAST * HIGHLAND SAVAGE * HIGHLAND THIRST * HIGHLAND WEDDING * HIGHLAND WOLF * SILVER FLAME * HIGHLAND FIRE * NATURE OF THE BEAST * HIGHLAND CAPTIVE * HIGHLAND SINNER * MY LADY CAPTOR * IF HE'S WICKED * WILD CONQUEST * IF HE'S SINFUL * KENTUCKY BRIDE * IF HE'S WILD * YOURS FOR ETERNITY * COMPROMISED HEARTS * HIGHLAND PROTECTOR * STOLEN ECSTASY * IF HE'S DANGEROUS * HIGHLAND HERO * HIGHLAND HUNGER * HIGHLAND AVENGER

Published by Kensington Publishing Corporation

HIGHLAND AVENGER

HANNAH HOWELL

ZEBRA BOOKS
KENSINGTON PUBLISHING CORP.

http://www.kensingtonbooks.com

ZEBRA BOOKS are published by

Kensington Publishing Corp.
119 West 40th Street
New York, NY 10018

All Kensington titles, imprints and distributed lines are available at special quantity discounts for bulk purchases for sales promotion, premiums, fund-raising, educational or institutional use.

Special book excerpts or customized printings can also be created to fit specific needs. For details, write or phone the office of the Kensington Special Sales Manager: Attn.: Special Sales Department. Kensington Publishing Corp., 119 West 40th Street, New York, NY 10018. Phone: 1-800-221-2647.

Zebra and the Z logo Reg. U.S. Pat. & TM Off.

ISBN-13: 978-1-4201-1879-7
ISBN-10: 1-4201-1879-X

First Printing: April 2012

10 9 8 7 6 5 4 3 2 1

Printed in the United States of America

Chapter 1

Scotland, spring 1480

Cold salt water matted her hair so badly Arianna could feel it pulling at her scalp. The rising wind did not help, yanking her hair free of its pins and whipping it around her head. It hurt when it slapped her in the face, something it did all too often as she made her stumbling way across the heaving deck of the ship in search of Adelar and Michel, but she had no time to fix it now. When she found the boys she intended to scold them until their ears burned.

The boys were far too careless with their lives, too innocent to be fully aware of the danger they were in. They thought they traveled with her to Scotland to live with her and her family, not really understanding that they were running for their lives. They were too young to heed any warning she gave them for long. Nor could they understand that they were the only part of her ill-fated marriage that she clung to.

There was someone on the ship who wanted her boys dead. Clenching her cold, wind-chafed hand over the hilt of her dagger, she swore yet again that she would do anything to keep them alive. She had thought that, by leaving France, she had escaped pursuit, but the ones after her boys had obviously set one of their men on the ship. She had every intention of burying her dagger deep in the man's black heart.

"Jesu! The little bastard bit me!"

The angry male voice sliced through the sounds of wind, rain, and creaking ship. Arianna turned toward that voice. Through the sheets of rain pelting down from the sky, she saw two men struggling to hold firm to two writhing, kicking boys as they dragged their small captives toward the ship's rail.

One dagger. Two men. Not very good odds, she thought as she moved silently but quickly toward them. Her boys were fighting valiantly but she knew they would lose the battle. They needed her help to save them.

She was not sure exactly who had hired the men and doubted she would have the opportunity to gain any answers from them. It did not matter. Arianna knew it was their uncle Amiel or the old, deadly enemy of the Lucettes, the DeVeaux. Or both, she thought, and nearly snarled. Amiel did not appear to care that he was now in league with a family that had caused the death and misery of so many of his own kinsmen. It should not have surprised and shocked her as much as it did. The man was trying to murder his own nephews to gain all they had inherited from their father. And, she strongly suspected, it had been Amiel who had killed their father, Claud, as well, murdered his own brother along with the mother of the boys. Dealing with an ancient enemy was a small sin next to those.

Just as she was within reach of the men, the wind slapped her hair into her face again. Arianna shook her head back and forth to throw off the cold, wet hair that nearly blinded her. As she did so, out of the corner of her eye she saw something that firmly grabbed her attention despite the threat to her boys.

Approaching through the rain was another ship. Unless some miracle occurred within the next few moments, something she had never been blessed with, that ship would soon ram the much smaller ship she stood on in the side. It was not only the boys she had to save now but herself as well. It began to look as if they would all soon end up in the rough, storm-tossed water.

Taking a deep breath as she sheathed her dagger, Arianna screamed as loudly as she could. Both men whirled round to stare at her. Still screaming, she pointed toward the ship bearing down on them. As she had hoped, the men were seized with the need to save their own lives. They dropped the boys on the deck and ran toward the side of the ship the other ship continued to aim for.

Aim for, she thought suddenly as she grabbed both boys by the arms, and knew it was exactly what the larger ship was doing. It was purposely heading straight toward them. There would be no stopping it. Her heart ached for the others on the little ship who were about to die at the hands of her enemy. She could do nothing to help them, however, and turned her full attention to the two small, shivering boys she held. There was a small chance she could save them and that was all she would allow herself to think about now.

"They were going to toss us into the sea," said Michel.

"Aye," she said as she dragged them over to the bow where she had earlier seen several empty kegs lashed to the deck. "I fear ye are about to end up in the sea anyway." She released them and used her dagger to cut the ropes holding the kegs to the ship.

"Then we will die," said Adelar.

"Nay. I willnae allow it." She glanced back toward the approaching ship and knew she had little time left to try and live up to that boast. Only the fact that it was battling the force of the wind-driven sea had kept it from already slamming into Captain Tillet's ship. "Do ye remember how to swim?"

"A wee bit," replied Michel in the mix of French and Scots accents that she found so endearing.

"'Twill do. I am going to get ye into the water, lads, and ye are to swim to shore." She turned the boys until they faced the shoreline they had seen earlier in the day but which was now hidden by dark storm clouds and heavy rain. "I will toss these kegs into the water and then both of ye will follow them. Ye are to grab hold of the kegs as soon as ye can. Soon there will be a lot of wood in the water so, if these kegs prove troublesome to catch, grab something else. Anything else that will help ye keep your heads above the water. Dinnae let your fears steal your wits. Fix your eyes upon the shore, hold fast to the wood, and kick your legs as I showed ye when I taught ye to swim."

"The sea is verra fierce, Anna," said Michel, fear

making his sweet voice tremble. "'Tis nay like the pond we learned to swim in."

"I ken it, my loves, but the skills I taught ye will do weel enough, be the water calm or rough. And ye only need to truly swim until ye can grab hold of a keg or some other bit of wood."

She hefted up a keg and looked down at the rough water. It was going to be a miracle if they got out of this alive. The chances of all three of them conquering the turbulent waters long enough to grab hold of a keg or other scrap of wood was very small. Unfortunately, the chances of them surviving when the larger ship rammed into theirs were even smaller. At least this plan allowed them to choose where and how they went into the water.

Glancing at the boys and then at herself, noting how they had all dressed to fight the chill of the air and protect themselves from the rain, she quickly set the keg back down. "Cloaks and boots off, laddies. Quickly now. Those things will be naught but anchors dragging ye under once ye hit the water." She yanked off her own cloak and boots and then hastily unlaced her gown, survival more important to her than modesty. "Put them into the keg. Hurry," she pressed, the increasingly terrified cries of the others on the ship telling her that time was rapidly running out on them.

It was all done swiftly, but Arianna's heart pounded out every passing moment like a death knell. After looping a length of rope around her waist, she secured the top on the keg and hurled it into the water. She rapidly tossed in a second and then a third. Kissing Michel on the cheek and praying it was not for the very last time, she dropped the pale, wide-eyed child over the side of the ship. Arianna did not hesitate to do the same with Adelar even though her heart was breaking.

She took one last look over her shoulder as she clambered over the rail. The other ship was so close she could see the hard faces of the men on its deck, yet the ship made no move to alter its deadly course. The way the men were bracing themselves told her they knew what was coming, had planned for it. Praying she and the boys could get clear of the looming destruction in time, she dove into the water.

Arianna hit the water hard, screaming in her head over the painfully frigid shock as she sank beneath the foam-flecked waves. Yet another threat, she thought, and wondered how many more trials she and the boys could endure. Fear and anger gave her the strength needed to push herself back up to the surface. Her eyes stung from the salty water while she frantically searched the waves for her boys. Panic was gnawing at her mind, screaming that she had thrown her beloved boys to their deaths, by the time she finally caught sight of them. Each boy clung tightly to a keg as the ocean waters callously tossed him from wave to wave.

She reached the third keg just before she reached the boys. Fighting against the strength of the storm-driven water, trying to ignore how the cold was leeching the strength from her body, she worked to lash the kegs together with the rope she had taken from the ship. By the time Arianna dragged herself up onto the odd little raft she had just made, she was shaking so hard her teeth clicked together. Then she heard the harsh, terrifying sound of wood splintering, the screams of doomed men cutting through the roar of the storm.

Looking over Michel, who was sprawled between her and Adelar, she yelled, "Paddle, Adelar! Use your hand and all your strength to paddle!"

It took a few more bellowed instructions but Arianna soon felt a slight difference in their movement through the water. They no longer just bounced along aimlessly amongst the waves, but moved with them. Pride clenched her heart as Michel carefully crawled on top of Adelar and added the strength of his thin arm to that of his brother's. She prayed they were increasing their speed enough to get out of the reach of the ones who had just sent two dozen men to their deaths in their cold determination to murder two little boys.

"Enough," she said in what felt to be hours later, her arm so weak and numb with cold she had to struggle just to pull it from the icy water. "The water itself will carry us the rest of the way to shore."

She pressed her cheek against the wet, rough wood of the keg and fought hard to push back the darkness creeping in at the edges of her mind. It was not only the battle to get the boys safely on shore, or the cold, sapping all her strength. From the moment she had realized that Amiel and the DeVeaux had put some of their men on the ship, she had barely slept at all, guarding the boys day and night. Arianna ached with the need to put all her troubles aside and sleep for days. A small, cold hand grasped her own and shook it. She opened her eyes enough to see Michel's too pale little face.

"Are the bad men dead now?" he asked.

"Aye," she replied. "The bad men who were on

our ship are dead, as are too many good men. The bad men on the bigger ship are not, however, and I dinnae think the DeVeaux will give up yet. Nay, nor Amiel."

"I am sorry. So is Adelar."

"For what?"

"We didnae truly believe you."

"Ah, weel, mayhap now ye will heed my warnings better. Aye?"

"Aye," said both boys.

"Good. Now, I want ye to cling tightly to these kegs. Ere the storm struck us I caught a wee glimpse of the shore. Do ye remember me showing it to you?" Both boys nodded. "The water should push us toward it now without much aid from us." She silently prayed there were not too many rocks between them and the safety of the shore for their crude little craft could not withstand any battering. "And do ye remember all I told ye to do if ye end up alone on that shore?"

"Ye will be with us, Anna," Adelar said, a touch of panic rippling in his voice.

"I pray that is so but I still ask ye if ye remember all I told you."

"Aye. We are to find your kinsmen, the Murrays, and tell them all that has happened."

"And who the bad men are," added Michel.

"Exactly. Now, dinnae fall asleep if ye can help it. Ye must cling fast to these kegs and be ready to swim to shore if the need arises. Slip your arm beneath the rope holding us together as that will help ye. I dinnae think it will be long now ere we stand upon solid ground again. These waves, for all they are a pure misery, are swiftly pushing us in the right direction."

Arianna hoped she sounded as confident of their success as she wished the boys to feel. She did not want them to sense her fear or the weakness that was making her very bones ache. Yet, as she reminded them of what they should do the moment they reached the shore, her mind kept whispering *if*. If some survivor from the wrecked ship did not come upon them and decide he needed their tiny craft more than they did. *If* the men hunting them did not find them. *If* they were not hurled upon the rocks in sight of land.

Her mind was so crowded with all that could go wrong, Arianna was tempted to stand up and scream, to bellow out her fear and anger up into the storm clouds. It was not fair, she thought, and winced at the childish whine she could hear beneath the complaint in her head. That did not change the truth behind the words, however. Michel and Adelar were several years away from even the hint of manhood, just boys and innocent of any great sin. Arianna knew she had not committed any great sins, either, although she could all too easily think of many a small one. Nothing that warranted death by drowning or watching two boys she loved as if they were her own sons die.

A part of her wished to curse God, but she sternly suppressed it. Being quick to anger was one of her many faults, but now was not a good time to give in to it. Now she needed to fill her mind and heart with earnest prayers, maybe even a few promises of some good deed she would do or something she would give up if He only spared the boys.

But it was hard to think clearly anymore. The blackness creeping over her mind was slowly conquering all her attempts to remain conscious. With the last of her strength she twisted some of the rope holding the kegs together around her wrist. She prayed it would be enough to hold her on the keg as she rode it to shore.

"Ach! I think e'en my bones are wet. This cursed rain has pounded its way right through my skin."

Brian MacFingal grinned at his brother. "Ye do look a wee bit like a drowned rat, Simon." He glanced up at the sky. "'Tis done now and I am thinking the sun will soon peep out to dry us."

The way Simon and young Ned glanced up at the gray skies and tried, but failed, to hide their doubt, nearly made Brian laugh aloud. He suppressed the urge because they might think he mocked them. At five and twenty, Simon was a strong, handsome man, skilled with sword and knife, but a lot of his boyish uncertainty lingered. Ned was but seventeen, all arms and legs, and none of them blessed with much grace. Brian remembered that awkward time all too well. He would not sting the boys' young pride with laughter.

"Trust me," he said, "the sun will soon be shining upon us. The clouds move away fast."

Simon nodded. "Aye, I can see that now. So, at least we willnae be poured upon as we collect our goods."

"Something to be thankful for."

"Do ye think we will gain as much coin from this ship's cargo as we did the last?"

"We should. In truth, I have recently spent many

an hour trying to think of a way to make this venture easier on us and on those bringing us the goods to sell." Brian frowned. "Yet, the secrecy of this venture is difficult to give up."

"Aye. The more people who ken about it, the more chance there is of our goods being stolen."

"That is the problem that weighs heaviest on my mind. But we are too far from the safety of Scarglas whene'er we make this journey. While our profits are good enough to compensate us for the trouble, 'tis nay always time we have to spare. The long journey home laden with goods also puts us at risk. Howbeit, I have nay found a safer way to do this."

"Mayhap we should just change the route we take a wee bit. It might add time to the journey, but we could seek shelter with trusted friends and kin each night."

Brian nodded. "That is also a plan I have been thinking on a lot. Yet, I wonder if that would then require us to share some of our bounty with the ones who shelter us, mayhap even have to protect us from time to time."

"Losing a wee portion of the profit would be better than losing the whole of it as weel as a few lives."

"It would. There is no arguing that truth."

And it was just that truth that kept Brian returning to the plan that included stops at places where they could shelter in safety. They would also be places where a few extra swordsmen could be gathered if trouble rode at their heels. Brian knew it all made sense but he had to fight to subdue his reluctance to lose even one coin brought in by this new venture he had begun. The money was helping Scarglas grow stronger. Even more important, it was helping him to gather enough coin that he might, one day soon, be able to get a piece of land for himself.

The mere thought of holding his own land or owning his own home twisted Brian's heart with a longing that grew stronger every day. He did not envy or resent his brother Ewan's place as laird of Scarglas. He also cared for every brother his father had bred, the illegitimate as well as the legitimate. Yet he ached to have something of his own, and there was always someone with acreage or a manor who was willing to sell off a small piece of the family's land because of a need for some coin. Marrying for a piece of land or house was another way, but he refused to leash himself into a marriage for such gain. The only other way to get some was to gain the king's favor, and the chance of a MacFingal doing that was very small.

Perhaps envy did prod him, he decided with an inner grimace. He not only wanted his own piece of land, he wanted what his brothers Ewan and Gregor had. Even what those irritating fools his cousins Sigimor and Liam Cameron had. He wanted his own home, his own family. He wanted a woman to come home to, one who actually cared if he came home at all. He wanted children. The only thing he would not do to gain the land he wanted was marry for it. His craving was also for a woman who truly wanted him, one to love him and the children they would have. Marrying a woman for money, a house, or land was not the way to get that.

It was a craving he kept to himself. Brian knew that, if he admitted to such a need, some of his brothers might take a moment to think carefully. If they did, they would soon realize he had no bastard children. Even worse, they might realize that he did not take as many opportunities to produce one as so many of them did. Brian had heard more than enough of the teasing his eldest brother, and laird, Ewan had endured for having "monkish" ways to know that he did not want to suffer it, too.

"Ye are looking verra solemn, Brian," said Simon as he rode up by his side.

"Just wondering if the storm has cost us anything," Brian said, and then frowned.

The moment the words left his mouth, Brian recognized the large possibility that there was some truth to them. When the storm had struck he had cursed the wet and chill of the rain and wind. Now he considered the fact that what had been annoying to them on land could be treacherous, even deadly, out upon the water. It would not beggar them if they lost the cargo, but several plans he had made to improve Scarglas would have to wait until the next shipment, which could be a long time in coming if he had to make new arrangements for his cargo.

It would also grieve him if the men he had come to know and trust were lost. He hated to think of the men losing their lives to the sea they had all loved so well. Brian pushed aside a pinch of guilt. He had not forced Captain Tillet to join him, nor any of the sailors with him. They had all wanted the coin such trade could earn them as badly as he did and had been happy for the work.

Brian shook away his dark thoughts. They would soon arrive at the small cove and he would have his answers, good or bad. He could only pray they were good ones.

"Weel, it appears God didnae listen to me today," Brian muttered when he dismounted on the small beach and surveyed the unmistakable signs of a shipwreck.

"Jesu, Brian, do ye think anyone survived?" asked Simon as he stepped up to flank Brian.

"There is always that chance. Search the beach," he ordered, and joined the eight men with him as they spread out to begin the search. "Look for both men and goods."

For two long hours they searched the shoreline as bodies and wreckage continued to wash ashore. The pile of salvaged goods grew but Brian's pleasure in that was severely dimmed by the number of dead they retrieved from the water. They found only five men alive, the burly Captain Tillet amongst them. The bruised and weakened men had been given blankets and were settled by the horses. For now, they would stay at Scarglas.

It was as he walked toward Captain Tillet, intending to ask the man what he wished to do with the bodies of his crew, that Ned grabbed him by the arm. He frowned at the youth, irritated by the interruption. Aside from the care of the dead, Brian needed to ask the recovering Captain Tillet what he had meant when he had claimed they had been attacked.

"Look there, Brian!"

The excitement in Ned's voice was enough to

make Brian look where his brother was pointing. "At the rocks?"

"Aye, but I saw something moving there. S'truth, I did! I am certain I caught a wee peek of someone watching us."

Brian bit his tongue against the urge to scold Ned for having too much imagination. The rocks were too far from the water for any of the crew to have hidden there. Nor was there any reason for one of Tillet's crew to hide from them. There was a very small chance that someone spied on them, but the cove was so well hidden, the nearest cottage too far away, for that to make sense. When Ned began to stride toward the rocks, however, Brian followed. As they rounded the rocky outcrop, Brian came to a halt and cursed.

"I told ye I saw something," said Ned.

"Aye, that ye did," agreed Brian. "A shame ye didnae see those knives, though."

Two young boys, wet, shivering, and wearing little more than rags, stood over a body sprawled facedown on the rocky ground. Both boys looked terrified but they held the knives in steady hands. Brian knew he could easily defeat them but he held his hands out to his sides and smiled at them. The way they protected what appeared to be a woman's body deserved such respect.

"We are nay here to harm, but to help," he said.

"Why should we trust ye?" asked the taller of the boys in an interesting blend of French and Scottish accents.

"Did ye trust the captain of the ship ye were on?"

"Aye, he was a good man."

"If ye look toward the horses ye will see how he fares."

"Michel, have a look, and tell me what you see," the boy ordered the smallest one in French.

Michel peered over the rocks and answered in French. "The captain is alive as are some of his men. These men have given them blankets, talk to them, and smile. The captain smiles, too."

"The captain was delivering goods to me. We are partners," said Brian, and then looked down at the body they guarded.

It was definitely a woman. Now he could see the long matted hair and the feminine curve to the legs bared by the torn clothing. Her arms were splayed out, reaching above her head, and Brian suspected the boys had dragged her up from the shore. One of them had obviously been clever enough to hide all signs of that, however, or they would have been found sooner.

"Is she dead?" he asked, and then cursed his bluntness when both boys lost what little color they had in their faces.

"Nay!" shouted the tallest one, while little Michel vigorously shook his head.

"Then ye had best let me see what I can do to help her." The moment the boys lowered their knives, Brian moved to crouch beside the woman, praying that he was not going to have to tell the boys that they had been guarding a corpse.

Chapter 2

Arianna fought against consciousness when it nudged at her. Despite her best efforts, it won the battle, rushing over her on a wave of pain. She struggled to breathe through the worst of the pain only to be distracted from that effort when her stomach cramped viciously with warning. Arianna groaned out a curse, forced her aching body onto its side, and let her body rule as it forcibly expelled all the water she had swallowed.

"I told ye she was still alive."

Adelar, she thought, and took a moment from her misery to give thanks. One of her boys still lived. When her stomach ceased to torture her, she would find out how Michel fared.

"Ye should listen to Adelar, monsieur. He is verra clever. Anna says so."

Ah, and there was Michel, Arianna noted even as more spasms overtook her. Both her boys were alive. She could die now. Not happily or peacefully, but gratefully.

Arianna was pulled from her blinding misery by

the rough touch of a man's calloused hands on her upper arms. Her bare upper arms. She wondered what had happened to her clothes but was too sick to truly care. She then wondered why the mere touch of a man's hands should ease her misery so much, the warmth of his big hands chasing away some of the chill that had sunk its teeth deep into her bones. A man's touch had never done her any good before.

"Done trying to rid yourself of your own stomach now, lass?"

The man's deep, gruff voice tickled something to life deep within her, something that had nothing to do with fear, pain, or sickness. Nor with the fact that her heart warmed at the sound of a fellow countryman's voice after being so long away from home. Arianna was not sure what that something was but instinct told her it could cause her a lot of trouble. She no longer had much faith in her own instincts, however, and she was too weak and too wretchedly sick to puzzle it all out anyway.

Her attempt to pull free of the man's grasp was thwarted by him with an ease that annoyed her. Before she could gather the wit to protest, she was rolled onto her back. Arianna found herself staring into a pair of dark blue eyes. It took her a moment to yank her gaze away from those fine eyes, just enough to notice well-shaped dark brows and an almost lush growth of equally dark lashes. Whoever this man was, he was unquestionably trouble. She did not have the gift of sight as some of her Murray kinswomen had, but she could foresee that much. Arianna wished she had the strength to grab the boys and run.

And was that not just her luck? she thought as he efficiently bathed her face. She washes up on shore—bruised and battered, her hair a gnarled, sand-dusted mess, her shift and stockings torn and filthy—and then spends far too long heaving her innards out on the ground. Is she aided by some kindly old crone? A plump, long-wed matron? A lowly servant? No. She is found by a man, a very handsome man. Arianna suspected that fate had chosen to ensure that no man would ever find her an object of his desire.

It was probably for the best, she decided as he sat her up and poured wine into her mouth. She would not know what to do with a man who desired her anyway. She had certainly failed abysmally with her late husband. Arianna rinsed out her mouth and spit, knowing she did so with more vigor and skill than any true lady should have. She decided to blame her brothers and a vast horde of male cousins for that indelicacy.

"Better?" the man asked.

"Nay," she replied, not surprised that her voice was so weak and hoarse as she was certain she had damaged it while heaving half the ocean out of her stomach. "I believe I shall just lie here and die."

"Nay," cried Adelar as he grasped her by the hand. "Ye must stay with us."

She smiled at the two boys looking at her with wide, frightened eyes. "I but jest, lads. Just allow me to rest for a wee bit and we will soon be on our way."

"On your way to where?" demanded the man still holding her in his arms.

"And who might be asking?" She wished her voice

were stronger for the weakness of it robbed her
words of all the cool haughtiness she had attempted.

"Sir Brian MacFingal," he replied, and nodded
toward the tall, thin youth standing behind him.
"That is Ned MacFingal, one of my brothers. Ye
were sailing on a ship I had hired to bring me some
goods to sell."

Arianna frowned at him, the name MacFingal stirring some faint recognition, yet she was too weary
and sick to clearly think of why it did. Or to care.

"I am Lady Arianna Lucette and these lads are my
wards, Michel and Adelar Lucette. We paid Captain
Tillet to bring us to Scotland so that I might take my
wards to my family." In her head, she suddenly
heard the echoes of the sound of the ship splitting
apart beneath the force of the larger ship ramming
into it and the terrified screams of the men. "Those
poor men," she whispered as she stared out at the
now calm waters. "Did they all die then?"

"Nay. Captain Tillet and four of his crew survived."

After sending up a prayer of thanks, she briefly
added prayers for the souls of the rest of Captain
Tillet's men. "A horrible way to die and so verra
needless."

"So, the captain wasnae mistaken when he said
they wrecked purposely," Brian noted.

"Nay, he wasnae. A much larger ship rammed
into the side of his, destroying it. The boys and I saw
it headed straight for us and got off the ship just
before it struck us."

"Ye jumped into the sea?"

"I believed we had a better chance of surviving if we

chose how we went into the sea instead of just waiting to be hurled in. We shed the heaviest of our clothing and used a few empty kegs to keep us afloat."

"Ah, so 'twas your clothing we found in one of the kegs," said Ned, and blushed when everyone looked at him. "They are safe and dry."

"That is good. Thank ye." Arianna began to recall shedding her gown, cloak, and boots, and then looked back at Sir Brian, refusing to be embarrassed by her state of ragged undress. "If we could but borrow a few supplies, we will be on our way. Once I am with my family again, I will see that ye are weel compensated for your aid."

"And that family would be?"

Brian waited patiently as he watched her mull over all the risks of telling him the truth. She was a mess. It was difficult to judge the color of her hair for it was wet, matted, and covered in sand. All he could tell, by the few hanks of hair that hung loose of the massive snarl, was that it hung to her hips if not farther. Her tattered clothing revealed that she was slim, her well-shaped legs surprisingly long considering how small she was. Despite the bruises and scratches on her too pale face, he could see that she would be a pretty little thing once she was cleaned up and healed.

Her best feature at the moment was her eyes, even underscored by the shadows of exhaustion as they were and a bit reddened by the sting of the salty water. They were large eyes, almost too large for her small heart-shaped face, and a beautiful amber color. Although clouded with pain and mistrust, he found that he had a very difficult time trying to stop staring into those eyes.

Arianna tried to clear the fog of weariness from her mind. She needed to think clearly. If she told this man she was a Murray, that would mark her as one of his countrywomen and might gain her more help. The Murrays of Donncoill were well known, however, as were all the branches of the clan. Admitting who she was could quickly turn her into a hostage for ransom. Recalling that her clan had enemies, she knew that becoming a hostage for ransom might be the least of the troubles she could face as she tried to reach her family.

She glanced at Michel and Adelar. They had done well so far, but asking them to care for her until she was strong again even as they traveled for many days, alone and unprotected, was too much of a burden to set upon their small shoulders. They were all also as good as captives of this man already, a man whose clan name still tickled at a memory in her tired mind. She could not be certain if it was a good memory or a bad one, or simply that the captain had mentioned it, but she was certain that, at least for a little while, she needed some help. Sir Brian MacFingal was the only choice she had.

"That family would be the Murrays," she said. "I am the granddaughter of Sir Balfour Murray of Donncoill. I am Lady Arianna *Murray* Lucette. My husband recently died and I am returning home."

"So, ye are kin to my brother Gregor's wife, Alanna, and, mayhap, my laird's wife, Fiona. Fiona was a MacEnroy ere she wed Ewan."

"Aye, Alanna is my cousin and I am kin to Fiona MacEnroy, too, but only through marriage, for her brother married my cousin Gillyanne." She frowned as the memory that had nudged at her mind slowly became more distinct. "So now I ken why the name MacFingal sounded familiar to me. That all happened ere I left to be wed."

"So ye see that it is best if ye travel to Scarglas with us and we can send word out to your family."

"Nay, I couldnae . . ."

"Brian!" Simon ran up to him and grabbed him by the arm. "I think we may have trouble soon. When I saw that ye and Ned had found others alive, I decided to wander farther down the shore to see if there were others who had pulled themselves up into the rocks. There are a lot of armed men headed our way."

Out of the corner of his eyes, Brian saw Arianna and the two boys grow deathly pale. "I think there is yet something ye need to tell me." He looked back at Simon. "How close?"

"They move verra slowly, searching, and have only just begun to do so. Half an hour, mayhap more, and they will be upon us. Fifteen men, I think. I cannae be certain for there is a chance a few have already moved from my sight or are still making their way in from the ship. I didnae linger to make sure of my count."

"Get the horses packed." As soon as Ned and Simon ran off to see to that chore, Brian stood up and pulled Arianna to her feet. "Are ye being hunted for some crime, m'lady?"

"Nay!" Adelar moved to Arianna's side and glared at Sir Brian. "'Tis me and Michel the men hunt for. They want us dead so that they can claim all that our father left to us."

"This is true?" Brian demanded, fighting the urge to steady Arianna when she swayed, still too weak to be on her feet for long.

"Aye," she replied. "They dinnae want to wait to see if my husband's family can get the boys declared illegitimate." When he just scowled at her, she added, "'Tis a long, sordid tale, Sir Brian, and I dinnae think there is time to tell it all right now. All that is important now is that those men want these boys dead so badly that they rammed Captain Tillet's ship, not hesitating to condemn us all just to kill the boys."

Silently cursing, Brian swung her up into his arms, ignoring her protests. As he hurried to the horses, he made and tossed aside several plans before reaching the one he believed would work best. It was a risky one, but he was certain it would succeed in confusing and dividing the men who would soon be hunting them. He was also certain that Lady Arianna Murray Lucette was not going to like it.

He was pleased to see Simon standing ready with the clothes Lady Arianna had stuffed into the keg, and set her down so that she could put hers on. She had a quick, clever mind, he decided as he thought on how she had saved herself and the boys. It would serve them well in the days ahead.

"Simon, Ned, ye take this wee lad with ye and the captain and his men. Ride straight for Scarglas." He pushed Adelar toward Simon even as the boy was still struggling to put his cloak on.

"Nay! The lads should stay with me," protested Arianna, pausing in her struggle to put her boots on.

"So that the three of ye can be an easier target for

your enemies?" Ignoring her muttered arguments, he looked at his brother Nathan and quickly explained why they needed to get the boys away from the shore. "Nat, ye take the others and the goods we have salvaged and make your way home in as twisted a way as ye can." He nudged Michel toward Nathan. "Ye will guard this lad."

"And what will ye do?" asked Nathan as he helped Michel get his cloak on straight.

"The lady and I will take three of the horses and head out as if we are racing for the Murray lands."

"As if? Where are ye truly headed then?"

"To Scarglas, of course, but by way of Dubheidland. I believe it may be time to visit our cousins the Camerons. Sigimor has become too tame. Leading this trouble to his door should get his blood flowing again."

Arianna watched the two men grin at each other and nearly cursed as she hastily laced up her gown, trying to ignore how uncomfortable it was to put anything over her wet, torn shift. She was tempted to curse at the men, too. They were obviously intoxicated by the idea of thwarting some foe, just like men everywhere. She had seen that expression far too often to mistake it. The fact that they would take up the challenge to protect a woman and two children as well as avenge Captain Tillet's drowned men only added to the sweetness of the battle. It was fortunate that she had seen another side to men as she had grown or she could easily think they were all bloodthirsty idiots.

She looked at Adelar and Michel. The boys looked as frightened and uncertain as she felt. She did not need to ask if they were as terrified of being taken from her as she was of letting them go. It was written all over their pale faces, causing tears to shine in their wide gray eyes. Although her legs protested the movement, she went over to where the boys huddled together as the men moved quickly to finish the preparations to leave. Arianna knew she had very little time to soothe the children, or herself.

"We should stay with you," said Adelar. "All of us together."

"We will be together again soon." She kissed each boy on the forehead.

"Do ye trust these men?"

"Aye, I think I do. Ye heard. They are my kinsmen through marriage and I have heard about them. The captain trusts them as weel. Go, my fine brave laddies. We will meet again verra soon and, mayhap, this will prove the safest way for us to get to my family. Heed weel the men who take ye with them."

Tears stung her eyes when both boys hugged her tightly. She stroked their hair and then clenched her hands into tight fists to stop herself from snatching them back when they joined the men. Arianna ignored the pain and weakness wracking her body and stood watching until they were out of sight. Doubts and fears churned her stomach but she struggled against them. In the end the decision to let the boys go rested upon one hard, cold fact. She was in no condition to keep them safe and would not be for a while.

"Come," said Sir Brian as he tossed her cloak over her shoulders, grasped her by the arm, and tugged her toward the three horses waiting for them. "We need to leave now."

"Why three horses?" she asked, placing a hand on the flank of the white mare he led her to.

"I want to be certain the men hunting those boys think they have three choices to make, that they need to break into three groups to track us all down." He looked at her. "Are ye strong enough to ride?"

Arianna nodded, praying she was not fooling herself. The very last thing she wished to do right now was get on a horse, riding hard in an attempt to pull some of her enemies away from the trails the boys had taken. She wanted a bath, clean clothes, a hot meal, and a soft bed. She even wanted to cease having to be so strong, having to silently endure all her fear, pain, and weariness. It would be so lovely, she mused as she pulled herself up into the saddle, if she could just fall to the ground and give in to her misery, perhaps cry loudly and messily like a child for a little while.

Brian mounted, checked the lead to the third horse loaded with several packs to mask the fact that it was riderless, and then glanced at Lady Arianna, who was securing her cloak more firmly around her body. She did not look as if she would stay in the saddle for long, but he had the suspicion that there was a core of stubborn, hard steel in the woman. All he needed was a few hours of hard riding out of her. As he kicked his horse into a steady gallop, he found himself hoping he could offer her a few comforts when they had to stop for the night.

After an hour of hard riding, Brian slowed their pace a little. The trail they followed was wide enough that Arianna moved up to ride at his side. He caught her glancing behind them several times.

"They wouldnae have reached the place we left for a while, and deciding what to do when confronted with three trails will hold them back for a time as weel," he assured her. "They willnae follow the whole way at such a hard pace, either. They are unfamiliar with the area and will need to keep a closer eye on their route to be sure they stay on our trail. Nor will they wish to ride their horses to death, if they e'en have them."

"I suspect they brought horses with them," she said. "The ship was verra large, much larger than Captain Tillet's, and they wouldnae have wished to chase me and the boys on foot if they thought we had escaped drowning. Your mon Simon may have left ere they were able to bring their horses to shore."

"Which will take more time. Good for us."

"True. The DeVeaux and Amiel may e'en have held back on bringing the horses to shore until they were certain a search or chase would be needed for 'tis a lot of work to do. They were looking for our bodies." She winced. "When they find the dead we had to leave behind they will ken that Michel and Adelar survived. I am so sorry those poor men died only to be left to the carrion."

"'Tis nay your fault. And I dinnae think the men hunting you and those boys would act verra kindly toward us once we said they couldnae have ye, so 'tis best we didnae wait there to confront them."

Arianna sighed and rubbed her forehead, but it did little to ease the pounding in her head. "Nay, 'tis why I ceased to seek any help. That and the fact that Claud's family didnae wish to believe that Amiel was

doing any wrong. They certainly refused to believe
that he would ever deal with the DeVeaux."

"Who is Amiel?"

"My husband's brother."

"Ah. So the boys inherit something *he* wants."

Explanations were needed but Arianna heartily
wished she did not have to give them. It meant revealing her humiliation, her shame. Unfortunately, the
man not only deserved the answers he wanted, he
might need them to better protect her and the children. She had learned enough from her family, and
from ruling over her husband's lands as he spent
much of his time dallying with another woman, to
know that even the smallest piece of information
could make a difference between life and death.

"At the moment the boys are my husband's heirs."

"At the moment? I assumed they are his heirs because he was wed before he married you."

"He was and he remained married even as he
took vows with me." She could feel the heat of embarrassment color her cheeks and almost welcomed
it for it chased away some of the chill lingering in
her body. "No one kenned it, but he had married a
girl in the village nearly six years before he married
me. He did not annul that first marriage, which
gave him the boys. Instead, he allowed all of us to
believe Marie Anne was his mistress and had me
train his boys. I kenned they were his sons, but I had
thought they were his bastard children, ones he
wished trained to a better life."

Brian bit back the curses stinging his tongue. He
could only guess at the depth of the humiliation
she had suffered. It was all too easy to recall the
anger and bitterness suffered by his father's wives

over the man's unfaithfulness. For this woman to discover that she was a mistress and not the wife she had thought herself must have been a hard blow indeed.

Then he thought on how she treated the two boys his family now rushed to a safe haven. Brian had no doubts that she cared for them and they for her. It said a lot about the woman that she did not turn her anger or heartache onto the boys. Few women he had known would be so kind and loving toward the children of a man who had so cruelly betrayed them.

"Yet you still call yourself Lady Lucette?"

"To do otherwise would only shame both our families. I may be angry with Claud for his deception, but he is dead now, as is his wife. Murdered by his own brother, I believe. And his family? They may have nearly cost the boys their lives by refusing to heed my warnings, but they were grieving the loss of their eldest son and still reeling from learning how many lies he had told everyone. My family had naught to do with it all save to offer me what they all thought would be an excellent match. There is naught to gain in letting Claud's lies be kenned save to shame all the ones who have done no real wrong."

"Including you and those laddies."

"Aye, including us. All I demanded of them was that, if they got the boys disinherited, that they gift them with the property held here and leave them with me. Then I left the problem of trying to sort out Claud's deceptions to the Lucettes and brought the boys here. It was foolish of me to believe, even for a moment, that that would be enough to end the threat to them."

"Your Claud was a coward."

"Why do ye say that?"

"He didnae have the stomach to tell his kin the truth. He probably feared he would lose his place as the heir because he wed a woman he kenned his family wouldnae approve of. Instead of fighting for the marriage he wanted, fighting for his sons, he lied and dragged ye into his life of lies without a thought as to how it would affect you. And ye were right to bring those laddies here. They will get the protection they deserve now."

That sounded very much like a vow but, before Arianna could respond to Sir Brian's somewhat impassioned speech, he kicked his horse into a gallop. She hurried to get her own mount moving to keep up with him. It was not easy but she forced herself to ignore the exhaustion and pain battering at her body. She just prayed that it would not be too much longer before he claimed it safe enough to stop for a rest.

She fixed her mind on what he had said about her late husband, Claud, and had to agree. Claud had been a coward, too spineless to stand firm on what he wanted honestly and openly. He had also been selfish, thinking only of himself. It embarrassed her to think of how hard she had tried to make their marriage a good one before she had discovered Marie Anne, the woman she had thought was his mistress. Discovering that Marie Anne had actually been his true wife had made her feel, briefly, relieved that she had not indulged in many of her grand plans to seduce him away from his mistress.

Arianna just wished the sense of failure she still carried would ease. She had not failed for there had never been any chance for her to succeed. Claud was the one who had failed them all and was still failing them. Instead of being there to help protect his sons, it was the woman he had lied to and betrayed who was fighting to keep the boys alive. Arianna fixed her gaze on Sir Brian's broad back and promised herself that she would win this fight. She also promised herself that she would never be so trusting and painfully naive again.

Chapter 3

"M'lady? M'lady! Wheesht, I didnae ken someone could sleep sitting up and with their eyes open."

"G'way." Arianna swatted weakly at the hands grasping her waist.

It was not until she was dangling in the air, those big warm hands at her waist all that kept her safe from falling, that Arianna became aware of where she was, who she was with, and that he was simply lifting her off the back of the horse. She breathed deeply, pushing away a sudden surge of fear. When he set her on her feet, gripping her shoulders when she swayed, she looked up at the sky. When had the sun sunk so low? she wondered.

"Are ye awake now?" Brian thought she looked so enchantingly befuddled despite the tangled hair and bruises, he had to fight down the urge to kiss her.

"I wasnae asleep," she muttered.

"Nay? I had to stop your mount, unclench your hands from the reins, and call to ye near to a dozen times ere ye spoke. Appeared much akin to sleep to me."

It certainly sounded so to her, too, but she was

not about to admit to it. Arianna could recall a few embarrassing tales her family loved to tell about her doing such a thing when she was a child, exhausted yet unwilling to stop whatever she was doing. She had obviously not outgrown the strange habit. The fact that Sir Brian had had to do so much before she had even become aware of his presence was proof enough of that. Sir Brian MacFingal was not a man any woman could easily ignore.

"Where are we?" she asked, praying he would not press her on her strange behavior.

Brian grinned, doing nothing to hide his amusement even when she gave him a narrow-eyed glare of warning. "We are where we can safely rest for the night."

She could not stop herself from glancing behind them. "Are ye certain?"

"As certain as one can be. Your enemy cannae ride in the dark any better or more safely than we can. The horses can be hidden by the trees and we can rest in a wee cave set behind those rocks."

Arianna grabbed the reins of her mount and followed him as he moved toward a large collection of stones set between the side of a rocky hill and a thick growth of trees and brush. They moved off the narrow, rough, drover's trail far enough that she suspected it would be very difficult for anyone on that trail to see the horses. The moon was on the wane so, even if the night remained clear, it would not shed enough light to make anything lurking in the trees visible unless someone rode very close or the horses made some noise that drew attention to them.

She inwardly shook her head. It did not matter.

They needed to rest and so did the horses. Without sufficient rest the horses would falter and she and Sir Brian would be hard-pressed to elude her enemies on foot. Arianna began to change her mind about that, however, when Sir Brian ducked into a small opening in the side of the hill only to return to her side a moment later and gesture for her to go in.

"Ye first," she said, hoping that she would soon gain enough courage to enter that hole in the earth.

"There are no animals in there," Brian said.

"Ye were nay in there for verra long. Mayhap ye should look again."

"'Tis but a wee shelter. There wasnae much looking I needed to do."

"Oh." It was not only a hole in the earth; it was a small hole, she thought with a shudder.

Brian studied her as she stared at the entrance to the small cave as if she expected some fierce, slavering beastie to leap out at any moment and go for her throat. He could sympathize with her reluctance to enter the shelter he had found for them. He was not too fond of such places, either. Unfortunately, she was not in any condition to travel any farther without some rest. He needed some rest, too, as did the horses. Then he studied her sad state in the fading daylight and nearly smiled. There was something he could tempt her inside with.

"There is water within, enough for ye to clean yourself," he said, and hid his sense of victory at the interest she immediately revealed, even though that interest was tainted with doubt.

"Inside that wee cave?"

"Aye. To the back of it. Runs in through some

opening in the rock when it rains and collects in a pool, a hollowed-out spot that was probably made by the constant wear of the water. 'Tis one reason I marked this as a resting place when I travel." He grabbed a pack from his saddle. "Come. I will start a fire and there should be something in here ye can wear so that ye can e'en clean your clothes. While ye clean up, I will settle the horses. That will give ye a wee bit of privacy," he continued as he grasped her by the hand and tugged her inside the small cave.

Once inside, Arianna stood very still, fighting her deep fear of such places, as Sir Brian made a fire. The moment the light of the fire spread throughout the small cave, she was better able to calm her fear. It was not as small as she had first thought, but, for a man of Sir Brian's height, the area in which he could move without risking a head wound was small. The rest of the cave slanted down toward the back until it shrank into little more that a mouse's tunnel. She heard the slow drip of water and immediately became all too aware of how ragged and dirty she was.

"Here. A pot of soap and a drying cloth." As soon as she took the items he held out to her, Brian draped a shirt over her arm. "A clean shirt. Ye are a wee lass so it should cover ye modestly enough. I will tend to the horses now, and brush away our tracks leading to this place. That should give ye time enough to clean up. Aye?"

"Aye," she answered. "Thank ye. I am verra eager to wash away the dirt."

She hurried toward the sound of dripping water, glancing back to make sure he had left the cave. It took all of her willpower not to just tear off her clothing, and she sternly reminded herself that she had need of them no matter how badly they were torn or stained. She could not ride about dressed only in a man's shirt and her cloak.

Tossing aside the last of her clothes, she stepped into the water, pleased to find it reached to her knees. She sat down in the water, uncaring of the slight chill it carried, and hurried to clean herself. Several places on her body were sore, causing her to wince as she washed, but she did not hesitate to give even those places a hearty scrubbing as well. Once her hair was washed, she dried off as best she could, squeezing and rubbing as much of the water from her hair as she could. It was not until she donned the shirt that she lost a little of her pleasure in getting clean once again.

The shirt was soft and clean but hung only to her knees, and she had nothing to wear beneath it. Arianna pushed aside her embarrassment and washed out her clothes. There was no other choice for her. She could not wear the clothes she had shed until they were clean. Ragged though her shift and stockings were, she was not sure they would be wearable even after they were cleaned, but if they could be salvaged, at least they would not stink of seawater, blood, and mud.

Arianna was spreading her wet clothes wherever she could on the rocks when Sir Brian returned with the packs from the horses. Before she could speak, he left again and she frowned. She ought to be helping him but suspected she was still too weak to be of much help. That angered her. Arianna detested the need to place her fate and care, as well as that of the boys, in another's hands.

"Foolish pride," she muttered as she searched

the packs for some food, determined to at least set out a meal for the man who was helping her.

The aches and weakness would trouble her for a little while longer. She would have to accept that. It was a miracle she and the boys had not drowned, that they had stumbled upon ones willing to help them so quickly. Her pride could take the bruising if it meant that they all survived. Arianna knew her pride had suffered a far worse battering at the hands of her late husband and she had gained little for it. So it could certainly withstand allowing a man to help her and the boys to survive. She had, after all, come to Scotland to seek the help of her family. Sir Brian was at least allied to her family through marriage.

"This may help to fill our bellies," Brian said as he entered and held up a rabbit readied for the spit.

Arianna stared at the catch in wide-eyed surprise. "I didnae think ye were gone long enough to go hunting."

"Didnae hunt it. Ill-fated creature hopped right into the midst of the horses. Fortunately, I am verra good at throwing a knife." He set the rabbit down and pulled a clever collection of iron rods from the pack, which he swiftly set up as a spit above the fire. "My brothers willnae be pleased that I took the pack with this in it." He winked at her and grinned. "It is a highly prized tool for one's travels."

A blush heated her cheeks and her heart actually beat faster in her chest, as Arianna reeled a little beneath the heady power of that smile. He is kin, she reminded herself firmly, but herself was all too quick to also remind her of the very tenuous connection of the MacFingals to the Murrays, despite his brother's marriage to her cousin. She had a lot of cousins. Arianna just nodded in a way she felt certain looked idiotic and then moved back from the fire to give him plenty of room to set up the spit. And to put some distance between her and a far too handsome man, she thought ruefully, silently accepting her own cowardice.

It troubled her that he could make her feel like some innocent maid who was caught up in her first time of flirting with a man. While it was true that she had had little experience with such games before marrying, she was now a woman who had been married for five years, betrayed, and widowed. She should be long past such blushes and flutters.

"Do ye ken how to cook it?" he asked.

"Aye. All the women in my clan learn how to cook. 'Tis believed it helps in kenning what is going on in the kitchens of the house the woman may rule one day, or if she weds a mon who cannae really afford such help," she replied, and then quickly shut her mouth, afraid that she was beginning to babble.

"A verra wise thing to do. I will leave ye to it for I need to clean up."

Arianna was astonished at how difficult it was for her to keep her full attention on cooking the rabbit as he walked away. She had never had any compelling urge to watch men so closely before. At times she had paused to appreciate a handsome face or a tall, strong body, but only for a glance or two. A part of her, however, was eager to closely watch Sir Brian MacFingal, to gaze for a long time at the way his tall strong body moved, the way his long, thick black hair gleamed in the light, or how his eyes lightened and darkened with his changing moods.

He did have a very handsome face, she mused. It was a strong face, its hard lines almost predatory when he was angry yet quickly softened by a smile. Those thickly lashed, dark blue eyes and the slight fullness to his lips softened the harshness of his features as well, but she had seen how fierce he could look when she had told him that Amiel and the DeVeaux wanted to kill the boys. It was that look that had prompted her to trust him with the lives of her boys. Her doubts about trusting the man were only faint ghostly twinges now, perhaps because her heart knew she had made the best decision for the survival of her boys.

She did not like being away from her boys, detested not knowing how they fared, yet was certain they would be protected. Just as she was certain she would be protected, that this man would do his best to get her somewhere safe and reunited with Michel and Adelar. That the occasional doubt she had did not linger puzzled her. It also worried her. She did not appear to be holding fast to her vow to be more wary, more cautious, about whom she put her trust in.

The sound of splashing water yanked her out of her thoughts. Had he shed his clothes to wash? Arianna was shocked that such a question would leap to mind. Worse, she badly wanted to look to get an answer to that question. Utter madness, she decided, and turned her attention to the pack that held the supplies. She put every scrap of willpower she could gather into settling all her thoughts on the simple matter of putting together a decent meal. The whispered suggestion that slithered through her mind that she was doing so to impress Sir Brian was ruthlessly suppressed.

* * *

Brian rinsed his clothes and spread them out. The rough shelter slowly filled with the tantalizing scent of roasting meat and something else. Lady Arianna had obviously decided to add something to the simple meal. By the scent of what she had made, he knew he would appreciate it but hoped she had not used too free a hand with his supplies. Gathering more while they fled her enemies would not be easy.

Turning to join her by the fire, he hesitated after only one step in her direction. She was busily using her fingers to comb out her hair, pausing now and then to gently untangle a stubborn knot or tend to the meal. Hints of red were revealed by the light of the fire, enlivening the thick mass of honey-gold hair that was so long it pooled a little on the ground by her slim hips. His fingers itched to take over the chore of untangling it.

He took a deep breath and let it out slowly. It eased the worst of a sudden fierce attack of lust but the sharp bite of hunger lingered. Something about the delicate Lady Arianna severed his control over his lusts, a control he had long prided himself on. From the time he had first looked into her soft golden eyes he had guessed that she could be trouble, but he had not truly considered just how great a temptation she could be to him. It could prove to be a very long journey ahead.

For a moment he considered seducing her. She was no maid, but a widow. Many men considered widows fair game. Then Brian grimaced. That was the reckless MacFingal part of him whispering in his ear. From what Lady Arianna had told him, she had little cause to trust men. Seducing her would certainly not aid her in trusting him.

"That smells verra fine, lass," he said as he moved to sit down next to her.

She tensed and he fought the urge to shift farther away from her. It might have been better if he had sat across the fire from her but he had not wished to stare into those captivating eyes of hers as he tried to eat his meal. Brian told himself it was best if he did not coddle her unease, either, for she had to depend upon him until she was safe with her family. He was not surprised when a little voice in his head scoffed at that excuse. It was a paltry one.

"I mixed some leeks ye had with the stale bread and a piece of rather old cheese. 'Tis naught," she said, trying not to be too pleased by his compliment. "Thought we ought to have more than just the meat." She cast a glance at his pack of supplies. "Ye carry a goodly store of food."

"Aye. I dinnae like to go hungry."

"Few do."

The fleeting, shy smile she gave him tightened his insides with the desire he was doing such a poor job of banishing. It was a puzzle that he felt any desire at all. Although she looked a lot better than she had when they had entered the cave, she was still all bruised and scratched. Her full lips were dried and cracked by the harsh salty water of the ocean and did not look all that kissable. Her injuries did not dim the beauty of her lithe, shapely form, however, or the glory of her long hair. There was no hiding the beauty of her eyes, either.

"Tell me all ye ken about the ones hunting ye and the lads," he said in an abrupt attempt to turn his wandering thoughts to something other than all the reasons he wanted her.

Arianna served him some food as she said, "I have told ye most of it. I truly believe that Amiel killed his brother and his true wife or ordered the killing done. He may have kenned the truth about Claud and Marie Anne even though the rest of the family didnae learn of it until shortly after the bodies were found, may have e'en hoped killing them both would keep that secret hidden forever. But Claud left a letter explaining how the boys were nay the bastards everyone thought them but his true heirs."

She shook her head and helped herself to some food. "I learned shortly after wedding Claud that his branch of the Lucette tree was, weel, verra blood proud. They were nay too certain I was their equal but they badly wished to have my dowry and the tie to my clan for it would ensure that the land they held in Scotland would be weel protected. The news that their eldest son, the heir to all titles and lands, had actually married a common wench, as they called her, appalled them. What little toleration they had shown toward Michel and Adelar faded away in a winking. They immediately set about the expensive and tedious chore of getting Claud's marriage annulled."

"But what of you? Did they nay care that they exposed ye to unwarranted shame and embarrassment?"

"Nay. They had already marked me as an utter failure as a wife for I lost the only child I conceived ere we barely kenned I was carrying one and I couldnae keep my husband away from his mistress." She shrugged. "They didnae ken that I had already learned the truth and was planning a way to get free of the mire I found myself trapped in. All that kept me from leaving the moment I discovered the truth about the boys, about Claud's lies, was that I wanted to find a way that saved us all, especially the boys, from gossip and the hurt it can bring."

"The boys all thought were your husband's bastards."

"Aye. I was given the care and training of them from the verra beginning. Michel was little more than a bairn. Marie Anne didnae appear to care much for them for she rarely visited them or took them to the bonnie wee cottage Claud bought for her.

"But none of that matters. Amiel is all that concerns me now. He doesnae want to wait until his family gets Claud's marriage to Marie Anne annulled, or, mayhaps, he doesnae want to lose the money it will cost to see it done. From the moment Claud's confession was read, Amiel began to plot to kill his own nephews. I truly dinnae think he kenned that Claud had left a confession but it meant he then needed to be rid of the boys, too, before he could grab what he coveted. He e'en joined hands with the DeVeaux to get it."

The way she nearly spat out that name told Brian all he needed to know. "An old enemy."

"Verra old and with a lot of Lucette blood on their hands. Matters between the Lucettes and DeVeaux had grown so deadly and dire that the king himself stepped in and forced them into a truce, promising some verra hard, and costly, punishments if the truce was broken."

"It didnae bring any true peace though, did it?"

"Nay, it just made the DeVeaux grow more secretive in their crimes against the Lucettes and the Lucettes even more subtle in their vengeance. I doubt any of them even recall what started the hatred or who; they just cling to it and make a habit of the old war. Amiel may have convinced people he had the right to kill Claud and Marie Anne because of the shame Claud had brought upon the family name, but not one of his clan will e'er forgive him for dealing with the DeVeaux."

Brian nodded; fully understanding that, for his family had suffered such a feud until recently. His family had not known peace for long and there had been one clan, the Grays, who had held to the old feud with a deadly tenacity. This tale held all the needed insults and pride that could end with the Murrays and the Lucettes locked in a feud, especially if Arianna's family discovered the full truth about how the family had treated her.

"What do the DeVeaux want?"

"Aside from simply getting some pleasure out of causing trouble for the Lucettes, I have no idea. I have e'en wondered if Amiel owed them something, some debt. Claud once told me that he held a wee bit of land the DeVeaux badly wanted, something he found greatly amusing. Amiel might have promised them that land in exchange for their aid." She laughed, a short, harsh sound holding little humor. "He may have e'en promised them me."

"Why would the DeVeaux want you?"

"My kinsmen tangled with the DeVeaux twice in the past and won each time, even gaining some land and coin from the family. All unforgivable sins in the eyes of the DeVeaux. From the moment I stepped upon French soil they kenned who I was and I ken weel that they watched me. The few times I traveled anywhere outside the Lucette lands I was verra careful, and made sure I was weel guarded." She quickly covered her mouth with her hand as a powerful need to yawn overtook her. "Pardon."

"Wheesht, we stopped because we needed to rest; ye far more than I. Yet here I am making ye answer question after question. Stay," he ordered as he stood up to fetch some blankets.

Arianna gave in to the urge to watch him this time. He moved with an easy grace, one that hinted at the strength and agility held in his tall, lean body. He was, she decided, a pure pleasure to watch. She wryly thought that he probably had to beat the lasses away with a stick. And, from what she was beginning to recall about the MacFingals, she doubted he bothered. The old laird, Sir Brian's father, had bred himself a small army of bastards and rumor implied that the sons, legitimate and illegitimate alike, were just as profligate. This was not a man she should be sighing after, she told herself firmly. If she ever dared to soften toward any man ever again, she would be certain he understood that she demanded constancy. It was often said that the MacFingal men were incapable of it.

Brian gently pushed her aside when she reached

for the blankets he had brought her. "Ye need to rest, m'lady," he said as he made them each a very rough bed with the blankets. "It is important that ye regain your strength as quickly as possible." He frowned when he saw that she had put away the remains of their meal while he had spread out the blankets and he pointed at the crude bed he had made for her. "Sleep."

She rolled her eyes and moved to the blanket spread over the hard floor. The two meager beds he had made were set very close to each other but she decided she would say nothing. Instinct told her that this was not a man who would force himself upon her. She did not ignore the possibility that he might attempt a seduction since she was a widow and close at hand, but Arianna was not worried about succumbing. If she was foolish enough to do so, however, she was no maid who could be forced into marriage to save the family honor. She was a widow of three and twenty.

The hard floor was not softened much by the blanket he had spread out for her. Arianna struggled to hide a wince as she settled herself down and pulled the second blanket he had left for her over herself. Despite the weariness that pulled at her mind and body, she stared wide-eyed at the flickering light of the fire dancing over the ceiling of their little cave. This was the first night in years that she could recall not bidding good sleep to her boys. Her arms ached to pull them close for that last kiss of the day.

Arianna knew that the Lucettes had thought her acceptance of the boys very odd, even considered it proof that she was not good enough for their son and heir. It had not really troubled her. From the moment the boys had been given into her care, she had loved them. The fact that she had suffered no jealousy over Marie Anne being their mother, over the fact that her new husband had a somewhat sordid past, should have told her a lot about her feelings concerning her husband and marriage, but she had ignored the whispers of caution that had slipped through her mind every so often.

What she had never been able to accept, or forgive, was how thoroughly the boys' parents had ignored their sons. Claud's family barely stopped themselves from spitting on the children in their disgust that their precious heir would sully himself with some common wench. But this did not seem as great a crime as the way Claud paid no heed at all to his own children. Her boys had been set aside or scorned by every person who should have cared for them. Arianna could not bear it if the boys thought she, too, had deserted them.

"Michel and Adelar will be safe, will they nay?" she asked softly as she listened to Brian settle down between his own blankets.

Brian could hear the fear she held for those children in her voice. He had to clench his hands into tight fists to resist the need to reach out for her, to comfort her. Her love for her false husband's bastards was something he could only admire.

"My kin will protect them with their own lives," he said. "As will my whole clan."

The words carried the force of a blood vow. Arianna knew her ability to trust had been badly damaged by Claud's deceit. Yet, she trusted in the words Brian uttered, the promise to keep her boys safe weighting every word.

"We are a false trail," she whispered, suddenly fully understanding his plan.

"Aye, and my dearest hope is that your enemy sends most of his men after us. We will lead them straight to their deaths."

Chapter 4

After making certain Sir Brian had left, Arianna groaned softly and rubbed her aching backside. Aside from a few fading bruises and the ugly remnants of some of the deeper scratches, she was fully recovered from her ordeal in the water. Since it had only been three days, she realized she had not been as injured as she had first believed. Spending three days in the saddle had left her with many a new ache, however.

She had not worried much about the riding for she often rode and had done so since she had been a small child. The aching in her backside and thighs told her that regularly meandering around her family's and then her husband's lands on a placid mare was a far cry from the riding she was doing now. Arianna hoped she toughened up soon even though she was not sure that a lady should want such a thing. Her husband had certainly made enough cutting remarks about how often she rode to make her believe men did not want their women to be toughened, either.

"But then he was ne'er truly my husband," she said as she moved to rub down her horse.

Her steps faltered a little when Arianna realized that the hurt and shame she usually felt upon confronting that harsh, ugly truth had eased. In the months since Claud had died and everyone had discovered the truth she herself had only just uncovered, the sting of the shame that had so crippled her had weakened. Anger, however, still flared hot whenever she thought on the matter.

"And I have every right to be furious," she told the horses as she moved to rub down the packhorse. "That cowardly bastard Claud used me, lied to me, and betrayed me and my clan. I wasnae his wife; I was his unwilling mistress. Aye, and he and his cursed family stole from us for they took my dowry and have ne'er offered to repay it despite the fact that I was ne'er married to their wretched son. And did his family e'er apologize for what was done to me? Nay!"

Warmed by her anger, she did not even try to push it aside as she had been doing for far too long. Arianna gave each of the horses a pat on the flank and then moved to gather wood for a fire. She had carried the weight of her false marriage and Claud's betrayal on her shoulders for long enough. She had also accepted the increasing derision and disregard of Claud's close family, wondering if they were right to think she was to blame in some way for their heir's folly in staying married to some woman they thought so far beneath him.

Her family would be utterly stunned by her forbearance. Arianna knew better. It had not been forbearance; it had been utter defeat and shame that had kept her so cowed that she did not even defend herself. Those weakening emotions had begun to possess her from the moment she had discovered that her new husband, the man she had thought she could build a strong marriage with, perhaps even a loving one, had a mistress.

That still stung. Arianna had wanted to experience that passion the women of her clan so loved to talk about. It was one reason she had married Claud even though it had meant she had to leave her home. He had seemed so kind, gentle, charming, and sweet. She had believed he would show her that passion. The few kisses they had shared before their marriage had hinted at it.

However, she had experienced nothing but discomfort and coldness in his arms. No fire, no tenderness, no secret whispers in the night. His kisses had been a lie. In truth, everything about Claud had been a lie. Claud had been cold and critical, always critical, from the moment the marriage had been consummated. When she had gotten with child and Claud had insisted upon leaving her bed, she had been relieved, only to suffer a crushing guilt for feeling that way.

Setting down the wood she had found, she began to build a fire as that thought reminded her of the child she had lost. Grief for the loss of the child she had wanted so badly, for the loss of that barely begun life, still cast a shadow over her heart. She had learned all about the healing arts, as was tradition for the women in her clan, and knew it was but nature's way, that there was a good chance there had been something wrong, that her husband's seed had not rooted correctly. Her mind accepted that but her heart still mourned. She could not completely shake free of the fear that something was wrong with her. After all, her husband had returned to her bed to try again, though not very often and with little enthusiasm, for almost a year, but she had not conceived again. Considering the fertility of the women in her family, that did not seem right to her. She also had to wonder how it was he could give Marie Anne two strong, healthy boys, yet give her no child at all.

"And once I discovered him with Marie Anne," she muttered, hesitated as a wide variety of bloodthirsty plans for her late husband's punishment went through her mind, and then shook her head, still embarrassed by how she had instead tried to lure him back to her bed. "I but thank God that madness didnae last long."

Annoyed by how her mind wanted to torment her with memories of her marriage, her humiliation, and her loss, Arianna concentrated on cutting up what was left of the last rabbit Sir Brian had caught. Tired of simply gnawing on rabbit cooked on a spit, she decided she was going to make a stew. It would still be yet another meal of rabbit but it might taste a little different, especially with what she added from the supply pack.

"And how that mon keeps that pack so full all the time is a true mystery," she said, and shook her head again. Sir Brian MacFingal certainly had a gift for foraging.

Determined not to be afraid as she waited for Sir Brian to return, she worked to make as tasty a stew as possible. It was not easy to ignore all the noises in the wood surrounding her, but she found some comfort for her fear in the calm of the horses. The animals would warn her if danger drew near.

She also tried hard not to worry about Sir Brian. The man knew a lot about surviving and hunting, she reminded herself. He had proved that admirably over the last three days. He had also shown that he knew the art of slipping through village and forest silently and unseen. Her curiosity about that skill had her biting her tongue against asking how he had acquired it. Arianna was not all that sure she wanted an answer to that question.

Glancing at the dark wood surrounding her, she wrapped her arms around her body and prayed he would not take too much longer to reconnoiter the area. There was a lot of danger in trying to hunt down the enemy and see what they were doing. Arianna could only pray that Sir Brian continued to be as good at sneaking around as he had proven to be thus far. The mere thought of losing him made her insides clench with terror and her blood run cold. She told herself it was just because she would then be alone with no one to help her fight her enemies but a little voice in her head whispered that she was lying to herself. An attempt to shut that voice up by admitting that she would not like to see a good man hurt, or worse, while fighting for her did not work either, but Arianna did not want to think much on why that was.

"He will be back soon," she said, and looked at the horses as if they should nod in agreement with her. "He will." She knew that if he did not return, she would not be able to stop herself from hunting for him, and that terrified her.

* * *

Brian paused just inside the trees, stroking the neck of his mount to ensure that the animal remained silent. He hated leaving Arianna all alone but it was important to keep a close eye on the enemy tracking them down. Unlike them, he could move more quickly and easily through the countryside for he knew it well. He also knew exactly where to position himself to watch the little village below without being seen, and what he saw now made him relax a little.

The men who had been following them were obviously going to settle in the village for the night. There was no doubt in his mind that the men he now watched were Arianna's hunters for they were certainly not his countrymen. There was no real need to hear them speak, either. The clothes told him what he needed to know. After working with Captain Tillet for so long, he now knew what they wore in France—something he had never imagined might prove very useful aside from helping him to decide what goods he wanted brought in.

He dismounted, secured his mount, and began to creep down the hill. Brian needed to get closer, needed to try and hear what the men were talking about. What he most hoped to learn was whether or not the men knew what direction he and Arianna were headed in. It also would not hurt to get a closer look at a few of them, he mused.

By the time he reached the inn, the men were inside. Brian hesitated, realized none of these men knew what he looked like, and slipped inside. Moving to a shadowed corner, he sat on a bench. One of the serving maids quickly appeared and he paid her for a tankard of ale. It gave him something to hide behind as he watched the ones who were so anxious to kill two children they would ride around a country they did not know just to find them. Brian wondered what tale they told when they tried to get information.

One of the men acted as if he was the leader, although the men with him showed him only grudging respect, and little of that. Brian wondered if the man was the Amiel Arianna spoke of for he could not believe the men would be so carelessly disrespectful of a DeVeaux, not if even half of what Arianna had told her about that family was true. If it was Amiel, Brian then wondered just how closely the man resembled the brother he had killed. He could see little about the man—who wore clothes more suited to a court appearance than to riding around a rough countryside—that would make one think him a man capable of killing his own brother, or hunting down his own nephews for the slaughter.

"I will pay for three rooms and the stabling of our horses," the man Brian thought was Lucette snapped. "I will take one of the rooms and the rest of you can decide who will sleep inside the inn and who will sleep in the stables with the horses."

"My lord," began one tall, almost too lean man.

"I do not believe I asked for your opinion on the matter, Sir Anton. Do as I say and leave Jacques here so that I might have someone to see to my needs."

That had to be Amiel Lucette, Brian decided. There was no one else who appeared to be leading the men. Some women might consider the man handsome, but his voice and manner would be enough to make most men want to kill him. The way the men eyed Amiel when the man was not looking their way told Brian that Lord Lucette was lucky to still be alive. Brian suspected only the man's alliance with the DeVeaux was accomplishing that miracle.

Everything about the man was thin or narrow, although Brian knew that did not have to mean that the man was some weakling. His hair was black and shoulder length, pulled back from his long, narrow face. There was a sullen curve to the man's full lips as well. He had the look of a spoiled child.

"I cannot understand how they keep slipping through our fingers," muttered Lucette, halting Sir Anton's attempt to slip away. "These barbarians should not be able to thwart us so."

It was a good thing he was speaking in French, Brian thought, or he would be dead. That sort of sneering insult was very akin to what many English aristocrats were fond of saying. Since Scotland and France had been allies more than enemies for many, many years, it surprised him that there was such distaste for his people among the French aristocracy. But then, most of the time all they wanted was extra men to fight their battles and to keep their old enemy the English beleaguered at home.

"This is their land, Lord Lucette," replied Sir Anton. "And their skill at fighting is well known, my lord. They have long made up some of our mercenary force."

"As arrow fodder so that good Frenchmen might stand back until it is safer. No, this puzzles me. I also think it was wrong for us to divide the men. We only need to catch hold of one of the men helping that bitch and my brother's get and that one would soon tell us where the boys are."

"Why should they? This is not their fight and they gain nothing from it."

"So why should they fight or die for either that red-haired bitch or those two common little whelps?"

"They may feel it honorable to assist a woman and two children."

Lucette waved a heavily beringed hand, sniffed the tankard of wine the maid gave him, and wrinkled his long nose in a clear sign of disgust. "I should not be so surprised that there is no good wine in this heathen land. If we had gained hold of Lady Arianna or one of the boys upon the beach, we would soon have had the lot in our hands. Those men would bargain with us. The message we received from Lord Ignace said this MacFingal clan has little money and is known to be very odd. That wench has no coin to pay them, does she? What coin she may have stolen from my family is undoubtedly at the bottom of the sea."

"No, she has no coin but she is very pretty."

"Not so pretty that one of these savage fellows would not turn her over to us for a nice, full purse. My brother certainly did not find her worth much in bed or he would have left that slut he married. Her dowry was a hefty one though, although this mess Claud left behind could cause the Murrays to demand it returned. And that is another good reason to see that she does not return to her family."

Lucette badly needed killing, Brian decided, and had to fight the temptation to try and fulfill that wish.

He began to get a clearer idea of what Arianna's life had been like with the Lucettes, and it was not good. Things she had said had let him know it had not been a happy time for her, but listening to this fool talk made it all chillingly clear. She had never been accepted.

"I will settle the men, m'lord. After a good night's rest, we can begin the hunt again. We should also have word from at least one of the other groups soon. I will send a man to the meeting place to see if word has come. If one of the others has managed to find the boys, we could end this and go home."

"Only the boys? Your lord wishes to catch the woman, too. I thought you knew that. His family is eager to pay back the Murrays for things that happened in the past and she would be a very good weapon to use. I cannot see the DeVeaux giving that up. That family lives for vengeance."

Sir Anton just shrugged and walked away. A few moments later a tall, broad-chested man joined Lucette. As Brian watched Lucette order the man to see to his food and drink as well as make certain a bath was prepared, he decided he would gain no more information now. Lucette's mind had turned to his own comforts. Brian was also running a risk by lingering too long. His family was not completely unknown in the area.

Despite the danger of being caught showing far too much interest in a party of visiting Frenchmen, Brian meandered by the stables. Hoping the stable hands would say nothing, he grabbed a shovel and began to clean out one of the stalls. When an older man came over to stare at him, Brian tensed but just winked and kept working. His tension eased when the man simply collected a bridle, sat down near him, and set to work on it.

"So what is your interest in these fools?" asked the older man the moment the stable was clear of Lucette's men.

"Mayhap I have just taken on a job here," Brian replied as he set the shovel aside and looked at the man.

The man gave a short bark of laughter. "Dinnae try to fool me, lad. I own this place. I do the hiring. Now, what is your interest in these men who think we are all naught but swine?"

"Ah, ye speak French."

"Mother was French. Father brought her back when he was done fighting one of their battles for them." His sharp gray eyes remained fixed upon Brian's face. "Ye are verra good at nay answering questions, m'lad."

Brian considered his answer for a moment as he studied the innkeeper. The man looked honest enough, his gaze straight and clear. The deciding factor, however, was that the man had not exposed him. One word and Brian would have been fighting for his life, a fight he might well have lost against so many. Lucette's men might not know who he was but they were strangers in his country, hunting three innocents with murder on their minds. They would have viewed anyone unknown as suspicious and a threat to their plans.

"Just here to try and discover how close they are to the bonnie wee lass I am trying to get to Dubheidland."

"Dubheidland, huh. Ye dinnae look like one of those cursed Camerons."

"I am from the dark side of the family."

"Ah, one of old Fingal's lads. Ye do have the look of him. Odd mon, that Fingal. Always was."

Since his father had been born and raised in this area, Brian was not surprised that the older man would know who his father was. "Aye, odd, but verra virile." He grinned when the man laughed heartily and slapped his knee.

"True. Verra true. Get out of here, lad. Get your wee bonnie lass far away. These men are nay good. Didnae like them from the moment they stepped in my door and will be glad to see the back of them. If business round here wasnae so poor, I would ne'er have let them in the door. They will gain no information here. I will see to it. Get her to Dubheidland. That braw laird will enjoy swinging a sword at a few Frenchmen."

Brian did not hesitate to obey the man. With a grin and a wink that made the man mutter something about Fingal breeding true, he slipped out of the stables and made his way back to his horse. He had not gained much information on how close Lucette was to finding him but what he had learned was not good.

They knew who might have taken Arianna and the boys. They even had developed a way to keep each group informed of what the other had discovered. That meant there was no stopping them from eventually riding to Scarglas. At least he knew the man would gain no help from the ones working at the inn.

He also knew he could not tell Arianna all he had learned. The moment she heard that her enemy had knowledge of who might be aiding her, she would be terrified about the fate of the two boys. She had enough to worry about. He would not add to her fears.

As he rode back to where he had left her waiting for him, he thought on what he had learned. There were more men with Lucette than he had realized. This was the first time he had seen them all together. At least, he hoped that was all of them. Ten men and Lucette himself. That was more than he could deal with on his own, especially when he also had to keep Arianna safe. It also meant that, if the men landing on the beach had actually split up into three groups, Lucette and his allies had brought a small army with them.

For a moment he was concerned about the others, his brothers, the captain and his men, and the two boys, but he easily shook off that worry. His brothers would be safe enough. The odds were far more even with the other two groups. It did not even matter that the enemy now knew who they followed for it was not easy to catch up with a MacFingal who did not wish to be caught. The number of men hunting him and Arianna, however, made it even more imperative that he get her safely to Dubheidland.

The way Lucette had spoken of how the DeVeaux wanted to get their hands on Arianna and why plagued his mind as he rode. He was no stranger to the need for vengeance but Brian only saw the need for it when a wrong had been committed. He had the feeling the DeVeaux wanted it only because some Murray had thwarted a plan they had made. The more he learned about the DeVeaux, the more he saw them and what they wanted as a far greater threat to Arianna and the boys. Lucette's wants were appalling, but simple. He wanted his nephews dead so he could return to France and take his place as the new heir.

If it was possible he would make Lucette and his allies believe that Arianna and the boys were already dead. Unfortunately, there was no time to concoct such a scheme. The ones following him, and those chasing his brothers, had undoubtedly already been given enough reason to believe otherwise, as well. The only way this could end now was with the deaths of the ones hunting her and the boys. Considering the number of men on his trail and adding in the ones who were chasing his brothers, Brian was certain that would only happen with a battle, and if he was going to have to go to battle, he wanted to do so on his own land with his brothers at his back.

"Ach, weel, Fither will be happy," he muttered. "He believes that the truce with the Grays has made us all soft."

"Brian?"

He heard Arianna's tentative, soft call and looked around. Brian frowned when he could not see her. Edging his horse a little closer to where he had left her, he finally saw the banked fire, the pot of aromatic stew, and the horses. He dismounted and a moment later found his arms full of the woman he thought about far too often, and far too warmly.

"I was afraid they had found me," she said against his chest, her small hands clutching at the back of his shirt. "Too long sitting here whilst the night crept in, I am thinking."

Brian stroked her back until her trembling eased. She was a tempting armful. He could feel the press of her breasts against his chest and his hands itched to stroke them. Even as a voice in his head warned him it was not a good idea, he placed his hand under her chin and turned her face up to his. Stealing one kiss would not hurt, he told that voice, as he lowered his mouth to hers.

Arianna watched his mouth come closer to hers and knew she should pull away. She knew it would not be a good idea if only because they still had a lot of miles left to travel together and this could breed some awkwardness between them. The temptation to be kissed by this man was too strong to resist, however. She may have been married for five years but, even counting the few stolen by young men before she was betrothed, she had experienced a paucity of kisses. And none of the ones who had kissed her had been as handsome as Sir Brian MacFingal. Not one of those kisses had made any grand impression upon her, either. She was curious to see if the man whom she found so intriguing, so fine to look at, would change her mind about the worthlessness of kisses.

The moment his lips touched her, Arianna knew this kiss would be different from any that had come before. His lips were soft and warm, that warmth flooding through her body. She slid her arms up around his neck, giving in to the urge to be held even more closely in his arms.

When he nudged at her lips with his tongue, she opened for him with caution. This part of the kiss had never really pleased her. Her kinswomen had assured her that it was wonderful if done by a man you wanted and one who had some skill. With but a few strokes of his tongue within her mouth, Arianna knew they had spoken the truth.

She quickly sank beneath the pleasure of the kiss. Her whole body was warmed by it and greedy for it. That warmth began to change, however, as he stroked her back and the kiss grew fiercer. A tightness began to grow inside her. Her nipples tautened and ached until she rubbed up against his chest in a vain attempt to ease the strangely pleasurable pain. Dampness pooled between her thighs, her woman's place beginning to feel slightly swollen, and a low throbbing ache started to form deep in her belly. Arianna wanted to crawl inside his skin.

Shaken by what she was feeling, she pulled out of his arms so quickly she stumbled. He reached out to steady her and she stepped back, away from his touch. Fear slid insidiously through her veins, cooling the heat he had stirred within her. Arianna had no idea what he had done to her, but it worried her. She needed to think and that would be impossible as long as she was in his arms.

Unable to meet his gaze as she recalled how she had been rubbing her body all over his, she turned to the fire and the meal she had prepared. "We best eat this before it burns," she said, and inwardly cursed herself, certain that she was acting and sounding like an idiot.

Brian frowned at her but said nothing. The brief glimpse he had gotten of her expression after she had leapt out of his arms, as if she had suddenly remembered that he was a leper, had been one of fear and confusion. He had not pushed her too far, or asked too much, so he did not really understand what he had done to frighten her.

For now, he decided as he moved to use a little of their water to wash, he would let her run. It was clear that she did not wish to talk about the kiss, either. He would grant her that silence for a little while. It would also give him time to think of the best way to approach her about her sudden retreat.

One thing he was sure of was that she had felt the same rush of desire he had. He was tempted to point that out to her and then ask her what ailed her, but knew that could be a very big mistake. Arianna had scars on her heart. She was not a woman a man rushed. Brian winced at the ache in his groin that told him his body was more than willing to rush her.

He would have to ignore it, something he had some experience in. Arianna was like some abused animal, cautious and easily frightened. Brian suspected she was unused to passion, may never have really experienced it. Nothing she had yet told him about that idiot Claud implied that he had been a good lover, or had even tried to be. Until Arianna could accept that she was a passionate woman and that he stirred that passion in her, he would have to tread very lightly. He would have another kiss soon, however, he decided as he sat down by the fire and watched her stir the stew. Forgoing the occasional reminder of what they had just shared with another a kiss would be wrong because he knew she could easily convince herself that she had felt nothing. That lie would not be allowed to stand.

Arianna served Sir Brian some stew and then sat down across the fire from him to eat her own meal. She could barely even look at him so deep was her embarrassment. The more she thought on the way she had behaved, the more she saw it as wanton behavior worthy of some tavern whore.

It did not help her peace of mind to discover that every time she stole a glance at him, she looked at his mouth. She could taste him on her lips and there was a greed within her for more. If this was passion, she was not sure she wanted anything to do with it. It was too strong and made her act in ways she never had before. Arianna did not like to admit it, but going to France to marry Claud was the most, and only, truly adventurous thing she had ever done, but even then she had not suffered any of the wild emotions one kiss from Sir Brian had stirred within her.

When she finally settled down on her blanket to sleep, she decided it was best if she stayed out of the man's arms. She had too much to worry about at the moment without venturing into the turbulent waters of passion. Regret was a sharp pain in her heart but she ignored it. Perhaps when her enemy was defeated and she and the boys were truly safe, she could venture down that road—if Sir Brian was still close at hand, she mused, rather liking the idea of that.

"Shall I kiss ye good night, love?"

She turned her back on him, not needing to look at him to see that he was grinning for she could hear it in his voice. Then again, she thought, perhaps she would just find a thick stick and hit him over the head.

Chapter 5

Brian glanced at Arianna, who was far too quiet. She had barely spoken a dozen words all morning. He could still taste the kiss they had shared. When the memory sent all the blood rushing straight to his groin, he quickly banished it. He set his mind back to puzzling out why she had fled his arms as if he was a threat to her instead of a man she desired. One thing he had never been to any woman was a threat. He never forced his attentions upon a woman or told lies to get what he wanted. And, he thought, a simple kiss should not have been so frightening to a woman who had been married for years.

Unless her husband had abused her. Brian frowned and glanced at her again, wondering if he had been wrong to think that it was simply a matter of Claud never having given her a taste of passion. He had seen what a man's abuse could do to a woman and Arianna did not show any of the signs. The biggest proof of that was that she had allowed him to separate her from the boys, from all the others, and make her travel alone with him, yet revealed only a natural wariness to begin with despite the fact that she only knew him by name. That wariness was already easing.

He returned to the idea that the late, unlamented Claud might have been a very poor lover. If the man had never roused the passion Brian was certain was in Arianna, she could easily fear such unknown heat and need. Even in the morning's harsh light, he remained confident that she had felt the same fire he had when she was in his arms. He might not have the wealth of experience some of his brothers had, but he did know when a woman responded to his kiss, and she had. That brought him back to what he had decided last night and that was that he was going to have to ease her fears because he had every intention of sharing another kiss with her and, if luck was on his side, a lot more than kisses. Brian just wished he knew how to do that. All the thought he had exerted on the problem before falling asleep had not given him any answers.

"We will stop soon, give the horses a wee rest, and take one ourselves," he said, already planning exactly where he would shelter. "Mayhap have a wee bit to eat."

"That would be lovely," Arianna said as she briefly met his gaze.

She quickly looked away again, setting her attention firmly on the trail they followed as it passed by beneath her horse's hooves. Just looking at Sir Brian was enough to make her blush. Her lingering embarrassment was born partly from how she had felt as they had kissed, all hot and aching with a need she was not sure she understood. Most of it, however, came from how she had reacted to the

flood of feeling that had swept over her from the
moment his lips had touched hers. She had leapt
away from him as if he were some leper. Young
maidens did that sort of thing, not mature widows
of three and twenty. In truth, she suspected she had
acted worse than even the shyest of maidens. She
should have found a way to end the embrace with
some dignity.

At least I did not swoon, she thought with a twinge
of self-disgust. Although it had been a close thing,
she admitted reluctantly. Claud had kissed her and
made love to her, but she now considered there was
the very good chance that Claud had simply been
dutifully mating with her. Claud had never once
caused her to experience such tumultuous feelings.
Most of the time she had just wished Claud would
hurry and get it over with, or stop. That had certainly not been what she had been wishing while she
had been kissing Sir Brian.

And that was really what had terrified her, she
thought, and finally accepted that harsh truth. She
was a coward. It was quite possible that Sir Brian's
kiss had stirred that passion her married kinswomen
all sighed over and she had always thought she
wanted. And what had she done when finally given
a taste of what she had craved? Run from it. Arianna
was not sure what she could do about that or if she
should do anything at all.

"I think this will be a good place to rest for a wee
while."

Brian's deep voice shattered her thoughts and Arianna looked around. They were in a beautiful spot
near a swiftly running burn. Wild violets covered the

banks of the burn and she could see bluebells winding through the trees.

"Despite all the troubles I still face, it gladdens my heart beyond words to be back here," she said as she dismounted.

"I have heard that France is beautiful," Brian said as he also dismounted and moved to stand beside her. "I suspicion your husband's lands were beautiful and probably verra fertile."

"Aye, they were, but they were nay like Scotland." She knelt down on the bank and inhaled the gentle scent of the violets. "I think I missed the land as much as I missed my family."

He grabbed some oatcakes and cheese from his pack, handing her some as he sat down next to her. He looked over the land as he ate, thinking it a particularly pretty spot, and knew he would miss Scotland if he had to leave it. Harsh in as many places as it was soft and peaceful, the weather temperamental, and the living often hard, it was still home. It was in his blood. He suspected it was in Arianna's as well.

"They didnae let ye come home at least once during the time ye were there?" he asked.

"Claud occasionally promised he would take me home to visit, but I soon saw that it was said mostly to quiet me," she replied. "I dinnae think he e'er wanted to come here. He e'en called this land barbaric when he thought I couldnae hear him. So did his family. And thus I was the wee barbarian they were forced to endure for the sake of the family's fortunes."

There was the hint of bitterness behind her words but he was surprised there was not more. Everything she told him about Claud and his family revealed that she had never been accepted, and she had endured that for years. She was due a hearty bout of bitterness. She had not only lost her family when she had been sent to France, but had been given nothing to take the place of them.

"I also think," she continued, "that, once I had learned of his mistress, they all feared that, if I went home, I wouldnae return." She shrugged. "I probably wouldnae have and they would have been humiliated by that."

Brian cursed under his breath. "They ne'er gave a thought to what that fool did to ye, did they? Ne'er once cared how ye suffered."

Arianna looked at him with surprise, his anger clear to hear in his voice. "Nay, I was but the wife and wives must endure, must they not?"

"The wives my kinsmen have taken would do the fools a sore injury if they did to them as Claud did to ye. Aye, and the family would have been sent running to the hills if they tried to make either of those lasses take all the blame for their son's betrayal of them."

She grinned. "Aye, that is how most of my kinswomen would behave." She suddenly frowned. "'Tis verra odd that none of my family came for me as I did write to them of what I was suffering. What Claud did should have enraged my kin." It was hard to understand that, to find a reason that would ease the pain she felt at their apparent desertion of her.

"Oh? And tell me, did ye hand that missive to one of your husband's people to have it sent on to your family?" He nodded when her eyes grew wide and she paled. "I suspicion those letters ye wrote were read ere they were sent on and any that spoke of the wrongs done to you were probably tossed straight into the fire." Brian clenched his hands into fists as he fought the urge to take her into his arms to soothe the grief and pain he could read on her face. "Ye had a large dowry, did ye?"

"'Twas rich enough and they were in sore need of it for they lived too weel."

It should not have been such a painful shock, she thought, as tears stung her eyes. She had certainly not been welcomed into the family. The man she had married had obviously never cared for her. Arianna now knew that, if she had had a child, that child would not have been completely accepted, either. She could not believe she had been so naive as to trust any of them. People who treated a person as they had treated her were not ones that should be trusted. Worse, she had accepted the possibility that no one in her family cared how she was treated, and for stirring that mistrust of her own kin in her heart, she would never forgive Claud's family.

"Weel, this shall anger my family," she murmured. "Ach, what am I saying? They will all be furious o'er how I was deceived, over how they were deceived as weel. Kenning that I was treated poorly by that whole cursed family and robbed of my dower, too, will send them into a killing rage."

"Do ye think they will want to fight the Lucettes?"

"They will wish to, but I think in the end they will only fight with words and demands for restitution. There is a connection through blood and marriage with the family, ye see. An old one. I was to be a renewal of that connection. There are some verra good people within the Lucette family. I wrote to them, as weel." She sighed. "I suspicion those letters also went into the fire and that is why I ne'er saw the ones I have met before, ones more closely tied to my clan."

Brian was just about to give her his opinion on the way the Lucettes had treated her when he heard the sound of approaching horses. "We must leave now," he said even as he grabbed her by the arm and tugged her to her feet.

"Do ye think it is them?" she asked, hurrying to mount her horse.

"Aye, I suspect it is. Move into the trees where the shadows will hide us. I wish to see to be certain. E'en if it isnae them, I think it best if we keep out of sight. We dinnae want them to be able to gain any information on where we have been."

"But if they pass so close to us, will they nay see us?"

"They are on the other side of the burn."

Once within the shadows, her gaze fixed upon the other side of the burn, Arianna leaned forward to lightly stroke her mount's neck. She closed her eyes to listen carefully and finally heard what Brian had. There were definitely horsemen approaching on the other side of the burn. She was astonished at the keenness of his hearing. She would have sat there in full view, probably not hearing the approach of anyone until they were right there staring at her.

Opening her eyes, she stared at the opposite bank and tensed as the riders came into view. She easily recognized Amiel. The man sat a horse with all the stiff arrogance he showed in his every dealing with people. Arianna would feel badly for the people who served the Lucettes if they had not, almost to a man, scorned her and the boys as completely as Claud's family had. They were certainly not blessed in the people who ruled them, but that did not fully excuse their unkindnesses. Claud had been neglectful, his parents the same, and Amiel would be cruel. She had seen that in him from the beginning.

It troubled her that Amiel remained on their trail no matter what Brian did. It was possible that the few people who caught sight of them as they traveled told Amiel and his men, but it was still a wonder that she and Brian had not shaken free of the man yet. It was almost as if Amiel knew where they might go, that he was not so much following their trail as forging along one he felt sure they would use.

Arianna looked at Brian, about to ask him what he thought, but he signaled her to follow him. As she did so, certain her every move thundered through the trees, she fought the feeling that Brian knew a great deal more than he was telling her. She then recalled that he had slipped away last night to spy upon Amiel but had not told her what, if anything, he had discovered. As soon as they were safely out of the hearing of her enemy, she intended to demand he tell her all he knew.

It was almost sunset by the time Brian signaled for them to halt. Very few words had been passed between them, speed and silence being more important. Arianna no longer believed they had shaken free of Amiel; they had only put a safe distance between them.

"Brian," she said as she dismounted, "I think Amiel kens what he is looking for."

"Aye, ye and the laddies."

He glanced at her and grimaced as he tended to the horses. She stood there staring at him, a frown on her pretty face and her hands fisted on her gently rounded hips. Arianna did not have to openly accuse him of lying with harsh words; her stance said it quite clearly.

"I think ye learned something whilst ye were creeping about last eve," she said.

"I ne'er creep."

She ignored him and continued, "And ye failed to tell me what it was. Amiel is too much the spoiled courtier to be able to keep so close on our heels through skill alone. Aye, and too vain to think anyone else might ken what to do better than he, so I doubt he heeds the wisdom of a good tracker."

"Arianna, let us tend to the horses and ready our meal," he said. "Then I will tell ye what I have learned."

She hesitated a moment before nodding in agreement. Her stomach slowly tied itself in knots as she worked, however. He had found out something that he did not want her to know. That stirred up all her fears for the safety of Michel and Adelar. By the time they sat side by side near a low, banked fire, sharing cold meat, bread, and cheese, she was so tense with fear that every bite she took sat like a stone in her stomach.

"The good news is that Amiel and his men are nay as skilled at tracking us as it may appear," began Brian. "The DeVeaux and Amiel did divide their men into three groups as we thought they would, but they have some way to keep each other informed of whatever is going on or what they have learned."

"They ken who is helping us." Arianna was not surprised to hear the fear in her voice.

"One of the groups following one of my brothers apparently did discover that, aye. A certain Lord Ignace. A DeVeau, I suppose."

"Aye. Youngest brother to the head of the family. Kenned to be clever and vicious, but that appears to be a common trait amongst the DeVeaux. Although"— she frowned in thought—"I think there is another called Ignace. A distant cousin. The name is verra popular amongst the DeVeaux. I rather hope it is that Ignace."

"Why?"

"Because I think he is just a winemaker, nay a warrior. Nay like the other one, the clever, vicious one."

"I cannae think they would send a winemaker after us. So it is probably the more weel-kenned one. And, he may be clever and he may be vicious but he is riding o'er land he doesnae ken, trying to gain information from a stubborn people, many of whom have no wish to aid any stranger."

"The weel-kenned Lord Ignace is rumored to be verra good at getting people to tell him what he wants to learn. Even the king has asked his assistance on occasion. I find it a little frightening that the king, who has dungeons and torturers of his own, would think Lord Ignace more skilled at forcing people to talk. One has to wonder just what he can do that will make people bend to his will when they wouldnae bend to the king's or his torturers'."

"True, but he still doesnae ken this land." Brian ran a hand through his hair. "I but pray that most people who are in his path ken enough to hide when they see him coming. He sent word to Amiel and I find their ability to do that of more concern. We dinnae e'en ken what the others are doing, nor they us, and our only plan is to get behind some sturdy walls as soon as we can."

"A verra good plan."

He reached over and took her hand in his. "Your lads will be safe, Arianna. Ye must trust me in this. No one, nay matter how clever or vicious, can catch a MacFingal who doesnae wish to be caught. Aye, we prefer to fight but we learned quickly that 'tis often best to flee a fight, at least until ye can choose the ground ye want to fight it on."

Arianna took a deep breath and let it out slowly as she struggled to push aside her fear. "Do ye think Michel and Adelar are already behind the walls of Scarglas?"

"Adelar most certainly. Michel may be, but it all depends on how twisted a route Nat had to take. I would not be surprised to learn that the DeVeaux have lost a few men, either."

"But, if they ken we dinnae have the boys, why are they still following us?"

"For ye." He sighed and put his arm around her shoulders when she paled. "They still believe that capturing one of ye will pull the others into their hands."

"I would ne'er hand them my boys," she said as she leaned against him, attempting to take some of the strength and confidence he showed into her heart and blood.

"I ken it but that doesnae mean they do. Amiel also believes that they need but capture one of us, wave a full purse beneath our noses, and we will give him ye and the lads."

"Nay, ye would ne'er do that."

The firmness of the belief behind her words warmed him. Brian knew the reputation of his clan was slowly improving but he also knew that many still scorned them as being no more than a pack of rutting fools. Arianna had faith in his strengths, in his ability to keep her and the boys safe, and he reveled in that faith. Too few offered it to one of his family.

"Nay. Never. Nor would any of my kinsmen." Deciding she needed to know it all, that it would help if she fully understood the danger she was in, he continued. "They also want you but nay just to bargain for the laddies."

"The DeVeaux want a Murray in their grasp?"

"Aye, ye were right to wonder on that. Your kin obviously left them with a fierce need for revenge."

"I ken it but that doesnae matter. Only Michel and Adelar matter."

He did not agree with that but said nothing. "What we need to remember is that that idiot Amiel isnae tracking us, he is riding to where he believes we are going. I willnae say that he doesnae get a wee piece of help along the way, but he isnae skilled at the chore he has been given. And, as with the DeVeaux, he does nay like this land nor ken it as I do, as my brothers do. I wish I could shake him off our tail, but I dinnae think I will be able to. Howbeit, I am fair certain that he willnae creep up on us and get you."

"And the DeVeaux will nay be able to creep up on your brothers and grab one of the boys. Aye?"

"Aye."

"All this for two boys who will soon be marked as bastards anyway. I just cannae understand why."

"And may nay ever do so unless we can catch one of them and make him tell us. I would wager, though, that nay all the men riding with Amiel and this Lord Ignace neither ken what they are doing anyway, nor give it much thought. They just do as they are told."

She nodded. "And men who ride with the De-Veaux ken weel the cost of nay doing as they are told. I am thinking that Amiel is much the same."

Brian slipped his hand beneath her chin and tilted her face up to his. "The lads are safe, Arianna, and I intend to keep ye safe as weel."

She knew even before he began to lower his mouth to hers that he was going to kiss her again. Arianna also knew that she should pull away from him now but she did not, could not. Despite her fear and confusion, she had not been able to stop thinking about that kiss they had shared, about how he had tasted and how good it had felt to be held in his arms. At least until her fear had reared its ugly head. This time she was determined to enjoy the kiss and then withdraw with grace and dignity.

Brian brushed his mouth over hers and, when she did not immediately pull away, he quickly deepened the kiss. His desire rose up with a force he had never known before, but he fought to keep it under control. Arianna was not some skilled courtesan or flirtatious, willing widow. He was beginning to realize that, despite her marriage, she was nearly as innocent of what could occur between a man and a woman as any sheltered, well-born maid.

It was not easy to go slowly, however. He wanted her as he had never wanted a woman before. His whole body tautened with the need to be flesh to flesh with her, to be inside her. Brian could sense her desire stirring to match his and that made it even more difficult to tread softly with her.

Arianna shivered as he caressed her waist and hips while holding her close. His kiss grew more passionate, more devouring, and she was soon welcoming that fire. When he slid a hand up from her waist to stroke her breast, she gasped into his mouth as pure delight streaked through her veins. That delight turned to need until she was crawling into his lap, and that was when the fear began to stir within her.

Try as she would, Arianna could not keep her heart and mind fixed only on the pleasure of his kiss, of his touch. She began to think of how thin she was, how small her breasts were, and how lacking she was in the curves a man craved. It was Claud again, whispering in her mind, reminding her of all that she lacked as a woman. And then she began to fear what she felt in Brian's arms, that it was too much, too soon, and destined to turn to scorn when he realized she was unable to satisfy him as a man needed to be satisfied.

She was not surprised when he cursed as she yanked herself free of him and leapt to her feet. Her hand on her mouth, she stared at him as he looked at her, frowning and dragging a hand through his thick hair. Her hands itched to do the same and she could not understand why that was. She was rapidly beginning to want to do all manner of things to him that she had never once considered doing with the man she had thought was her husband. Or any other man, either.

"I willnae hurt ye, lass," he said. "Ye but need to say nay and I would release ye without question."

"I ken it."

And she did. Her fear was not born of any thought that he might force himself on her. She knew in her heart that he never would. Her fear was born of the fact that she would give in to this desire he stirred within her, one he appeared to share at the moment, only to see that look of disgust Claud had worn every time he had left her bed. Arianna knew that if she saw that look upon Brian's face, it would tear the heart right out of her.

"Yet ye flee me with a look of fear upon your bonnie face."

"'Tis nay ye I fear." This was not going to be easy to explain, perhaps even humiliating, but she knew she owed him some explanation for her strange behavior. "I dinnae wish to disappoint you."

"How could ye disappoint me? I may nay be the randy fool many of my kin are, but I am nay without some experience. I ken ye feel desire when we kiss, the same desire I do."

"Aye, but what about after ye try and satisfy that desire? I am nay good at that."

"How can ye ken that? I am fair sure your husband wasnae verra much of a lover to you," he began.

"Nay, because I was such a poor bed partner. He would rise from our bed and tell me often what I lacked in the art of pleasing a mon. I couldnae bear to see ye look at me like that, so I think it best if we cease with the kissing and the wanting of more." She took a quick step back when he surged to his feet and glared at her.

"I am nay that bastard Claud," he snapped.

"I ken it. But . . ."

"Nay. Sit. We will eat and then rest and then continue on our journey."

She cautiously sat down, watched him pace the little clearing for a moment, and tried not to tense when he sat down beside her. It was clear she had angered him and she was not certain how to soothe that anger. In fact, she wondered if she should. If he remained angry with her there would be no more kisses. The thought of that made her heart ache and she inwardly cursed.

"I am nay Claud," he said again as he handed her his wineskin and began to unpack more oatcakes, cold meat, and cheese. "I see now that he wanted to make ye question everything about yourself, lass. I would have thought ye kenned that by now, that ye would see that whate'er he said was just more lies."

Her mouth full of cider, she just nodded. It was hard to meet his gaze, but she forced herself to do so. Arianna just wished the conversation were not so embarrassing. Losing oneself in the heat of a kiss while held in the arms of a very handsome man was one thing, talking about it was quite another. It was only now that she realized she knew very little about what went on between a man and a woman as Claud had done only what was necessary to get her with child. She knew there was so much more but not what that more was, despite the talks she had heard from the married ladies in her clan.

"There are two ways for a mon to grind a woman down beneath his boot. He can beat her with his fists or he can pick away at her with cruel words until she has no pride left and no will to stand against him. Ye need to accept that Claud used words to crush ye and accept that whate'er he told ye was wrong, was just used to make certain ye caused him no trouble. Weel, that and as a way to make ye shoulder the blame for his own mistakes."

"I do ken that," she whispered, for she had begun to question Claud's cruelty to her from the moment she had discovered he was not truly her husband.

"If he didnae find pleasure in the bedding of ye, it was all his own fault. I can feel the passion in ye, Arianna. 'Tis sweet and hot. He caged it because he didnae want it. Ye have to free it. Ye have to cease thinking ye have some lack that will leave a mon cold. Believe me, cold is the verra last thing I feel when I have ye in my arms."

"Tell me, how would it make ye feel if, when a woman rose from your bed, she made sure ye kenned that ye had failed to satisfy her desires? What if that woman was your wife and she told ye that every night?"

Brian did not even want to think about it, knowing it would eat at his soul if something like that ever happened. "It would burn its way into my heart and mind as it has yours. Only ye can push it away, toss it on the midden heap where it belongs. I would tell ye what else I would probably do but fear it would sound too much like I was just trying to get ye to do as I want."

"And what would that be? What would ye do?"

"I would eventually find myself a woman and find out if the wrong was in me or in the one who claimed I failed her. And if the wrong was in me, then I would do what I could to fix it because I would ken that I had the passion in me, that I just needed to learn a few skills to share it with another.

Now, eat. We need to rest and, I think, ye need to wrestle with a few ghosts."

Arianna ate and settled down in her blankets without saying another word. Her mind was too busy with thoughts about what he had said to try and converse. She was also disappointed with herself. She did know what Claud had been doing with his constant insults and quiet cruelties, but she was having a lot of trouble shaking free of the power they had held over her. It had held her in its tight grip for far too long.

She could all too easily recall the heat of Brian's kiss and the way his hand upon her breast had made her blood run hot. A part of her was demanding she allow herself a full tasting of the pleasure he promised her, while another part cringed from the possibility that he, too, would find her lacking.

Courage was what she needed. Arianna was determined to find that courage, the strength to banish the fear Claud had bred in her, and accept what Brian offered. She was a widow and could indulge herself without fear of much censure. By the time they stopped for the night again, she wanted to be ready to find out the truth. She wanted to prove all Claud had made her believe of herself as a woman was no more than another one of his lies.

Chapter 6

An inn. From the stupor of exhaustion she had fallen into, Arianna roused herself enough to smile. For almost two days she and Brian had done little more than ride, take a short rest, and ride some more. The inn was a little worn down but it looked like the finest castle to her. For at least one night she would be sleeping in a bed beneath a roof. Even better, she might be able to eat something besides rabbit.

"'Tis nay verra fine but 'tis clean and the food is good," said Brian as he helped her down from her mount. "There is but one wee thing we need to agree on ere we go inside."

"And what is that?" She frowned when he did not immediately answer, even looked a little nervous, and then guilt swept over her. "Oh. I fear ye will have to wait for my share of the cost until I can reach my family. All my coin went down with the ship. Do ye have enough coin e'en without me adding something?"

"Dinnae fret o'er the cost. I have enough. Nay,

'tis just that we will be getting only one room. That is what I needed to speak about."

Brian hoped she would not think he was making them share a room so that he could get her into a bed and into his arms. He wanted to, no question about that, but he had to wait until she was ready to be there. His body was tied up in knots only she could untie, but he could wait until she was ready. He just prayed that would not take too long.

Arianna struggled to think clearly enough to understand exactly what he was saying. The man had revealed a desire for her but she did not believe he was a man who would trick or force any woman to share her favors with him. He could not know that she had decided it was time to cast aside her fears and let him show her what passion was. Something she would have done by now if they had stopped for more than the briefest of rests.

Perhaps, she thought, it was a matter of a lack of coin despite his claim that he had enough, but that did not make much sense, either. If he had so little coin he would not have even brought her to an inn. She rubbed a hand over her forehead, deciding that thinking about it was just confusing her, not gaining her one single answer. She needed to stop bouncing around on top of a horse and let her mind clear.

"Why are we getting only one room?" she asked.

"I dinnae think it would be safe for us to be separated. If the need to flee this place comes, we can do it more swiftly if we are together. There will be two pairs of ears to catch every sound, two sets of eyes to catch sight of any threat or, at least, to see a little more clearly. And there would be no time lost if trouble came, no need for one of us to try and warn the other."

"Oh, of course."

Arianna was not sure why she was worried about sharing a room at an inn with the man since she had been alone with him for six long days. She had already shared a cave with him, and slept close around a fire with him. And she had also decided to let the desire that flared between them have free rein, which would certainly be more easily done if they were sharing a room. Yet, strangely, the thought of sharing a room with him, a room with a bed, had her stomach tied up in knots. Suspecting that was Claud's poison affecting her, she did her best to push aside that tension.

"But . . . what will ye tell them?" she asked. "How will ye explain why the two of us need only one room?"

"I doubt we will be asked the why of it. Molly isnae one to ask many questions," he replied as he took his pack of supplies from the back of the horse.

Before she could ask him how he could be so certain of that and ask just who Molly was, he grasped her by the hand and pulled her toward the scarred door of the inn. Arianna could think of many reasons why he was so sure the innkeepers would ask no questions and none of them pleased her very much. The one reason that troubled her the most was the possibility that he had brought other women to this inn and often enough that the innkeeper would feel he knew why she was at his side. The thought that she had decided to give herself to a man who frolicked all too often with women was not a comfortable one.

She was opening her mouth to actually ask him if this was some favorite trysting place when a very round woman with a large wart on her chin stepped in front of them just inside the door of the inn. Arianna was glad of the interruption. Asking Sir Brian about his trysting habits was not a good idea. It was truly none of her business where or how often he did his trysting, she told herself firmly. All she wanted of him was to show her that she could not only feel passion but make the man in her arms feel it, too. She was fairly sure it was all a man like him could offer her anyway. From what she recalled of the tales of the MacFingals, none of them understood the word *constancy.*

"Ye are a MacFingal," the woman said in a surprisingly deep voice as she placed her big, work-worn hands on her ample hips. "Dinnae tell me which one," she snapped when Sir Brian opened his mouth to tell her his name. "I am trying to learn who be who as ye seem to be coming round here more often."

That did not sound good at all, Arianna thought. She had an image of Sir Brian wandering in and out of the inn with a long line of buxom, willing women. It was not something that should bother her. He was simply her protector and might yet become her lover, a man who was helping her get to her family and safety while showing her all about passion. But it did bother her. A lot. That was not good for it implied that she felt a lot more for him than gratitude or lust, saw him as far more than an honorable man and one of a clan that was helping to keep her and her boys alive until they could be

safely placed under the protection of her family.
She could not allow herself to become entangled
with a man.

"Aha!" The woman slapped him on the shoulder.
"Sir Brian."

"Verra good, Molly." Brian grinned. "'Tis nay so
verra easy to tell us all apart."

"Nay, true enough. There are a lot of ye lads and
ye are all, to a mon, big, handsome devils. I am
thinking your fither left a verra strong mark on all
of ye, aye?"

"Aye, he surely did."

"Just how many of ye are there? More than those
rogues the Camerons?"

"A lot more. The old Cameron laird died after
breeding a mere dozen or so but our fither is still
verra much alive." He winked at her.

Molly laughed, a loud, raucous sound, and
slapped Sir Brian on the arm again. "Rogues. Naught
but a lot of handsome rogues. Ye lot and those thrice-
cursed Camerons. So, ye will be wanting my best
room, aye?"

"Aye, I would and, Molly? If anyone comes looking for us, we are nay here and ye have ne'er set
eyes on us."

She nodded. "Helped yourself to someone's
daughter, have ye?"

Arianna was just opening her mouth to answer
what she saw as a slur upon Sir Brian's honor when
he gripped her arm so tightly she feared there would
be bruises left behind. She understood the silent
warning. What she did not understand was why he
would want the woman to think he was such a man,
one who would spirit away someone's daughter for a

tryst at a lowly inn. Unless he *was* such a man, she thought, and scowled at him. He did not see her disapproval, however, for his gaze was fixed upon Molly. Since she had already decided a MacFingal could not be constant, the one thing she would insist upon if she ever became interested in marriage again, she was also being very contrary to take umbrage at Molly implying the same thing. Arianna inwardly shrugged, and scowled at him again.

"Any Frenchmen come here, Molly my beauty, and I want to ken about it."

"If ye havenae already slipped away, eh? Weel, best ye pay me all I will be due right now. I am getting too old to be chasing young laddies down the road. The will is there but nay the strength." She slapped her knee and laughed.

A look of confusion and then anger passed over Sir Brian's face before he joined in with Molly's laughter. Arianna recognized that look. She had seen it often enough on the faces of her kinsmen. Sir Brian had just heard something he had not understood, had thought it over, guessed what was meant, and was not at all pleased. Some of Sir Brian's brothers were probably going to get a hard lesson when he next saw them. She ignored how relieved she was over the indication that Sir Brian was not some lecher who made regular visits to the inn with a different lady on his arm every time.

When the woman named her price, Arianna was prepared to call it nothing less than base thievery. But then Sir Brian laughed, flung his arm around the woman's wide shoulders, and began to bargain with her with a skill that many of her kinswomen would have envied. It quickly became evident that this was exactly what the woman wanted and thoroughly enjoyed.

It also became quickly evident that Molly considered Arianna of as little interest as she did the packs Sir Brian carried. She did not know whether to be amused or insulted and decided she was a little bit of both. The MacFingal *laddies* obviously used this inn as a trysting site with some regularity even if Sir Brian did not. Molly had decided that Arianna was just another woman one of the MacFingals would enjoy for a little while and then blithely discard.

The room they were led to came as a pleasant surprise to Arianna. The inn looked worn on the outside, but Molly clearly took great pride in keeping the inside very clean and well appointed. There was a large, high bed with ample pillows and linen, plus two chairs and a table set before a small fireplace. A wooden privacy screen in the corner undoubtedly held what was needed to clean up, perhaps even the chamber pot.

"A maid will be up soon as I have requested a bath," said Brian as he put his packs down on the bed.

"A real bath? Heated water and all?" Arianna wanted to push him down onto the bed and kiss him senseless.

"Aye." He grinned. "Molly drove a hard bargain for it but I thought we both deserved one. All I ask is that ye dinnae linger until the water chills."

"Nay, I swear I shall leave ye some of that heat." She looked around the room and then frowned. "Where will the bath go?"

"Right before the fireplace. As soon as it is brought

up, I will go down to see about a hot meal and give ye some privacy."

Even as she was thanking him there was a rap at the door. A boy entered with the round wooden tub followed by two maids with buckets of heated water. It was obvious that Molly kept some water readied for such requests.

"I believe Molly must get enough of my brothers and cousins here to ken that having water ready for a bath is worth the trouble," Brian whispered in her ear. "The woman kens how to keep those who use her inn coming back time and time again."

"Verra wise."

It took several trips by the maids to fill the tub, and Arianna was doing her best not to get impatient. The moment they set two buckets of water in front of the fireplace so that extra heated water could be added or some could be used to rinse, Arianna began to unlace her gown. When the door shut behind them, she almost tore her clothes off. A sigh of pleasure escaped her as she sank her body into the hot water. It had been too long since she had enjoyed a hot bath.

Despite the temptation of it, she savored the way the heat eased all the aches in her body for just a short time and then began to wash. She scrubbed her hair until it squeaked, wrapped it in a large drying cloth, and then began to scrub the dust of travel from her body. There was no denying how much she had missed pampering herself in such a way, and she promised herself that she would do very little traveling after this journey was at an end.

Realizing that some of the heat was already fading from the water, she climbed out of the tub and dried herself off. Since she would have to allow Brian the same privacy he had allowed her, she dressed in the gown Brian had bought for her in the last village. Once he was done, she would wash the one she had been wearing in the bath before it was emptied. She was in the midst of rubbing her hair dry when a rap came at the door.

"'Tis Brian, Arianna."

"Come in. There is an extra bucket of heated water by the fire," she said as he came into the room. "I used the other one to rinse with. I will go into the hall while you bathe."

He frowned. "I am nay sure that is a good idea."

"I will stay right outside the door." She extracted a comb from the pack. "It will take me a while to do my hair. That will keep me busy and I will be close enough for ye to hear me if there is trouble."

Brian did not have a good argument against her plan so he let her go. He firmly told himself that Molly would never allow anyone to drag Arianna away without at least making an uproar. After assuring himself that she was staying just outside the door, he stripped off his clothes and climbed into the tub. He washed his hair and bathed as quickly as he could, not wishing to leave her alone and unguarded for long.

It was not until he was dressing that he looked around the room, at the one bed, and knew it was going to be a very long night. After the talk they had when she had fled his arms for the second time, neither of them had mentioned the incident again. There would have been some awkwardness if they had not been working so hard to stay out of Amiel's clutches. There had been little time for rest, let alone kissing or talking. Now, however, they were both clean, would soon have full bellies, and then they would be climbing into the same bed.

He wondered if she had thought about all he had said. Brian wanted to believe he had been clear spoken and his words wise but he was not sure of that. Attempting to convince a woman that she was beautiful and desirable when she had been told for years that she was not was not easy. He had certainly never confronted such a problem before despite having knowledge of how damaging words could be. If he were wise, he would get another room so that he did not have to spend the night sharing a bed with a woman he desired and could not touch.

There was no other choice, he decided, after considering it for a moment longer. He had to keep her close to him to be able to keep her safe. Brian only briefly considered sleeping on the floor. After days of sleeping on the hard ground he was not about to give up the chance to sleep in a bed. If she insisted on keeping some distance between them, he could roll up the blankets and place them between their bodies. He could only pray that he could get some sleep with her so close at hand yet so unreachable.

The moment he let her into the room, she hurried to rinse out their clothing. She was draping their wet clothes over the chairs she had set before the fire when the boy and the maids returned to empty the bath. As he sat beside Arianna on the bed watching her braid her hair, he tried to sense if she was nervous or afraid. When all he could see in her face and posture was a quiet contentment, he began to relax. She might not be ready to let him become her lover but at least she was not going to cause any trouble about them sharing the room. He was getting a little weary of suffering for that idiot Claud's many sins against her.

As soon as the youth carried away the now empty bath, two maids arrived with the food Brian had ordered. The scent of warm bread and roasted chicken made his stomach growl. Brian smiled faintly when Arianna laughed and then he dragged the table over to the side of the bed.

"I didnae think on how we would have need of those chairs for our meal," Arianna said as Brian sliced off large pieces of the chicken and set them on her plate.

"Our clothes needed the washing. Eat up, love. We will be back to oatcakes and the occasional rabbit all too soon." He grinned when she groaned but then turned his full attention to his meal, unable to ignore the needs of his stomach any longer.

Arianna looked at her shift and sighed, then hoped that Brian could not hear her behind the privacy screen where she had gone to change for bed. The worn, roughly mended shift was not something to wear to entice a man—even if she knew how to be enticing. The only improvement in her appearance for days was that she was clean. She now wished she had saved the plain linen shift Brian had bought along with the extra gown instead of immediately donning it. It might be a very plain shift, but it was unstained and not mended.

She shrugged. It was all she had and she would not allow that to stop her. Tonight, in that big soft bed, she intended to conquer her fears, to silence Claud's insidious whispers in her mind. Arianna knew it was too soon to completely banish the man and rid herself of his poison, but she could prove to herself that the one who had failed in their marriage bed had been Claud, not her. It did not matter that the whole marriage was a lie, for that did not change how he had left her believing that she was a failure in the art of love. Tonight she intended to find out if that was true. Taking a deep breath to shore up her courage, she stepped out from behind the screen and started to walk toward the bed.

The sight of Brian already in the bed, propped up by pillows, his broad chest bared to her view, made her steps falter. Arianna tried not to stare at his chest but it was hard to resist. The man had a broad chest taut with muscle and adorned with only a small patch of dark hair. His skin was smooth and faintly swarthy in color. It also showed her that she was about to take on an awful lot of man as a lover. Someone so handsome and virile might not be the best choice for her first attempt to discover if she could be a passionate lover.

Stiffening her backbone and refusing to allow uncertainty to change her mind, she climbed into the bed. Lying close by Brian's side, she imitated his pose and stared up at the ceiling. Now all she had to do was say something that would let him know she was ready to test the passion that flared between them. Unfortunately, her mind offered her not one suggestion. She had never really requested Claud's attentions and lying on her back staring up at the ceiling was all he had ever really required of her.

Arianna decided that she could lie there all night staring at the ceiling, her mind empty of any clear yet subtle hint of willingness she could give Brian, or she could act. A timid part of her whispered a third choice, that she could just forget the whole thing. Arianna ignored that timid side of herself, rolled onto her side and came face-to-face with Brian. She had been so lost in her own thoughts that she had never felt him turn toward her.

"I have been thinking about what ye said, ye ken, that last time we kissed and I, weel . . ."

"Ran away?" Brian fought down the eagerness he could feel building inside, the anticipation that had his body already taut with need.

"Weel, aye." Arianna reached out to stroke the broad, smooth chest she could not stop admiring. The way his skin felt beneath her hand sent a shiver of delight through her.

"I remember it all verra weel. Have ye decided ye will now cast off the chains Claud wrapped ye up in?" In his head, Brian was close to begging that that was so.

"Aye, but . . ."

He wrapped his arms around her and pulled her close. "Nay, dinnae say *but*. Dinnae torment a poor mon, love. Aye or nay."

"Aye, but when we are done, if I do it all wrong or verra badly, can ye just politely tell me what I did wrong and how I might improve?" She knew any criticism, any cold words from him, would crush her.

"'Tis clear there are a few chains left to shake off. Love, ye may lack a skill or two yet but I doubt ye can do this badly. I have tasted the passion ye have inside. Ye just have to set it free."

Before she could argue that and tell him that it could not be that easy, he kissed her. Arianna sank into his arms without hesitation. The fact that she loved his kisses, reveled in the heat of them, was one reason she now dared to go further than kisses. She stroked his broad shoulders and back and beneath her hands the heat of his skin sank into her, warming her blood. By the time he broke off the kiss, she was so swept up in the desire racing through her that it took her a moment to be aware of the fact that he was yanking her shift off her.

"Ye wish me to be naked?" she asked, and wondered if she had truly just heard him call Claud a horse's arse. "Are ye certain I should be naked?"

"Aye, I want ye naked and I want me naked. I want us skin to skin. I want to feel your soft heat touching me everywhere it can touch me."

"Oh."

She was flushed with an odd mixture of embarrassment and anticipation. He tossed aside her shift and slowly pulled her into his arms. Fear crept in when he stared at her naked body and she fought it, seeing no condemnation in his gaze. She dared not trust her own judgment in thinking he looked hungry for her, even approving what he saw, but the lack of cold dislike in his gaze was enough to ease the fear that was trying to chill the warmth of her desire.

When their flesh touched, she shuddered from the pleasure of it. He was hard muscle covered with surprisingly soft skin. Arianna wanted to rub herself all over him.

"Oh," she whispered again. "Oh, my."

He laughed against her throat but his amusement

rapidly faded beneath a pounding urge to taste, to touch, and to possess. Brian fought to control the need tearing at him. Arianna needed more than some frantic coupling. She might not be a virgin but she was wounded in heart and mind. He had to make absolutely certain that her desire was stirred into a greedy fever and that she was fully aware of the fact that he burned as she did. Even though he doubted his skill at such things, he also knew that he had to give her a lot of flattering words, praise for her beauty, and her passion. Claud had given her nothing but insult and humiliation, and Brian was determined to keep the man's cursed ghost from sharing this bed with them.

Arianna could not catch her breath. She was panting like a hard-run hunting dog. Beneath Brian's caresses her flesh burned. When he stroked the aching tip of her breasts with his tongue, she barely stopped herself from screeching in shock at the pure heat it sent through her body. She did not have to urge him to do it again, which was good, for she was unable to speak coherently. Instead she wove her fingers through his soft, thick hair and held him close as he licked, nipped, and suckled her breasts until she thought she would go mad from the pleasure it brought her. He kept telling her how good she tasted, how soft her skin was, how much he wanted her, and even how beautiful her breasts were, his words stirring her as much as his touch. The almost constant sound of his deep voice held her entranced and, even though she doubted the truth of his flattery, it pleased her.

The tension of what she now recognized as her need for him curled hot and tight in her belly. When

Brian slid his hand between her thighs she fleetingly stiffened, uncertain about the intimate caress she had never experienced before. He said nothing about the reddish curls sheltering her womanhood, only murmured compliments about the heat she was gifting him with. The way he stroked her, dipping his finger in and out of her in imitation of what he would soon do with the hard length he rubbed against her thigh, had her arching into his touch. And still she wanted, needed, more.

It was not until he began to join their bodies that a little of passion's haze began to clear from her mind. With Claud this was what had been the most tedious and embarrassing part and the one that had then become painful. She had barely begun to go rigid, bracing herself for the stinging pain, when Brian was inside her. Arianna blinked in surprise, holding very still until she was certain that there had been no pain and would be no pain.

When he rose up on his forearms and touched his lips to hers, Arianna flung her arms around his neck and kissed him with all the passion swirling inside her, and a touch of gratitude. He thrust his tongue into her mouth, stroking her with his tongue in the same rhythm he used to move his body in and out of hers. She was filled with him, stretched further to hold him than she had ever been with Claud, yet there was still no pain. He tugged her legs around his waist and she gasped in delight as he plunged even deeper within her.

She could hear herself making soft noises as he moved within her, rubbing against her where their bodies were joined in a way that increased the pleasure he was giving her. The knot low in her belly grew tighter and tighter with each thrust of his body until it was nearly painful. She was just beginning to wonder if she could ever make love without pain when that knot snapped, filling her veins, her heart, even her mind with the purest bliss. Arianna was faintly aware that she called out his name. A heartbeat later, he thrust deeply, held fast there inside her, and his body shuddered as he spilled his seed.

Though weak, in a way she thoroughly enjoyed, Arianna held him close and savored the lingering flush of pleasure. She liked the damp warmth of his breath against the curve of her neck, liked the damp touch of sweat coating his broad back, and especially liked the faint trembling that afflicted him for several moments after he collapsed in her arms. With Claud she had been glad when he had abruptly left her arms, but she wanted to cling to Brian, wanted to hold him deep inside her for as long as possible.

This was what the women in her clan had sighed over, had tried to get her to understand. This was passion, that deep, wild hunger that her husband had never given her. Even better, this was a passion that was shared. She suspected she was not completely free of her doubts that she could please a man, but for right now she was certain that the man in her arms had been pleasured most thoroughly. The cure for the wounds Claud had given her was probably not complete but she did not care for she was certain that the healing had begun. If she was not so tired she could not even keep her eyes open to appreciate the beauty of the man sprawled in her arms, she would have gotten up to dance around the room.

"I did weel, aye?" she whispered as she allowed exhaustion to finally claim her.

Brian slipped from her lax hold and dragged himself out of bed to fetch a damp cloth. Once he had cleaned them both off, he crawled back into bed and pulled her into his arms. He took a moment to enjoy the sight of her naked body from the fullness of her rose-tipped breasts to the gentle curve of her waist. He especially liked the lean strength of her legs. Even more so when they were wrapped around him, that strength used to hold him close while he buried himself deep within her wet heat.

It was hard to understand how a woman like her could think herself unable to please any man she chose to gift with her favors. Her passion ran hot and wild once she stopped running from it. Claud had tried to kill that sweet heat, left it unsatisfied and then denigrated her. If the man were not already dead, Brian would have been willing to go to France to kill him.

He touched a kiss to the top of her head and smiled against her silken hair. "Och, aye, love. Ye did weel. Verra weel indeed," he murmured before allowing himself to follow her into sleep.

Chapter 7

Arianna woke to soft, warm lips upon her cheek and a big calloused hand stroking her breast. For a moment, she thought herself back in her marriage bed but then the last dregs of sleep released her mind. Claud had never been affectionate like this. Her eyes widened as she abruptly recalled everything that had happened before she had fallen asleep.

She was curled up in bed with Sir Brian MacFingal, naked and wrapped in his arms. She had taken a lover. She had taken a big, strong, handsome lover many women would envy her for. She had also enjoyed every minute of it. That still astonished her as much as it pleased her right down to her toes. Claud had been very wrong. She was not cold.

Even as she began to smile, fear crept in, rapidly dimming her pleasure. Arianna could not deny that she had finally tasted that pleasure her kinswomen all talked about, but had Sir Brian really experienced the same pleasure? She had felt him spill his seed inside her but Claud had done the same.

When she had foolishly given her opinion that that showed he had found pleasure with her, he had laughed. Claud had then told her that a man could rut with a hole in the ground, which he had said was a good thing for she was not much livelier. Had she misjudged the depth of the pleasure Brian had experienced?

When those soft, warm lips touched the corner of her mouth, she recalled something else Claud had often said. She had once attempted to kiss him in the morning upon awakening and he had roughly pushed her away, claiming that in the morning she had breath akin to the bottom of a garderobe shaft. Arianna clapped a hand over her mouth and pulled away from Brian.

Brian tensed and looked at Arianna where she now balanced precariously on the far edge of the bed. His annoyance over what had appeared to be a rejection despite all they had shared before falling asleep turned to confusion as he studied her. She did not look as if she now regretted what they had shared, nor did she look angry. She looked nervous and just a little afraid, rather like someone who expects some sort of blow to fall at any moment.

"What is wrong?" he asked, fighting the urge to reach for her for, if she backed away again, she would topple right out of bed and onto the floor. He was also getting tired of the way she kept fleeing his arms.

"I need to clean my teeth," she said, her hand still over her mouth muffling her words.

"Why? Ye did it ere ye climbed into bed and ye havenae eaten anything since then."

"'Tis needed. Claud said I had foul breath in the morning."

"Nay, ye dinnae." If Claud were not already dead and buried, Brian thought yet again, he would gladly kill the fool, but only after beating him soundly first.

"How could ye ken whether I do or nay? We have-nae kissed. Claud ne'er kissed me in the morning if we woke together for he said that my breath when I first woke rivaled the stench of the garderobe."

"Claud was an idiot. Ye were sleeping with your mouth open, lass. If ye had breath that foul I was close enough that I would have smelled it. When will ye believe that the mon was probably angry that he didnae have the courage to tell his family the truth, that he had gotten himself caught up in a tangle of lies, and 'tis verra clear from all ye tell me about him that he wasnae a mon to shoulder his own blame. So, he spat his anger out at ye. I cannae say it enough. That was all it was, lies meant to beat ye down."

"He ne'er hit me," she said, cautiously remov-ing her hand from her mouth.

"Aye, he did, and weel ye ken it, though ye seem to forget it quickly. All my words of wisdom cast aside like sad refuse," he murmured, and almost smiled at her glare for it showed she still had her spirit. "He struck out at ye often, I am thinking. With words. Ye ken weel that they can hurt and scar as easily as fists."

Arianna stared at him as she thought over what he had said. She had been casting his words from her mind, not really thinking much on them. Words *could* scar. She knew that in her mind, but deep in her heart Brian's wise words had not yet taken hold. Constant criticisms could beat one down as thoroughly as fists. Claud was always criticizing her when he was not ignoring her or burdening her with all the work he should have been doing himself. The way he had so flagrantly favored his mistress over his wife had also left its scars, if only because such actions silently strengthened every criticism he had flung at her. Arianna was not sure how she could heal those scars for his sharp insults and unending criticisms still whispered through her mind. She had, after all, thought she had cured herself of Claud's criticism of her worth in the bedchamber yet, with the rising of the sun, had fallen into the same old trap.

"Are ye certain he lied?" she asked, tentatively moving closer to him.

"Jesu, lass, I would tell ye if it was so bad that ye should clean your teeth ere I kiss ye. Foul breath in the morning curses us all from time to time and 'tis nay something to fret o'er but, I swear to ye, yours isnae foul."

Brian pulled her into his arms and kissed her. She tensed as if she feared he would begin to gag and push her away, but quickly softened in his arms. The way she fit so snugly there, her silken flesh warm against his skin, had him hard and hungry for more of what they had shared last night. When she twined her slim arms around his neck and pressed her lithe body even closer, he decided there was no harm in lingering in bed for a while longer.

His body soon let him know that there would be no lingering. Despite his efforts to control his desire, it rose up fast and greedy. To his delight so did Arianna's. Her body welcomed him with all the heat any man could want. He could sense her pleasure in her every sigh as he drove them both to passion's heights. They reached that pinnacle together, her husky voice crying out his name music to his ears as he emptied himself inside her.

It was a long time before he found the strength to pull away from her. The heat of her surrounding him and the way she idly caressed his body with her small, soft hands, as if she truly liked the feel of him, had him eager to remain joined with her. That need had never been there with any other woman and Brian knew he should seriously consider what that meant. Later, he thought, as he gave her a quick kiss and moved to get out of bed.

In truth, it did not really matter if he ever sorted out all he was feeling for Lady Arianna Murray Lucette. She was not for him. She was better born and far richer than he was, used to the finer life he and his kinsmen were only beginning to see glimmers of. The widow of a French *comte,* a woman born of a clan connected in some way to half the clans in Scotland, both notorious and influential, was too high a reach for one of the youngest of the eleven legitimate sons of Fingal MacFingal. It was true that his brother Gregor had married a Murray, but Alanna had been a maid and they had traveled together. The need to honor her with marriage after that overcame any other considerations as to whether Gregor was worthy of the lass or not. Arianna was a widow and those demands would not be directed at him when he finally got her settled with her family. There was no maidenhead to be lost here.

He grimaced as he slipped behind the privacy screen to wash up and relieve himself. His clan was a jest in many ways, made up of his father and all the sons he had bred in and out of the marriage bed. It was the result of a man being angry with his true family and clan and, like some spoiled child, deciding to make his own. The only claim to fame they might have was that his father was a prodigious breeder of sons. The acknowledgment of their ability as fighters was growing, but slowly, and it did not even begin to equal the place of honor so many Murrays held. Considering how many of his brethren acted, they were more notorious than honored.

No, Lady Arianna was not for him. Brian just wished that he did not want her so badly. He had the brief thought that he could probably tie her to his side with the passion they shared, or even a child, but quickly shook it aside. Her clan had already climbed free of the mire of their rough beginnings. He could not drag her down into that again and it would be a long time before his clan got much beyond the struggle to just survive. He was going to have to keep their affair no more than a sharing of pleasure, and keep his heart from yearning for more. The problem was, he feared he was already far past that.

The moment Brian stepped out from behind the privacy screen, Arianna dashed behind it. She had donned the shirt he had given her for it was easier to find than the shift he had tossed aside in the night, but it was not very modest since it barely reached her knees. Then she realized it was more than simple modesty that made her rush to hide behind the screen, that she feared he would retreat from her once he clearly saw how little her thin body offered a man. A man liked rounded curves, flesh on a woman's bones to cushion his body, and found the reddish hair covering her privates to be common and gaudy.

She softly cursed. It was Claud whispering his denigrations in her head again. She had never been vain but she had always believed herself to be moderately appealing to a man's eyes. Until Claud. Until he had found fault with everything from her face to her feet, some of the criticisms poorly disguised as kindly suggestions on how she might improve herself. By the time she had caught her first sight of the buxom Marie Anne, Arianna had been quick to see just how much she lacked compared to her husband's mistress. It had also given his family and his people all the excuse they needed to show her their scorn. Brian had now seen her naked and she had seen no hint of the disdain Claud had always shown her, but the fear of it lingered.

What had she allowed him to do to her? Arianna began to think that the scars his cruel words had left ran far, far deeper than she had believed. It was embarrassing to realize how much she had let him say to her without retribution, and how much of it she had taken to heart. She should have been stronger than that, should have believed more strongly in her own worth. What frightened her was that, if she did not hold a strong belief in her own worth, how would she find the strength to rid herself of Claud's poison?

Even worse, if she did not believe in her own worth, how could she hold fast to a man like Sir Brian MacFingal? And she admitted to herself that she did want to hold on to him, tightly. For a moment she feared she was letting her first taste of passion trick her into thinking there was more to what she felt for him than lust, and then she shook that doubt aside. What she felt for the man had been born from the moment she had opened her eyes on that beach and looked into his. Everything that had happened since then had only strengthened it.

"So much for keeping my distance and allowing this to be no more than a simple affair," she whispered angrily as she finished relieving herself and then began to wash up.

"Are ye all right?" asked Brian.

"Aye, just talking to myself. I will be ready in a few moments."

Brian frowned at the screen. He had not been able to understand what she had said but the anger behind the words had been clear. Anger was not what he wanted her to be feeling after they had made love. Before he could ask her what she was angered by, a loud banging came at the door.

"Frenchmen, Sir Brian," said Molly the moment he opened the door.

"At the inn?" He moved to pack their things, already planning how to slip away.

"Will be soon. My youngest lad came to tell me they were asking for a good inn to stay at and had been directed here."

"Ye have a back way out of here?"

"I do, and I have already told the lads to have your horses readied and waiting for ye behind the stables." She glanced at Arianna as she ran out from behind the screen still lacing up her gown. "This is about more than ye taking some lass for a wee bit of pleasure, isnae it?"

"A lot more, but I havenae the time to tell ye. 'Tis life or death, hers and two wee laddies. I would suggest that ye keep those burly lads of yours close and armed. This isnae some group of simple travelers."

"That be what my lad said as he wasnae sure we would be wanting them staying here. Come with me. I will show ye the best way to slip out of here."

Brian grabbed a pale Arianna by the hand, cast a last longing look at the bed, and followed Molly. He had hoped they could rest for a little while. He had also hoped to savor Arianna's passion in the comfort of a bed a few more times, if only to make it very clear to her that she was not only desirable, she also satisfied him.

In truth, she satisfied him in ways he had never felt before. Not only did she stir his desire to heights it had never reached in another woman's arms, she left him far more sated than any other had, too. Brian knew it was going to be very hard to let that go.

As they slipped through the back garden of the inn and to the rear of the stables, Brian could hear the voices of Amiel's men. The stable boys were clearly trying to delay the men, holding them outside the stable with a long, torturous bargaining over the cost of caring for so many horses. He was tempted to go and see what he might learn, but one look at the fear on Arianna's face had him pushing that idea aside. He could not take the risk when she was so close to her enemies.

He kissed Molly on the cheek and then lifted Arianna up into the saddle as he said, "I thank ye, Molly.

Best ye get back inside the inn to greet your new guests."

"Aye. Dinnae worry. If ye can slip out of town without them seeing ye, ye should be safe for a while. Sent one of my lads to tell a few maids that there was a party of rich Frenchmen here. I am thinking those men will soon be too busy to come a-hunting ye and the lass."

Brian chuckled and began to lead Arianna on a winding route that kept them sheltered by the buildings. As long as he and Arianna could get away without any of Amiel's men catching sight of them, they would have time to put some distance between themselves and their pursuers. He was a little surprised they had stopped for a rest when it was so early in the day. It was an action that confirmed his fear that Amiel knew where he was headed, was not tracking them as much as hoping to get between them and where they needed to go. The man was treating it all more like a journey to visit someone than the hunt it really was.

When the line of buildings ran out, Brian paused, leaning over the neck of his mount to look up and down the street. They would be in the open for a while and he needed to make certain none of Amiel's men were on the watch for them. What he saw made him grin.

At least eight women, dressed in all the finery a poor whore could afford, were gathered near the stables, flaunting their wares. The men who had not yet entered the inn were all watching the women, some already making their choices clear. Brian just wished the women would get the men inside the inn quickly.

"Are they watching for us?" asked Arianna.

"Nay. They are watching the women Molly sent her son to fetch. A bonnie little flock of birds. I but wait to see if they can get all the men to go inside the inn. If they dinnae do so soon, we shall have to take our chances and go that last distance to the trees anyway."

"I ne'er would have thought of such a thing as a distraction. Especially not when 'tis barely the middle of the day."

"Time doesnae matter to a hungry mon, lass." He grinned when she made a soft sound of disgust. "I but keep wondering why Amiel has stopped so early in the day."

"He probably just wants a good meal and a bath. Now that he kens who ye are and where ye may be going, he thinks he can take this journey at a leisurely pace. Amiel ne'er liked to do anything that appeared to be work."

"Ah, one of those men who craves the title but expects everyone else to do the work that comes with the privilege. It looks as if the lasses have finally convinced the men that they will get better service inside the inn. I suspicion Molly told her lad to ask the ladies to do that."

"Why would she have to ask? Where else would they be able to service the men?"

"In the stable, in the stable yard, in the alley, or near anywhere else where they might stand, sit, or lie." He glanced at her blush-reddened face and grinned. "I think ye have been verra sheltered, love." He looked back toward the men. "The last of them has been dragged inside. Best we move. I would love to just gallop out of here but there may yet be one sharp-eyed fellow amongst Amiel's men, and two people galloping out of town would draw attention."

The next few minutes were the longest Arianna had ever suffered through, at least since she had been in the water clinging to a keg. She sat tensely on her mount, expecting a cry of discovery to go up every step of the way. By the time they reached the shelter of the trees, she ached from sitting so stiffly in her saddle. She gritted her teeth when Brian began to kick his mount into a faster speed, and followed his lead. Galloping over the countryside was not what she had planned to do today but she would endure.

She prayed those women kept Amiel and his men very busy but did not suffer for doing so. If Amiel even thought he had been tricked, he could turn vicious, and attack the women, Molly, and her sons. It would be a sad way to reward Molly for all her help.

The thought of those women made her recall what Brian had said about where the women could entertain the men. Arianna began to realize that, although her kinswomen had hid nothing about the ways of men and women in marriage, she had been allowed little other knowledge. She had known that her brothers and male cousins went into the village to dally with the maids, but the few times she had thought on it, she had envisioned rooms and beds as the places where the dallying occurred. It was obvious that she still had a lot to learn about the world.

It was late in the day before Brian allowed them to stop for a rest. He had wanted to use the hours Amiel and his men might spend at the inn to get as far away from the man as possible. It would be better if the man decided to stay the night at Molly's inn but

Brian knew he could not count on that. Amiel could have simply stopped for a meal or an ale before planning to continue on. There was only one thing Brian could be sure of and that was that Amiel would get no useful information from anyone at Molly's. Even if the woman did not have some affection for his clan or Sigimor's, she would never betray regular paying customers.

He watered the horses and then took out the small sack of food Molly had stuck in his pack before joining Arianna where she had collapsed on the ground beneath a tree. "Nay much farther, love, and ye will be able to rest for more than a night."

"In a true bed?"

"Aye, in a true bed. And ye can have yourself another bath without worrying about leaving some of the heated water for me."

"I would like to sleep, just sleep, for a few days." She sat up straighter and began to eat the food he had placed in her lap. "S'truth, I have badly wished to do that since I first kenned that my lads were in danger on Tillet's ship and began keeping a close watch on them."

"Ye can get some sleep at Dubheidland although I am nay sure it can be several days' worth."

"Are ye certain your cousin willnae object to our staying there, especially when we are bringing this trouble with us? This isnae his fight."

"Lucette wants to kill two bairns simply to fill his purse. Trust me in this, Sigimor will want the mon dead for that alone."

Arianna nodded. She recognized such a man. Her kinsmen would feel the same. It would not even matter if the man were an ally or an enemy, simply that he meant to hurt children because of greed. She had heard a few odd tales about the laird of Dub-heidland, ones told her kin by her cousin Alanna and then told to her in what few letters she had received from her family. At least the Lucettes had allowed her to receive those letters, she thought bitterly, wondering if they had read them all and then destroyed ones they didn't like, just as they had done with the ones she had tried to send those she loved.

Then she tensed. "Brian, I think I have an idea on how Amiel kens where we might go, how he might not need but a whisper of our passing to ken who we might try to get help from."

"I suspect it is because he has the coin to loosen a few tongues. I fear there are many in this part of the country who ken us weel, the MacFingals and the Camerons."

"Do ye recall how we thought the Lucettes read the letters I wanted to send to my kin, destroying any they thought were too critical of them?" Arianna could tell by the dark look growing on Brian's face that he was already seeing what she just had. "What if they also read all the ones my kin sent to me, if only to be certain they destroyed any they believed could cause some trouble for them? Ones that might ask me to come home for some reason or ones asking when they might visit me. Or they looked for information on my family, mayhap to find a way to get some more money from them."

"And thus they would ken every place ye had kin or allies, or nearly so. That is, if the ones who wrote to ye would speak of such things, tell ye what tales they have heard of concerning other kin and allies."

"Ye mean they would gossip." She grinned briefly.

"'Tis what it is. And, aye, near all my kin love to tell tales. That is another reason your name and the Camerons seemed so familiar to me. The Mac-Enroys, as weel." She sighed. "My family wished me to ken where everyone was and so 'tis verra possible that whoever read my letters has learned it, too. A lot of information about my clan and all we are allied with was in those letters. Amiel was always around and, as Claud's affair with Marie Anne continued, the elder Lucettes became more and more disgusted with their heir. If Amiel began to aid them in keeping a close eye upon what news passed between me and my kin, then . . ."

"Amiel learned about us all and but needed a few clever judgments as to who ye were with."

She rested her head against the rough trunk of the tree. "I suppose Amiel could have a cunning that I ne'er noticed before."

Brian nodded and finished his food as he thought over the possibility that the men hunting for Arianna and the boys had come with knowledge of the places she would try to run to. If Amiel had had a plan to murder his brother for a long time, it made sense that the man would learn all he could about his brother's wife. Yet Brian did not think Amiel had plotted against his brother for that long. The man he had watched in the inn did not have that sort of patience. That meant that Amiel had simply taken advantage of information already collected on Arianna and the Murrays.

The reason for the collection of such information on allies was varied and none of them revealing anything laudable about the family Arianna had married into. None of the reasons mattered at the moment, either. All that was important was that Amiel and the DeVeaux knew too much. He and Arianna could evade the men pursuing them, but never fully shake free of them.

"Ye are verra quiet," she said, watching him closely. "I am sorry. None of us saw any reason to be verra cautious."

He took her hand in his and kissed her palm. "Ye have naught to apologize for. The Lucettes are allies and ye all thought the family of your husband would be safe. Why wouldnae ye be free in what ye said to each other?"

"In a way I can understand why they carefully watched what I said to my family, mayhap e'en why they watched what my kin said to me. Yet, why make a record of it all as I begin to think they did? What need would they have had to keep such information at hand?"

"They may nay have had any true plan for its use, just a wee thought that it might be useful at some time. Whatever plan they had doesnae matter now. 'Tis Amiel's knowledge of it all that we must consider now."

"We cannae lose him. I suspicion your kinsmen cannae lose the ones after them, either."

Brian wrapped his arm around her shoulders and pulled her close to him. "My kinsmen will be fine. They may ne'er lose the ones on their trail, but they can and will evade and outrun them. As can we. My kin have something we dinnae have as weel, something that gives them an advantage."

"Oh, aye? And what would that be?"

"More men."

"Ah, true. Would it help if we hired more men? I

can afford it. Weel, once I am back with my clan and can get some coin in my hands, I can."

"I did think on that, but nay. We are verra close to Dubheidland. Best if we continue as we have. I still believe we have a better chance of slipping round these bastards if we are alone. I will be rid of the third horse once we reach Sigimor, though. I dinnae believe it fools anyone any longer."

"If they can send word to each other and ken all else we think they do, then nay, it doesnae fool them at all. They ken where the boys are being taken by now."

She shivered, and the way Brian held her a little tighter only slightly warmed the chill of fear. It was a fear that ran too deep to be banished. With each passing day, each new scrap of information on their enemies, her need to see Michel and Adelar grew until it was a sharp ache inside her. It was not just because she missed them, which she did, but a need to see with her own eyes that they were safe. She also needed to see that Scarglas could keep them safe. Although she trusted in Brian's word on that, her heart needed the proof her own eyes would give her.

"Dinnae worry so, love." Brian brushed a kiss over her mouth and stood up.

"Easier to say than to do," she muttered as she took hold of the hand he held out to her and let him tug her to her feet and into his arms. "'Tis hard for many to understand considering who Michel and Adelar are, but they are *my* boys."

"Ye had the raising of them, fostered them in many ways." He pressed a kiss to her forehead and then led her over to the horses. "Ye also have a heart too good to hold the wrongs their parents did to ye against them. It will nay be long now before ye are with them again, a sennight at most. There may e'en be word about them waiting at Dubheidland."

Arianna prayed there was. It would be enough for her to calm her fears about the boys for a while. Her arms ached to hold them, but if she knew for certain that they were safely behind the walls of Scarglas, she could endure their absence for a few days more.

Chapter 8

"Wait here, lass."

Arianna frowned at Brian as they both dismounted. "What do ye plan to do?"

"Slip into that wee village ahead and find someone to take word to your kinsmen," he replied.

"Ye think that must be done now?"

"Aye. There are ten men after us, lass. Ten. If they have sent an equal number in all three directions we tried to lead them in, then we have a small army running about the country hunting those lads of yours." He winced when she paled and wished he had held to his decision to keep that information from her.

She gasped and grasped him by the arms. "Michel and Adelar?"

"Are better protected than we are and, ye must trust me in this, lass, my family kens weel how to sneak about and hide themselves and anything of value they have, including other people. I can promise ye that verra soon after my kin rode away from that beach those lads wouldnae have been recognizable e'en to you and a plan was already made to hide them if the need arose. And do ye ken what else my kin can do verra weel?"

"What?" Arianna desperately wanted to believe him if only to push back the fear that was now making her thoughts scatter and her heart pound. "What can they do?"

"Fight." He kissed her on the forehead. "We survived for years surrounded by enemies, which my fither was verra skilled at making. Some of those enemies were verra determined to see us all dead. They failed. As my fither liked to say, he may nay have been the best of fithers and was a worse husband, but he had done a fine job of teaching his lads how to survive. And he did. We are all verra, verra good at it."

She rested her forehead against his chest for a moment as she finished beating down her fear for her boys. His plan had been a good one, still was a good one. The fact that there were a lot more men hunting her, Michel, and Adelar than they had believed did not change that. The utter confidence underlying his words helped her get control of her fear as well. She recognized that sort of arrogance for her kinsmen had it. Brian knew his strengths, his abilities, and those of his kinsmen. It was a good arrogance, too, for it was one that would not blind him to what he could *not* do, to what would be just reckless to even try.

Stepping back a little and releasing him, she took a deep breath, let it out slowly, and nodded. "Go then. Since I am nay sure of exactly where I am, I am nay sure which of my kin is the closest . . ."

"I am. Once Fiona let us ken who her clan was

allied with, we found out all we could about them."
He gave her a quick kiss. "I willnae be gone long."

"Just be careful."

She watched until he was out of sight. The ease
with which he disappeared into the shadows of the
scattered trees gave her even more confidence in
his assurances that he and his kin had the skills she
and the boys needed to stay alive. It was not easy to
understand the life he had led for it was so vastly
different from anything she had known, but she
could see that he spoke the truth. MacFingals knew
how to survive and treated a skill at stealth as just
one more weapon. Although her family had known
a reasonably peaceful life during much of her growing years, she suspected they had such skills as well.

Arianna turned her attention to the horses. It
had been a long, long day of riding hard, taking
tortuous routes, and hiding until it was safe to continue traveling. The time taken to send a message
to her kin was dangerous as they could not be certain just how close their enemy was, but it was necessary. They were going to need all the help they
could get to stop these men.

It appeared that Amiel and the DeVeaux had
brought a small army to hunt down her and the
boys. She should have known that but had never
taken much notice of how many men Amiel had
with him the few times she had seen them. Even if
she and her allies were able to cull those numbers,
Amiel and the DeVeaux had undoubtedly brought
enough coin with them to pay others to fight for
them. There were always plenty of men around
with no loyalties and an eagerness for coin.

The fact that she had dragged the MacFingals

into this battle made her feel so guilty it hurt, but she had had no choice. She believed Brian's assurances but, even knowing that the men were more than willing to help, it did not ease the guilt by much. If not for the children, she would have just fled on her own to her family. Unfortunately, the boys were the very reason she was even in this fight.

She also knew that, if caught, she could be used in an attempt to draw the boys into Amiel's hands. Everyone at Claud's holdings had known that she was more of a mother to those two boys than Marie Anne had ever been, in the eyes of Michel and Adelar as well as her own. Amiel gained nothing from hunting her save to use her as bait to entrap the boys. She doubted that the fact that the De-Veaux wanted her to exact an old vengeance against her family would matter all that much to him. The way she had thwarted his plans to kill the boys from the very beginning undoubtedly had added her to his list of ones he wanted dead, however.

It was difficult to understand the man. If he had just had a little patience she was certain the elder Lucettes, his and Claud's parents, would have succeeded in having the marriage of Claud and Marie Anne annulled, robbing the boys of all chance of inheriting anything. They just needed to pay the right people to see it done. The distaste many of the aristocracy would have for heirs who carried such common blood would also aid them. All Amiel had had to do was wait.

Unless, she mused, the man could not afford to wait. It all came back to whether or not Amiel was in debt to the DeVeaux. Those men could well have pushed him to act immediately once Claud was dead. That was somewhat reckless of the DeVeaux, who usually preferred more subtle, and deadly, ways of gaining what they wanted. Hunting two boys and a woman like hounds after a rabbit was not very subtle.

None of that mattered, she decided with a sigh. Once the game had begun it could not be ended. The crimes of Amiel and his DeVeaux allies were rapidly adding up. It was not easy to gain any justice when one accused a highborn man or woman of a crime, but the DeVeaux were no favorites if the king and the murder of a *comte*, an heir to even higher titles, was involved. Accusations, especially one of the murder of a very highborn Lucette, could prove costly to them. There was also the matter of sinking a ship.

Arianna cursed softly and rubbed her fingers over her temples. Just attempting to puzzle it all out was enough to make her head throb. Even though she saw it all as senseless, needless, and reckless, there could be any number of reasons for their actions, which Amiel and the DeVeaux would consider quite reasonable. In the end it did not truly matter why they were so intent upon killing two innocent children, just that they were. Every thought she had about being the DeVeaux's latest prey should only concern how to keep Michel and Adelar safe, as well as all of those who sought to help them.

Sitting on the ground near the horses, she decided that Brian's forays to look for the enemy or do something that might turn them off their trail were becoming more difficult to endure. Arianna did not like being left behind with the horses. She did not like being left alone while Brian was slipping about through the wood or creeping through villages doing what was needed to keep her alive and get her to a safe place. Arianna was not accustomed to feeling so helpless, so much like some useless, delicate maiden who could do no more than sit and wait for a man to save her. Or so much like a burden, she thought, wincing.

If her brothers or cousins found out, she would be tormented and teased by them. A Murray woman did not sit about like some helpless, spineless female without the wit to lace up her own chemise. Murrays were strong women, women who fought beside their men. They did not allow others to fight their battles for them while they huddled safe and hidden with the horses, she thought, leaping to her feet.

After taking three steps in the direction Brian had gone, Arianna cursed again and sat back down. Murray women also knew when to sit and wait even if they did not like it much. She had to just accept the fact that she did not have the skills that Brian did. Even more important, Amiel and the DeVeaux knew what she looked like and had undoubtedly described her very well to each one of their men. All they would need would be one glimpse of her and she would become no more than a sword at Brian's throat.

So she would sit and wait. And pray, because each time Brian left her sight she feared he would be hurt. Arianna did not want to think too hard on how she would feel if that happened, but did not really have to. The way her heart clenched at the mere thought of it told her all she needed to know. She was falling in love with the man, or already had. It was not something she wanted to look at too closely. Brian was kind to her, made love to her as she now knew a man should make love to a woman, but he spoke no words of love or even hinted at a future beyond that of getting her safely back to her kin.

For a moment she wondered if his kindness and the passion he made her feel were why she imagined herself in love with him. She had never experienced such things in her marriage and could be fooled. Then she shook her head. It was more, much more. What she was feeling for him went deep. Arianna feared that when he left her with her family and walked away he was going to be taking her heart with him.

Brian ignored the sultry invitation of the tavern maid as he made his deal with the young shepherd Tam. It had taken him longer than he liked to find someone he dared trust with a message to Arianna's kin. He had almost decided to wait until he got to Dubheidland. If Lucette and his men were not so close or so certain of where he was taking her, he would have. He suspected his family may have already done so but he could not be certain of that.

"Dinnae worry, mon," said Tam, who would be taking his wool to market soon and so made a perfect choice for a messenger. "I will be leaving here ere the sun rises and I will see that this gets into the hands of a Murray. I have dealt with them before, ye ken. They deal fair and always pay what be due me."

And that, thought Brian, was why he could trust this man. Such things were important to someone with goods to sell. A bribe came only the once but a man who bought your goods every season and paid well was not worth risking for that one brief moment of having a heavy purse. He gave Tam the message and counted out the coin promised into his dirty, heavily calloused hand.

"Beware Frenchmen," he warned again as the man gulped down the last of his ale.

"Wheesht, only a fool wouldnae do so."

Brian was still chuckling when the man left and the tavern maid sidled up to him again. She was pretty enough, fairly clean, and buxom, but he had no interest in her. He made that clear as gently as possible but there was still the hard glint of anger in her eyes when she finally walked away. As he finished his ale, he prayed Lucette did not stop here. Brian was not very concerned about his ability to evade the man but the maid had watched his dealings with the shepherd. He could only hope she had some loyalty to those in her own village.

He was slipping out of the village as easily as he had slipped in when he saw the shepherd ambling toward a small, worn cottage. After one quick glance at the man, which Tam returned with the same subtlety, Brian drawled, "I am thinking the maid in that tavern doesnae like to hear the word nay from a mon." He could tell by the way the man's body tensed that Tam understood the warning.

"Nay," replied Tam, never taking his gaze from the dirt path he walked. "My cousin is a vain bitch. Best someone reminds her what a sin that is."

Brian was a little surprised when Tam turned around and headed right back to the inn. He felt a little guilty that the girl might suffer from a harsh hand just because he was a suspicious sort, but shook the guilt aside. Tam had not questioned what Brian had meant and the man knew his cousin better than Brian did. And, if the woman said too much to the wrong people, it could not only put Lucette hard on his trail but it could get Tam killed.

He quickly continued sneaking out of the village, eager to get back to Arianna. It would be the last time he left her alone, he thought, even though he knew that might be a very hard vow to keep. Brian did not like leaving her behind with the horses, always too aware of how easily Lucette or one of his men could find her. Arianna was not completely helpless but she would be no match for a grown, armed man intent upon capturing her. Unfortunately, he could not take her with him on these small forays because she might be seen and her looks were the type people noticed and remembered.

Which made it so difficult to understand how she could have come to believe all the poisonous lies Claud had told her. Brian had to admit that he did not understand women very well. Arianna was beautiful yet saw nothing but faults when she looked at herself. It was similar to what his brother Ewan's wife Fiona had suffered. With her honey-gold hair and violet eyes, Fiona was a beauty yet she had fretted endlessly over the small scars marking each cheek. Ignorant men were the reason for that for the same ones who had once wooed Fiona had quickly turned from her when she was no longer perfect. With Arianna it had been but one ignorant man who believed he had the right to punish her for his own weaknesses. There were a lot of men out there who would be better for a sound beating, he decided.

It would gall him to have to do so, but Brian

wished there was someone who could give him some advice on a way he could make Arianna more confident in her worth. His cousin Liam came to mind as that man had been very skilled with women and with sweet words that left them smiling and flushed with pleasure. Unfortunately, Liam was now married, and to a Murray lass, worked his own lands, and probably had yet another child on the way. There was little chance that the man would be at Dubheidland.

So he would just have to keep making love to Arianna until she believed in her power to make a man desire her, he thought with a grin. She was hesitant, always awaiting that blow from harsh words, but she quickly grew passionate when he got her into his arms. Brian was more than willing to keep her there until she accepted that she was not only a desirable woman, but also a passionate one that any true man would be pleased to hold.

He reined in his mount at the very edge of the place where he had left her. A heartbeat later she stepped out from behind a tree and smiled at him. The welcome in that smile struck him hard. It was one of the things he ached for. He could almost see her greeting him with it as he entered their home, the scent of a good meal in the air, and laughing children clinging to her skirts.

It was not to be. He fought to smile back at her, hiding the stab of disappointment he felt like a sword wound to the chest. Lady Arianna Lucette could only be his for a little while. She was a titled lady, one who would undoubtedly be sought after by many men once they knew she was free. He was certain she would be dowered again, even if she did not get back what the Lucettes had taken, and the falsity of her marriage would be well hidden.

Brian walked toward her and told himself he would not weaken; he would not marry for the land he craved. Some of that refusal came from pure pride, but he now knew that there was a good chance it could prove impossible to make Arianna believe he wanted her for any other reason if she did gain a new dowry or regain the old one. He would just make sure that he completely sated his need for her before he had to let her go.

"Brian?" Arianna backed up as he walked straight at her, until her back was pressed up against the tree trunk. "Is something wrong?" she asked, despite the fact that the look on his face did not speak of anger.

"Nay." He placed his hands on the tree trunk on either side of her face. "I just want you."

Before she could respond to that, he kissed her. The hunger in his kiss quickly invaded her blood. She wrapped her arms around his neck, returning his kiss with all the passion he stirred within her, and welcomed the weight of his body as he pressed against her. It was not until she felt the cool of the air upon her breasts that some of the haze his kisses always clouded her mind with cleared away and she realized he had unlaced her gown. She was now bare-breasted before him, her bodice down to her waist, in the full light of day.

"'Tis the middle of the day," she protested, the heat of a blush rapidly spreading over her face, but he held her arms back when she tried to cover her breasts with them.

"Nay, 'tis a wee bit later than that." He teased the hard, rosy tip of her breast with his tongue, savoring the taste of her and the way she shuddered in his arms. "Sweet. Beautiful." He accented each word with another lick of his tongue. "Enough to make a mon crazed with want just by looking at them."

Arianna found that her lack of belief in the words really did not lessen the power of them. Her embarrassment over being so exposed in the light of day faded beneath his flattery and caresses. When he slid a hand beneath her skirts and up her thigh, she did not stop him or even mutter one word of protest. Nor did she do any more than gasp faintly when he roughly tugged off the small linen braies she wore beneath her skirts, a strange habit she had gotten from the women in her family and which Claud had loathed. Brian paid no heed to them as he tossed them aside leaving her open to his touch. She ached for him to touch her there, opening to him willingly as he stroked her with his long fingers.

When he began to tug up her skirts, she murmured, "I will get a blanket."

"Why?"

"To put upon the ground so that we can, weel, we can finish this."

"We can finish it right here," growled Brian.

"Here?"

"Love, do ye recall me saying that those lasses crowding around the Frenchmen at Molly's inn didnae need a bed?"

"Aye."

"Lying, sitting, or standing up, I said."

"Aye. Standing?"

The word ended on a gasp as he placed one of her legs at his waist and buried himself deep inside her. Arianna clung to him, returning his fierce kiss with a ferocity of her own, as he pounded into her. It was rough, uncivilized, and the most exciting thing she had ever done or felt. Even the grunt of approval he made when she wrapped both her legs around his waist fed her desire. She heard herself make a very similar noise when he grabbed her by her backside to hold her steady as they fought their way to passion's precipice and plunged over it together.

It took Arianna several minutes to regain her sense and by then Brian had laced up her gown. She blushed when he handed her the small braies he had taken off her, but he still made no comment on them as she quickly turned her back to him and put them on. It was difficult to believe what she had just allowed him to do. The warmth of the pleasure they had just found in each other's arms eased the shock and embarrassment she knew she ought to be feeling, however.

"I found a mon to take word to your kin," Brian said as he handed her the wineskin.

"And ye trusted him to do it?" she asked, and then helped herself to a long drink of the sweet cider.

"Aye. He was headed off to market to sell his wool and a couple lambs. Said he has dealt with Murrays before and they always treat him fair. And pay."

"Ah, aye, that will make him do as ye want. Too many dinnae do that. The Lucettes owed money to everyone. My father always said that if ye cannae pay for it then ye dinnae need it. Said the poor mon selling his wares cannae afford to wait until ye decide to pay him."

"Being one who has wares to sell, I greatly appreciate that sentiment."

"Did ye save much of what had been on the ship?"

He shrugged. "Enough. It will have to be looked o'er carefully before I can say for certain how much I have lost. And then there is the matter of Captain Tillet and whether we can continue to work together. He lost his ship and most of his crew and those are nay easy to replace."

"And the fact that Amiel and the DeVeaux thought nothing of destroying a ship full of people just to get to me and the boys tells one a lot about those men, doesnae it?"

"Aye, they badly need killing."

"There is a part of me, the one that understands a parent's pain, that feels badly for the Lucettes as I believe they are about to lose another son."

"The last of the heirs?"

"Nay, there is a third son. Quiet, loves his books and studies, and often suffered beneath the taunts and fists of his elder brothers. Yet, even though I didnae have much to do with Paul, the few times we met he seemed a much gentler, more thoughtful sort. It just might be that, in the end, the people who depend upon the Lucettes will win if he becomes the heir."

"I dinnae believe there is any *if* about it."

"Nay, for if Amiel doesnae die, he could remain a threat to Michel and Adelar." She brushed down her skirts and started to walk away.

"Where are ye going?"

"I need a moment of privacy."

"Ah, weel, dinnae go far. And dinnae take too long. I would like to be back on our way soon."

"What joy."

He laughed and went to make sure everything was secure on the horses.

Arianna had just finished cleaning herself off

and putting her braies back on when she heard a sound that made her whole body grow tense and alert. She hastily buried the damp scrap of linen she had used beneath some leaves and crept toward the sound. It was hard not to curse aloud when she saw Amiel and his men cautiously wending their way through the forest. He was like a particularly painful burr one could not shake off one's leg.

As silently as she could she moved back toward where she had left Brian. The moment she felt she could move faster without being heard, she hiked up her skirts and started to run. Every step of the way she expected to hear a cry announcing that they had seen her. She was panting by the time she reached Brian.

"Amiel?" he asked even as he threw her up into the saddle and quickly mounted his own horse.

"Aye, he and his men are coming through the wood."

"Damn that woman!"

"What woman?"

"A tavern maid who didnae like taking nay for an answer."

"What was she asking?"

"Sorry, lass, no time to talk on that and I fear the rest of this journey to Dubheidland is going to be fast and hard."

Even as he spoke he spurred his horse into a gallop and she did the same, softly cursing Amiel and his allies to the darkest pits of hell.

Tam stared down at his cousin. She was badly bruised and had obviously been roughly used. When he had seen the Frenchmen riding quickly out of the village he had gone right back to the tavern to confront his cousin again. Although he was angry that she might well have caused trouble for a good man and put his own life in danger, he had to wince in sympathy over how badly she had been beaten.

"Ye didnae heed my warning at all, did ye, lass?" he said.

"I didnae tell them about you, if that be what worries ye," she muttered, her swelling lips making her slur her words.

"But ye told them about the mon, didnae ye? Vain bitch. The mon has a woman. 'Twas nay an insult for him to say nay to what ye offered."

"And when has a mon having a woman e'er stopped them from having another?"

"Ye deal too much with the bad ones, lass. And this isnae just any woman the lad has. He has himself one of those Murray lasses I have told ye about. Did ye e'en get paid for betraying a mon who ne'er did ye harm?" He cursed when she just glared at him through her one unswollen eye.

"I didnae intend to tell them."

"Then how did they ken ye had anything of worth to tell?"

"He asked about the mon and I think I did something to let him see that I kenned something." She eased herself up on her small, rough bed until she was sitting, and accepted the tankard of ale Tam held out to her. "Next I kenned I was escorted up here thinking he wanted a tumble and got this instead. So, aye, once the fists started landing on me I told him about the mon. But I ne'er told them about ye and what ye were to do for him."

"Are ye certain?"

"Oh, aye, I am certain. Ye may be a pious bastard who cannae mind his own business, but ye are blood and I kenned verra quickly that if I told them about ye, ye would soon be dead." She stared down at her hand, bruised badly by her vain attempts to defend herself. "Do ye think I have caused the deaths of that mon and his lady?"

"I dinnae ken." He watched a tear roll slowly down her bruised cheek. "I only met the mon and talked to him for a wee while. But, he is a MacFingal, cousin to those red-haired devils the Camerons. If anyone can get away from those Frenchmen 'tis a mon like that. I am thinking that all ye did was make him have to work a wee bit harder at it."

"Weel, mayhap I will drag myself to church and pray for them a wee bit."

"I am thinking that might be a verra good thing to do."

Chapter 9

Every bone in Arianna's body was loudly complaining as they raced toward Dubheidland. She fought the urge to look behind them to see how close her enemy might be. At times her back itched as if it sensed a weapon aimed at it.

Just as she was about to give in to the urge to look behind her, Brian made an abrupt change in the direction they were traveling in. She was forced to keep her full attention on following him. It was a rocky, winding trail they now followed, one that severely slowed their pace, if only for fear of maiming their horses.

For a moment, panic choked her, as she grew certain they would soon be caught, but she forced the fear down. Brian moved as a man who knew the land well. The ones chasing them did not. This upward winding, treacherous trail might slow them down more than she liked but it would slow down the enemy at their heels even more.

"Your cousins dinnae want anyone to come visiting,

do they?" she muttered as she struggled to guide her mount over the tortuous path, annoyed that she had none of the skill at it that Brian revealed.

Brian laughed softly. "Nay, they dinnae, but the more common route used to get to Dubheidland is a wee bit easier. This one is hard but shorter. A lot shorter. On the other side of this pile of rocks and heather the land is much easier to ride over. We shall have a straight, swift ride right to the gates of Dubheidland."

"Straight and easy also means open, doesnae it?"

"It does, but we would have ridden onto open land even if we had gone the other way, too."

"What if the others have learned to follow the other path, the easier one? Will they get ahead of us?"

"Nay. As I said, 'tis only a wee bit easier. Sigimor doesnae like to make any route to Dubheidland too easy. And, truly, this is much shorter. Dinnae fret, love. We will win the race."

Brian hoped his brave words proved true. It was going to be a very close-run race no matter which path that fool Amiel forced his men along. Worse, he and Arianna were on tired horses and were tired themselves. Brian knew Amiel, his horses, and his men were undoubtedly as weary as they were but that did not ease his concern by much.

The way Amiel kept finding them, remained so close at their backs no matter how convoluted a trail Brian chose, worried him. He began to suspect that Amiel, fool though he was, had finally had the wit to hire a Scot or two to lead him and his men. Or one of Amiel's men had. There were always those who would do anything for a few coins. A good tracker, one who knew the land, would explain why he and Arianna had been unable to lose Amiel despite all the twists and turns he had taken them on. In the beginning it may have been luck but good luck was never this persistent. Amiel might have known where they would head from the start but he should not have been so continuously good at finding the trail they took to get to that place.

Brian chanced a quick glance at Arianna. She looked weary but kept her attention fixed firmly on the dangerous trail they rode over. Small and slender though she was, she was revealing an astonishing strength so far. That strength was rapidly waning, however. He could see that in the paleness of her face and the shadows under her eyes.

What she needed was a few nights in a soft bed and a lot of nourishing food. She had not even been given time to recover from nearly drowning before being forced to run for her life. Another night at Molly's inn would have helped her but they had not been allowed that needed respite. Brian could only hope that they found it at Dubheidland.

Determined to get her to his cousin's keep unharmed, Brian turned all of his attention to the chore of reaching safer ground as quickly as possible. It was not a trail that allowed any speed, however, and he cursed it continuously as they struggled to get over the hill. When they finally got to safer ground, he paused for a moment to breathe a sigh of relief, not surprised to hear Arianna echo it.

"This does look much better," Arianna said as she nudged her mount up alongside his. "Is that Dubheidland in the distance?"

"Aye. A straight run."

"Some of which looks to be uphill."

"But nay as rocky as the hill we just rode over."

Before she could say any more, Brian tensed. A heartbeat later she knew why. The sound of horses approaching from their left was unmistakable. Amiel was obviously pressing his men and horses dangerously hard. She and Brian had not gained much of a lead at all.

"Ride, lass." Brian leaned over to slap her horse on its flank. "Straight for those gates," he yelled as they both picked up speed. "Dinnae look back and dinnae stop nay matter what happens."

Following Brian's example, Arianna leaned low over her mount's neck as she kicked it, prodding it to as fast a pace as it could provide. She prayed that the exhausted animal still had the strength left to get to those gates and safety. A cry from behind them told her that they had been seen, but she ignored the need to look toward the sound. She could hear her brother Neacal's voice telling her to keep her gaze fixed upon the direction she was headed in, that looking back would only slow her down. With shelter so close at hand she was determined to win the race.

She was close enough to see men moving on the high, thick walls of the keep and hear shouting coming from within when the deadly hiss of an arrow passing close by reached her ears. Arianna tensed, fear swiftly chilling the blood in her veins, but nothing struck her, she heard no cry of pain from Brian, and her horse did not falter. Shouts and curses came from behind her and there were no other arrows fired at them. Amiel had obviously reminded his men that he needed her alive. Her death gained him nothing. The DeVeaux wanted her and Lucette needed the boys.

The man was an utter fool if he thought she would sacrifice her boys to his greed. Even if she did not think of Michel and Adelar as hers, she would never trade the life of a child for her own. Amiel's ignorance gave her a small advantage. So long as she remained free, her life was not truly in danger. The same could not be said of Brian, however, so she would continue to act as if the men chasing them wanted her dead. Not later, after she had given them what they wanted, but now.

"Almost there, love!" Brian yelled, able to see Sigimor's men on the wall so clearly that he recognized a few. "'Tis Sir Brian MacFingal! We are coming in!"

"Ye have a tail, laddie!"

"Cut it off!"

This time when Arianna heard the sound of arrows slicing through the air her heart did not leap up into her throat. The deadly weapons were not aimed at her and Brian but at their enemy. She followed Brian through the high, iron-studded oak gates only to abruptly rein in her mount, barely avoiding riding straight into a group of mounted men.

"I see ye brought me a wee gift, Brian," said a huge, red-haired man.

"I need at least one of them alive, Sigimor," yelled Brian even as he dismounted, grabbed another horse and joined with the men riding out through the gates, their horses at full gallop and their swords drawn before they had even cleared the gates.

"Such poor manners ye have, lad, to give me a gift and then tell me what to do with it," she heard the man Brian had called Sigimor yell back.

Brian's reply to that was lost in the roar of a battle cry erupting from all the men racing toward Amiel and his men. Arianna turned in her saddle to look out the gates, not surprised to see Amiel and his men immediately turn and flee, leaving two arrow-ridden bodies on the ground behind them. Arianna suspected those two dead men had been the ones closest to her and Brian.

"A horse! Go fight!" cried a high, sweet, childish voice.

Arianna turned back to look at the people gathered in the bailey. A small, red-haired boy was running toward the gates, a wooden sword held high in his tiny hands. Hard on his heels was a very pregnant, black-haired woman. One tall, lean man was quicker, catching the boy up in his arms and laughing as he disarmed the child.

Not sure what else to do, Arianna dismounted only to have to hang onto the saddle and lean against the horse when her legs threatened to collapse beneath her weight. Out of the corner of her eye she saw two black-haired little girls, armed with wooden swords as well, attempt to creep around the people gathering in the bailey. Before she could open her mouth to say a word, yet another tall, handsome, red-haired man caught both little girls by the back of their gowns and pulled them to a halt.

Just as Arianna was about to test the strength in her legs, the very pregnant, black-haired woman stepped up to her and smiled. The woman was, in a word, beautiful. There was only welcome to be seen in the unusual silvery gray eyes as well and Arianna found herself returning the woman's smile with a tired one of her own.

"I am the laird's wife, Lady Jolene Cameron," the woman said.

"English? Are we at peace with England then?"

"Who knows. It changes from one day to the next. Nay, I am but a poor English lass caught up by Sir Sigimor's great charm."

Arianna did not need the laughter of the men around them to tell her that was a jest. The laughter brightening the woman's eyes told her that. She also realized she had just been rather rude to the poor woman, who already had to deal with an enemy at the gates.

"I am sorry," Arianna said, and held out her hand. "I am Lady Arianna Murray." She stuttered to a halt as she shook the woman's hand and realized she did not want to be known as a Lucette any longer. The word had stuck in her throat. Relief swept over her and she knew it was past time she had let go of the name that had never truly been hers and had no pleasant memories attached to it.

"Well, I imagine you have had a very long and arduous journey, if your entrance into Dubheidland is any indication." Jolene slipped her arm through Arianna's. "Allow me to escort you inside. I suspect you would welcome a bath, clean clothing, and food."

"Och, aye, I would. Thank ye. I apologize for the trouble." She rubbed her forehead but it did little to ease the throb of exhaustion. "We just couldnae seem to shake them off our trail."

"They will be shaken off now."

The woman spoke with such confidence, Arianna was forced to believe her. She set her mind to simply walking without stumbling. Now that she had stopped running, she was all too keenly aware of just how exhausted she was.

"'Tis verra wrong of me, but I wish they were nay just shaken off; I wish they all end up dead."

"Nay, after what they have done to you, that you would wish it is no surprise. I understand that feeling very well, having had to run from an enemy myself. 'Tis how I met my Sigimor, but that is a story to tell you after you have rested. I suspect you have not had much rest from the running."

"Nay, verra little." She looked around when Jolene escorted her into a bedchamber. "Oh, this is verra nice," she murmured, eyeing the big bed and wondering if she had the strength to get over to it and collapse upon all those soft coverings.

"I have already ordered a bath for you." Jolene urged her toward the bed. "Sit and I will gather some clothes for you."

Arianna sat as stiffly as she could, afraid she would fall over and go to sleep if she did not. More aches were making themselves known in her body and she had to fight back a groan. She accepted the tankard of drink Jolene gave her with a smile—one sip enough to tell her it was a deliciously spiced cider—and watched the woman move quickly around the room to collect some clothes for her.

"This isnae your bedchamber, is it?" she asked.

"Nay, this is the one Sigimor's sister Ilsa uses when she comes to visit. These are her things. They may be a little long but I think they will fit you well enough." Jolene set the clothes down on the bed and turned to direct the youths and maids in setting up the bath for Arianna.

"They will be all right, will they nay?" she asked Jolene after they were alone again in the room and Jolene began to help her shed her clothes.

"Of course they will. There did not appear to be too many men chasing you and my husband likes a good fight. Or, considering how fast the men after you were fleeing, a good chase. Oh, my, such bruising you have. I will fetch some salve for them."

Before Arianna could protest, she was in the bath and Jolene was hurrying out of the room. Arianna sank down into the hot water, realized Jolene had sprinkled some gently scented herbs in it, and allowed it to soothe the aches in her body. She was dangerously close to sleep when Jolene and an older woman hurried back into the room.

The two women had her washed, dried, dressed in a fine linen nightgown, and seated before a full plate of food before Arianna could protest. "Ye shouldnae be doing so much," she said to Jolene as the woman finally sat down in a chair and faced her across the small table. "All this dashing about cannae be good for the bairn."

Jolene laughed and poured herself a tankard of cider. "I am fine. This child is due soon and well settled within me. You, however, look like you had better eat your fill quickly before the need to sleep conquers you."

"I am verra tired, I admit." Arianna began to eat the

tender venison on her plate. "I should tell you what this trouble is that I have brought to your home."

"No need. We got a message from Ewan and he told us some of it. Brian can tell us the rest. Oh, and I am to tell you that Michel and Adelar are safely tucked up behind the very high, very strong walls of Scarglas."

"Oh, thank God," Arianna whispered, and then burst into tears. "I am sorry. I dinnae ken what ails me."

Jolene handed her a linen cloth. "Relief and weariness. Have a good cry and then finish your food."

Arianna laughed and wiped the tears from her face. "I have just been so afraid for them. This isnae over yet but at least I now ken that they have been taken somewhere safe, somewhere that has the men to protect them."

"Oh, the men of Scarglas will keep them very safe indeed. You can put your mind at rest about that. Old Fingal might be a rutting old goat and the oddest fellow I have ever met, but he cares for children. No man will be allowed to harm them."

Not sure what to say about that remark concerning Brian's father, Arianna concentrated on finishing her meal. She could feel the hard pull of exhaustion and knew she would not be able to stay awake much longer. If she were not careful she would be falling asleep sitting in the chair in that strange way she did when she became too tired.

By the time she finished her meal she had become almost too tired to chew any longer. "I wish I could remain awake to greet Sir Brian when he returns, but I dinnae think I will be able to."

"Nay, I can see that." Lady Jolene took Arianna

by the arm and led her over to the bed. "Rest. You still have a bit of a journey to complete and you need to sleep when you can. Sir Brian will understand. I suspect he will be doing just as you have done as soon as he returns."

The moment Arianna was tucked up in the bed, she knew sleep was but a breath away. "Thank ye, m'lady," she managed to say before she gave in to the overwhelming urge to rest.

"Weel, he doesnae have as many men as he once had, but I think 'tis time to end the chase," said Sigimor as he reined in and glanced up at the sky.

"I was hoping to end it here," said Brian as he halted by Sigimor's side. "At least then we could travel to Scarglas without having to watch our backs every step of the way."

"Mayhap that is where he flees to."

"Aye, 'tis possible. 'Tis also possible that once he and his allies get a look at Scarglas they will decide it isnae worth the trouble just to gain a little revenge and that fool a title. I willnae put any wagers on that though. Chasing the lads here to Scotland when his parents already work to disinherit the boys was madness. I doubt this or a look at Scarglas will clear any heads."

"Sigimor," called Fergus, "what shall we do with the bodies scattered about?"

"Pick the three along the trail clean of anything that is worth something and leave them for the carrion," Sigimor told his youngest brother. "The two left outside the keep are already dealt with." He turned his mount back toward Dubheidland and left his brothers to deal with the gruesome chore as he headed back to his keep.

"There were a few more of them than there were the last time I saw them all together," said Brian as he rode beside Sigimor.

"Hired a few men, aye?"

"I think so. Amiel may have kenned where we were headed but there were too many times when he was right on our trail yet I was nay following the one everyone kens about. He could only have done that with the help of some mon who kenned the land."

Sigimor nodded. "And the others who are searching for the lads may do the same. Ye could find yourself in a true battle once ye get to Scarglas."

"Aye, but we can deal with it. We have before."

"We can talk on that after ye bathe and then join us for some food. I suspicion ye will be in dire need of some rest, too."

"Oh, aye." Brian cursed as he realized how he had left Arianna alone. "I should have seen to Arianna instead of leaping onto a fresh horse and joining ye in the chase."

"My Jo will see to her. And, if the lass is as weary as ye look, I wouldnae be expecting her to greet ye when ye return."

Sigimor proved right and Brian was not surprised to hear that Arianna was already asleep when he returned. He suffered a brief disappointment over the fact that she revealed no concern for his safety but easily shook it off. They had been chasing Amiel and his men, him and about twenty well-armed

Camerons. Arianna had enough sense to know there was little danger for him.

After bathing and donning clean clothes, he made his way down to the great hall. He wanted to sleep but his belly told him he needed some food first. Once in the great hall, he kissed Jolene on the cheek, ignoring Sigimor's scowl as he did so, and then sat down next to his cousin to fill his plate.

"Lady Arianna was so tired I feared she was about to fall asleep even as she ate her meal," said Jolene as she sat down across the table from him.

"She may weel have if ye hadnae gotten her into bed quickly." Brian told them of how she had fallen asleep on her horse and grinned when they laughed. "She hasnae had much time to recover from nearly drowning." Between bites of food he told them everything that had happened before and since he had found her on the beach.

Jolene shook her head. "I cannot understand how men can do such things just for the sake of gain. One begins to think that no child who might inherit something of worth is ever safe."

"There is that to consider. This is unnecessary though, for his family will surely get the boys disinherited simply because their mother was a common wench."

"Amiel may ken something they dinnae," said Sigimor as he sprawled in his chair and sipped at his wine. "Mayhap the lass wasnae as common as they thought. Some lord's bastard daughter or the like. There may be someone who will fight the Lucettes on their plans to mark the boys as bastards."

"Hadnae thought of that," said Brian. "Yet, if she

was better born, surely that fool Claud would have openly declared her his wife."

"Nay. Blood-proud people dinnae like the fact that someone is a bastard, especially since many of them spring from common stock. 'Twas just a thought. When this is done, however, I would have a wee look at what is happening concerning those lads and their inheritance if I were you. Even if they are marked as bastards, a deal leaving them something of worth may be made to get that marriage annulled."

"Aye, that will be done if only because Arianna also demanded something be given to the boys. Since the elder Lucettes must be pleased the boys are now out of France and Arianna has implied she willnae shame them with the truth of what their son did, she might just get what she asked for."

"Clever lass. A little blackmail can be a good thing." Sigimor caught his wife's disgusted look and winked at her. "Your brother sent out word to the Murrays once the lads were safely at Scarglas."

"I sent out word as weel."

"Then help should be on its way. But, I think ye need to seek your bed, cousin. If I felt as weary as ye look, I would be snoring with my head on the table right now. We can talk on this in the morning."

"I was thinking we should continue on our way in the morning."

"Then 'tis even more important that ye get some rest."

"Where was Arianna put then?"

"In Ilsa's old bedchamber," replied Jolene. "I have put ye in the one across from her."

"Nay, I will stay with her," Brian said, and could hear the force of demand in his voice despite how softly he spoke.

"Brian, she is not some simple wench. She is a lady, and a Murray."

"I ken that. I also ken she is a widow, so 'tis nay as if I sully some cherished innocent."

"I know what men think about widows, but that does not mean it is acceptable to treat them like you would some tavern wench. They still have a good name to protect."

"I dinnae treat her like that but I willnae leave her alone, either."

"Do you mean to marry her then?"

"Jo, m'love, leave the mon be," said Sigimor.

"But . . ." Jolene began.

"Nay. Go on with you, Brian. Ye will see that she is safe and cared for. Sleep weel and we will talk in the morning before ye leave."

Brian quickly escaped the great hall before Jolene could say anything else. He knew it was wrong to be so open about the fact that he was Arianna's lover, but the thought of not sleeping at her side forced him to be blunt. Jolene could not know that he did not have much time left with Arianna before he had to hand her over to her family. He was not going to waste one single minute of the time they had left in bowing to the proprieties.

He entered the room Sigimor's only sister had once occupied and smiled as he closed the door. Arianna was little more than a lump beneath the blankets. Brian shed his clothes and crawled in beside her, pulling her into his arms. She murmured his name and pressed close to him.

"Brian?" she said, although he could see that she was not really awake.

"Aye, love." He touched a kiss to her forehead.

"Ye are unhurt?"

"I am hale and so are all of Sigimor's men. I fear Amiel managed to escape, though."

"Bollocks."

Brian looked down at her face, saw that her eyes were closed and the hand on his chest limp, and laughed softly. Arianna could not only ride a horse while asleep, she could carry on a conversation. He knew she would not recall a word of it, however.

He tucked her head under his chin, and rested his cheek against her hair. The herbs from her bath teased his senses and his body stirred with need, but he was so tired it was easy to quell the urge to make love to her. The need to sleep with her in his arms troubled him a little as it showed him he was not keeping the distance between them that he should. No matter how often he told himself that he had to stay close to keep her safe, he could not fully believe it. They were now inside a strong keep with a strong force of men to watch over them and fight an enemy that tried to get to them. Brian knew, in his heart, that he simply liked to hold her close as he slept.

The part of him that wanted to keep her rose up and he tried to banish it. Even if he could convince himself that she would be happy with him, that she felt more than passion for him, it would be selfish of him to try and hold on to her. He could not give her all the things she could find with another richer, better-born man. Arianna deserved a life of ease, surrounded by the finer things, and there would be little of that if she stayed with him. Even with the improvements made to Scarglas and the money he had saved, it would not equal what she had had as a child of the Murrays or the wife of a *comte*.

Brian closed his eyes and held her a little closer. There was still some time left to them and he did not want to shadow it with thoughts of all they could not have together. For now, he would enjoy all they could share. He also swore that by the time he set her free, she would know her worth and be bled of the poison Claud had fed her for years.

Chapter 10

Fire flowed through her veins as Arianna crawled her way up through the fog of sleep. It took her only a moment to understand why she felt so hot and needy. Brian's dark head was against her breast, his lips and tongue stirring that almost painful pleasure in her breasts. She groaned softly as she threaded her fingers through his thick hair, holding him close and silently inviting him to do as he pleased.

She shifted beneath his stroking hands and heated kisses. There was a small part of her that was still shocked by how wanton Brian could make her but her delight in the passion he blessed her with easily soothed that shock away. Until she felt the touch of his mouth upon that part of her where she ached for him the most.

"Brian," she gasped as she tried to squirm away from him, but his hands on her hips held her firmly in place.

"Hush, loving. This will please you."

Arianna remained tense as he kissed her there

and teased her private flesh with his tongue. The women in her clan had occasionally mentioned such loving to her when her day to marry drew near, but she had been very certain that such an intimacy was not for her. As her desire, dimmed by her shock, roared back to life with a vengeance and she opened herself to his kiss, she decided that she had been hopelessly naive.

Each stroke of his tongue, each gentle nip and kiss, and even the way he caressed her thighs with his big hands, drove her wild. The need for his body to be joined with hers rapidly reached the point where she could wait no longer for him. Arianna heard her demand that he put himself inside her in a voice so thick with desire she barely recognized it as her own. She grabbed hold of his broad shoulders as he kissed his way back up her body with a slow greed that she had no patience for.

The moment he began to ease himself into her, she wrapped her legs around him and used them to push him deeper. She held him close as he filled her, fighting to hold back the need for release tightening inside her with every thrust of his body. Although she savored everything he did to her when they made love, Arianna enjoyed this part the most. This was when they were as close as two people could ever be. This was when they were one.

That realization was enough to cut the last tie she had on her control. Her release raced through her with such force, she cried out his name as her body shook from the strength of the pleasure he gave her. She was briefly aware of Brian thrusting fast and hard several times before he growled out her name and trembled in her arms as he found his own release. As she welcomed the warmth of his seed, she sank beneath the weight of the bliss pouring over her.

It was not until she felt the cool dampness of a cloth gently bathing her groin that Arianna began to return to her senses. Embarrassment threatened to swamp her and she struggled against it. It was not easy to defeat, however. Arianna had no trouble being touched there or having Brian enter her there, but kissing her there? Looking at her most private of parts? There was no denying that it had made her wild with desire, but now that desire had cooled, and she was left with the knowledge that she had shown none of a lady's modesty or restraint. Shame over that was a worm trying to bore into her heart and mind and destroy the lingering pleasure she cherished over all they had just shared.

Brian tossed aside the cloth he had cleaned them both with and quickly rejoined Arianna in bed. He pulled her into his arms and kissed the hollow where her shoulder met her neck, enjoying the small shiver that went through her body. Despite that he was all too aware of the tension in her.

"Ye think too much, love," he said, and was surprised at how her breasts moving against his skin as she took a deep breath and let it out slowly actually roused a spark of desire inside him. Obviously his body was a glutton when it came to the passion he found in her arms.

"Quite possibly," she muttered. "Yet, weel, it was wonderful, but . . ."

"But naught. We are nay more than two adults taking pleasure in each other."

"I ken it." She flopped onto her back, clutching the covers over her breasts and rubbing a hand over her forehead. "'Tis just that I dinnae ken who I am when the desire overcomes me."

"'Tis a blessing when it is so strong, nay a sin or a worry."

She grimaced. "I am nay surprised a mon would say that. It ne'er happened with my husband."

Brian propped himself up on his elbow and looked at her. "He wasnae your husband. I think he wasnae much of a lover, either. Nay with you anyway." He cursed his unruly tongue when she grew pale, distress darkening her amber eyes to a deep brown. "Arianna, I am a fumbling idiot. I . . . ."

"Nay." She placed a finger against his lips. "Ye speak the pure truth. He was neither my husband nor my lover. I dinnae ken why I have such a difficult time remembering that. 'Tis only when we reached here that I ceased adding his name to mine, yet that shocked me when I did it. Ye would think that, since I can still hear things he said to me, that I would be able to recall that my marriage was a lie."

"What do ye mean ye can still hear things that he said?"

Brian experienced a stab of emotion he easily recognized as jealousy and firmly told himself not to be an idiot. Claud had been no husband to her and, despite what attempts she had made to make her marriage a good one while still ignorant of the truth, Arianna had not loved the man. There was no ghost of some great love or lover for him to fight. What he had begun to see more clearly was that he just had to fight the poison the man had fed her for years. Claud Lucette had taken a bonnie, lively woman with confidence and strength, and turned her into a woman who questioned herself at every turn. Brian heartily wished he had been the one to kill the fool.

"The mon is in my head." She blushed, certain that she must sound like a madwoman to him. "A part of me remains angry and defiant o'er all he did to me. Yet, the whispers of his insults and criticisms continue to haunt me. I then feel an utter fool that I ever listened to him only to ken that his words found some way to set down root in my heart and mind. Curse it, I am making no sense at all."

He pulled her back into his arms and rested his chin on the top of her head. "Aye, ye make sense. I ken exactly what ye mean and have done so for a while. The mon poisoned ye."

"Nay, he . . ."

"Poisoned ye, slowly, for every day of the five long years ye had to suffer the lying fool. I told ye, words can be a sharp weapon and he used them against ye with a dangerous skill. Ye were barely a woman when ye wed him, and taken from a loving family to be sent to a place where no one cared for or respected ye. He used the uncertainty ye must have felt about your place there to make ye even more uncertain."

And that still hurt, she realized as she nodded.

"Ye should have been supported by your mon, all who didnae treat ye right being severely punished. Instead, he stabbed at ye with cruel words day after day, and there was no one there to help ye shed the poison he fed ye all the time. The bastard hasnae been dead long. Ye just need more time to push out of your heart and mind all the venom he put in there. There are a few things ye need to remember at all times that will help ye do that."

When he did not immediately tell her what those things were, she lifted her head to look at him. "What are they?"

"That he was a coward and he wasnae your husband. He kenned he was a coward, too, but couldnae accept that truth so he blamed ye for all that was wrong in his life. His every dealing with ye was a lie. I think he quickly kenned that ye were a clever lass with spirit enough to cause him some trouble so he did all he could to kill that spirit. He also kenned ye had wit and he needed to keep ye under his boot so that ye wouldnae turn that sharp wit to looking for why your marriage wasnae as it should have been."

"Weel, I have finally cast off his name," she murmured.

"'Tis a start. Now ye just have to cast off the rest of his lies."

Arianna opened her mouth to speak and abruptly forgot what she was about to say. She looked around the strange bedchamber they were in. It was another moment before she recalled where they were.

"Brian," she gasped, "ye had best slip back into your own room. The Camerons will rise soon and ye dinnae wish to be caught creeping about the place."

"I am in my room," he said, and had to bite back a smile when she looked at him with her eyes wide with shock.

"I walked here last night?"

"Nay, lass. We have the same bedchamber. I was

offered my own but told them nay, that I stay with ye."

A flush of embarrassment warmed her cheeks despite her pleasure over his statement. "The Camerons will think I am naught but some faithless creature, one with few morals. I mean, I am but newly widowed and even widows past their mourning time are more discreet than this."

Brian kissed her and then rested his forehead against hers. "Love, they dinnae care."

"How can ye ken that? I met Lady Jolene. I recall her now and she was verra much the lady born and bred."

"That she is, and yet she is wed to Sigimor, who is nay a gentlemon of the court. And I can promise ye, she was nay even a widow and I doubt she remained chaste in his company for long. She wed him thinking it but a ploy to protect her."

Distracted, she asked, "Was it?"

"Nay. Sigimor wanted her. He let her think what she wanted but had no intention of letting her ever leave Scotland or him again. He wanted her to stay and did all he could to make sure she did."

Arianna had the sudden urge to ask Brian if he wanted her to stay with him, but hastily bit back the words. Not only would that leave her open to hearing him try to explain why he did not want to keep her, but he deserved better than her. He deserved a woman who was whole, who could give him children, and did not carry all the wounds she did from a marriage that was little more than five years in hell.

"A sneaky mon. My family would appreciate

that," she murmured, and then recalled what he had been doing when she had crawled into bed to sleep. "Oh! How could I forget what happened? I cannae believe I could be so thoughtless. Were ye hurt? Was any Cameron hurt?" She frowned when he laughed.

"I kenned that ye wouldnae recall it but we talked briefly on this when I got into this bed last night. None of us were injured. We trimmed the number of men Amiel had with him but we didnae catch him. The dark stopped the chase ere we could. So, there will be fewer men hunting us when we leave, if there are any at all. Sigimor and I think they may go to join with the others now."

She sighed at the thought that she had to get back on a horse so soon but knew it was necessary. "Then we had best rise and eat so that we might leave and get to Scarglas ere we have a whole army to try and slip around."

"We can wait one more night, lass."

Brian could see the faint shadows beneath her eyes and knew she still needed to rest. If Amiel was headed to join the others at Scarglas, he was well ahead of them now. There would be no catching the man and no overtaking him so there was no real need to rush off to Scarglas. Arianna probably needed a few more days of rest before she fully recovered from all she had endured, but he could afford to give her the one more night. And, selfishly, he wanted one more night with her with no worries about who might slip up on them or how quickly they could get to their horses and flee. He pulled her close and began to kiss her neck.

"Um, should we not get up and break our fast?" she asked even as she tilted her head to the side to allow him better access.

"We will. After."

"But we just did that."

"Och, lass, ye must ken that a mon is ever hungry for a woman as sweet and hot as ye are. Morning, noon, and night." He paused just before kissing her mouth. "Are ye sore from all the riding?"

Arianna briefly considered saying she was for it was scandalous to roll about beneath the covers with a man she was not wed to when she was a guest at someone's home. Then she cast her unease and fear of censure aside. Time was short for her and Brian and she was not going to allow anything to steal away the first truly peaceful moment they had shared. There would be no one riding hard on their heels, no one forcing them to run out the back of the keep, and no one forcing them to do more riding than she ever wanted to do again. There was also the fact that, if the falsity of her marriage to Claud ever became common knowledge, she would be marked a whore anyway, unfair though that was, so why not at least commit some sin she could have fond memories of?

"Nay," she said, and pulled his face down to hers so that she could kiss him with all the renewed desire she could feel growing inside her.

"I think ye should marry that lass," said Sigimor as he handed Brian a big tankard of ale.

Brian scowled at his cousin. He had suspected

something different when the man had pulled him into his small ledger room. A discussion about what he should or should not be doing with Arianna was an odd choice for Sigimor. It was not any of the man's business, either, but he knew telling Sigimor that would not deter him.

"Sigimor, I have naught to offer such a lass," he said.

"Ye have yourself."

"Weel, that willnae keep her properly housed, fed, clothed, or in jewels."

"Dinnae think she cares much for those things. Of course, she will want to keep those lads. Is that it?"

"Of course not. Sigimor, she would sit higher at any table than I do and has spent the last five years as a countess. We both ken the Murrays are powerful, admired, and nay too poor. Some are cursed rich. 'Tis true that her marriage turned out to be a lie and the mon she thought was her husband was a cold, callous bastard, but she still had all the luxury such a position can give a woman. I cannae e'en afford to leave the keep where I have a small room and little privacy. Mayhap I could build a wee cottage in the village but nay more than that. Nay, she needs to go back to her family."

"Ye are an idiot. Jolene was the daughter of an English Marcher lord. Didnae see that stopping me, did ye?"

"Weel, ye are a laird and rule Dubheidland. I am a younger son to a mon some think may be utterly mad and have more brothers than any mon should, most of them bastards."

"Mayhap ye ought to try and see what she wants."

"Women dinnae always choose wisely." He ignored Sigimor's snort of laughter.

"Do ye nay want her for more than a lass to warm your bed then? But then I am thinking ye ken weel that she will be marked if the news of her marriage being naught but a lie gets round."

"She is nay like that," he snapped. "'Tis nay as ye try to make it sound."

"Yet ye will offer her nay more than a few nights and then send her home?"

"Aye, because I cannae offer her more. I am nay good enough for her, and her family would be quick to say so. I dinnae think she need worry about the news of her false marriage causing her trouble, either, for the Lucettes will wish to keep that as quiet as possible if only to keep the Murrays from wanting their blood. And before ye mention Gregor, the only reason Gregor has himself a Murray lass is because they traveled together and she was a maid. He ne'er would have even tried to reach so high otherwise. There really wasnae much choice if she was to hold fast to her honor and he his. 'Tis just good that they wanted to be together. If I already had a wee piece of land, a nice wee house, and some coin, I might try to woo Arianna, but I dinnae have any of that yet."

"Brian, if ye wait until ye have all ye think she wants or needs, ye will be sitting alone in your fine wee house with your nice full purse, looking out at your wee piece of land, and wishing ye had ne'er let her go, but it will be too late. Aye, and she will be set somewhere with a new husband and five or six children at her skirts."

That was a thought that chilled him to the bone but he quickly pushed it from his mind. "I think I would rather discuss what to do about these cursed DeVeaux and Amiel." He sighed when Sigimor just stared at him. "I will think on what ye have said but may we now talk on the threat that still hangs o'er her head? I think that is of a more immediate importance."

"As ye wish."

Sigimor began to give his opinions on what Brian should do about the ones hunting Arianna and the boys, most of them dealing with the many ways they might be killed. It took Brian several minutes to push all of Sigimor's words concerning the possibility of keeping Arianna for his own right out of his mind and he knew it was because his cousin was advising him to take what he wanted anyway. He forced his thoughts to remain fixed upon ridding them of the threat posed by Amiel and the De-Veaux. It was all the future he could allow himself to think about.

Arianna watched Lady Jolene settle herself in the chair by the fire. She poured the woman a drink of cider and served her. As she poured one for herself, she tried to discern any scorn or disapproval in the woman's eyes or actions but saw none.

"You did not have a good marriage, did you?" said Jolene as she helped herself to one of the honey-sweetened oatcakes on a tray set between them.

"Ah, nay, I didnae." Arianna was not comfortable with the topic and wished she had not returned to her bedchamber where Lady Jolene had so easily found her alone. "Did Brian nay tell ye all about the trouble there has been?"

"Do you mean how the man lied to you and how this brother of his wishes to kill those boys, maybe even give you to an old enemy of the family?"

"Aye. I was hoping to get to my family before any trouble reached us, but that plan failed. I felt a wee bit guilty about it but decided no one could have kenned that the enemy would be willing to sink a whole ship just to kill the boys."

"Nay, that would have surprised most anyone. You were very fortunate to fall into the MacFingals' hands. They are a rough lot of men, a little wild, a little uncivilized, but good men despite that."

"Aye, they are. Brian assured me again and again that his brothers would get my boys safely to Scarglas and they did, boys they had no blood tie to and who were trailing right behind them men willing to kill anyone just to get them. To do so does show how good the men are. Rough ways and a wee bit of wildness doesnae matter."

"Then mayhap you should consider keeping Brian."

Arianna nearly choked on the bite of oatcake she had just taken and had to take a quick drink of cider to clear it away. "Sir Brian has shown no interest in my keeping him."

"Nay? He insisted upon sharing this bedchamber with you even though there was no need for such protection while you are here. What I saw when he did so was a man who did not wish to sleep alone."

"That doesnae mean he wants to keep me. We both ken that men can bed and sleep with women all the time and nay wish to actually keep them."

"Men also do not find it easy to speak of such things."

"So I must ask him if he wishes to stay with me? I must be the one to set myself up for the blow that will come when he says nay, thank ye kindly?"

"Quite possibly. It depends on how much you would like him to stay with you. Do you care for the man, Arianna?"

"I wouldnae be scandalizing the whole keep by sharing his bed if I didnae."

"True, but I was not speaking of passion. Sir Brian MacFingal is a very handsome man. Near all the MacFingal men are. I was rather hoping you would be honest about what lies in your heart."

"I think I love the man."

"Only think?"

"I have spent the last five years of my life with a mon who told me, near every time he spoke to me, that I was riddled with faults from how I looked to how I could please no mon in the bedchamber. Then comes Sir Brian and suddenly I ken what my kinswomen spoke of when they spoke of desire, loving, passion. I dinnae ken if that clouds my mind or nay. 'Tis verra hard to tell what is in your heart when ye are feeling things ye ne'er have, strong things that overwhelm ye from time to time."

Jolene nodded. "I can understand that. Yet 'tis my belief that a woman would not feel such things unless a piece of her heart was already involved."

"Nay, she probably wouldnae." Arianna shook her head. "I am trying to keep my heart closed to him."

"Why would you ever do such a thing?"

"Because, e'en if he convinces me that all Claud said was a lie—and that will take some time I fear—I couldnae tie him to me anyway. It would be unkind. 'Tis bad enough that I will be marked a whore if the falsity of my marriage becomes widely known. Considering how people look at the MacFingals now, I dinnae think they need such a woman as part of their clan." She ignored Jolene's muttered opinion of that as being nonsense. "Also, I am fair certain I am barren."

Jolene reached across the table to place her hand over Arianna's clenched hands. "Are you truly certain?"

"I lost a bairn. I had but just realized that I carried one and then it was gone. We did try again but I ne'er quickened again. Then Claud had a physician come in to look at me and that mon said I couldnae carry a child."

"Yet you did get with child once and I cannot believe miscarrying so early would damage anything. Were you very ill? Bleeding a great deal?"

"Nay, I dinnae think there was anything particularly wrong in the way it happened, only that it happened at all." Arianna slipped her hands out from beneath Jolene's and wiped a tear from her cheek. "We did try for a year after I lost my baby but naught happened and, after that full year of trying, there were times Claud would try again, usually after his parents made some remarks about his absence from my bed or the lack of an heir. And Claud gave Marie Anne two fine sons so it wasnae a lack in him."

Jolene sat back and crossed her arms over her chest. "A physician can be wrong. I believe very few of them actually know anything at all about babies and birth and women. They all tend to strongly dislike having anything to do with us. And 'tis not so uncommon for a woman to lose the first child she quickens with. Tell me, how old is the youngest of the two lads?"

"Five, near to six."

"So for the entire time you were trying to carry this Claud's child, he was still bedding his mistress and yet she never got with child again?"

Arianna blinked and thought that over for a little while, trying not to let that flicker of hope in her heart grow too large. "I dinnae think so. Do ye think Claud somehow lost his, um, virility?"

"It happens. There are many fevers and such that can steal it. All works as it should but the seed is dead. I should not give up hope of having a child so quickly."

"The trouble is, Jolene, the only way to be certain I am nay barren is to get with child. It would be best if I do so while married but, if I marry and do prove barren, then I have cheated the mon who married me. Wheesht, I could even be accused of having lied for I would have married him kenning there was a chance I would give him no children."

"Then perhaps you ought to try without concerning yourself about the marrying part of it all." Jolene grimaced. "That sounds very devious."

It did, but the idea stuck in Arianna's mind as she

and Jolene began to talk about their families. It was still there when Brian climbed into bed with her a few hours later and pulled her into his arms. She could not shake free of it, her craving for a child refusing to allow her to give up the idea. Arianna then swore upon her very soul that, if she did find herself carrying Brian's child, she would not use it to drag him into a marriage he did not want. From what she had heard, the MacFingal clan had no problem at all with having bastard children, and a lot of them. If she was going to test whether she was truly barren or not, there was hardly any better choice than one of the notoriously virile MacFingals.

"We must be back on the horses on the morrow, love," he said as he removed the chemise she wore and tossed it on the floor.

Arianna grimaced at the thought. "'Tis the last of the journey though, aye?" She slid her hand down his taut stomach, enjoying the smooth warm skin and play of muscle beneath it, actually eager to explore a man's body for the first time since the embarrassing attempts she had made in the first weeks of her marriage.

"We are done when we reach Scarglas and ye may linger there as long as ye like before going anywhere else." He hoped she would choose to linger for quite a while before she left to rejoin her family even though he knew it could make parting with her even harder than it would be now.

"Good. I suspect it will be a verra long time before I wish to get back on a horse."

Brian was about to ask just how long she thought that might be when she curled her long, slender fingers around his erection. He groaned and held her tightly, shifting his hips in a silent plea for her to caress him. When she answered that plea, stroking him, even slipping her hand between his legs to toy with him there, he lost all ability to think.

Arianna was enjoying the power she had over this strong man, surprised at how her touch was affecting him so strongly. She was just wondering what else she could do to keep him groaning and muttering flatteries for a while longer, when he suddenly pushed her onto her back. His lovemaking became fierce, his passion a wild thing that demanded she join in that wildness. When he joined their bodies, there was little gentleness in the way he moved, but she did not care. Her passion easily rose until it equaled his, and she was soon urging him on with her words and her body. The release that tore through her had her crying out his name, clinging to him as if she was falling and he was the only thing she had left to hang on to. When his release came, his seed filling her, he gripped her so tightly she knew there would be a few bruises and she did not care.

Still trembling from the force of the passion they had shared, Arianna opened her eyes and looked at the man sleeping so soundly in her arms. She thought of how often he had spilled his seed inside her and that tiny flicker of hope in her heart grew a little bigger. If there was the slightest chance that she was not barren, then passion as hot and wild as what she shared with Brian had to leave her with child. It would cause a lot of trouble if she ended up back with her clan, with child and no husband, but she did not care. If Brian sent her away, did not wish to keep her, at least she would have a piece of him to cherish. Arianna just hoped that was good enough for, with each moment spent in his arms, she knew she never wanted to let him go.

Chapter 11

"I think ye ought to let me send some men with you."

Brian sipped his ale and looked at his cousin Sigimor, who was sprawled in his huge chair at the head of the table and rapidly emptying a bowl of sliced apples. "Nay, I told ye last night that isnae necessary. The men were routed, their numbers culled, and some even wounded. If they were still close at hand your men would have found them by now. Arianna and I can slip round them if our trails cross before we get to Scarglas."

"Wheesht, ye could probably slip right through the midst of their camp while they dine. But, if ye had a few men with ye, ye could at least stop to cut a few throats ere ye flee. Reduce the number of men hunting the lass even more than we did when we chased them out of here. That would be a good thing to do."

"A fine plan," Brian said, and shared a grin with his cousin, "but I believe I will hold fast to my own. Every instinct I have says they are all gathering to try and grab those boys. There is also a chance her family may have already arrived there to look for her. We have to get to Scarglas to see what is happening there. Aye, and Arianna needs to be at Scarglas, needs to be back with the lads so that she cannae be taken and used against the boys."

"I have nay kenned the lass for long but I do ken that she would ne'er betray those lads to save her own life."

"Nay, she wouldnae, which is a thought that chills me to the bone. Howbeit, if she was held as hostage to get those boys, I think those lads would quickly try to trade themselves for her and naught short of chaining them up would stop them. 'Tis true that I only saw them together for a short time, but e'en though they call her Anna and they have no blood ties, she is their mother."

He repeated what he had told Sigimor about how he had found her upon the beach, the boys guarding her, and even how they had acted when parted, but this time he stressed how the boys and Arianna had acted toward each other. Then he explained more fully how the Lucettes had treated the boys and Arianna. Brian made no attempt to hide his anger over that, either, and could see that his cousin shared it.

Sigimor nodded. "Aye, ye are correct. In their eyes, she is their mother. 'Tis no surprise. The lads were nay cared for by their true parents nor by those blood-proud fools they should have been able to call family. Only to be expected that the three who were so scorned by all who should have cared for them would join together, make their own wee family. They were all each other had whilst trapped in that keep where no one was kind to them."

Tapping his knuckles on the table as he frowned in thought, Sigimor continued, "I am also verra surprised that the lass's kin didnae come to fetch her and break a few heads in the doing of it. E'en if they all still believed the marriage was a true one, that clan wouldnae abide one of their own being treated as poorly as Lady Arianna was. I ne'er asked, but did the lass ne'er send them word?"

"She did but I believe every missive she wrote was read by that fool she thought she had wed or his parents. If they didnae like what was said, they destroyed it. We also think they read all that was sent to her, may even have destroyed a few of those. It would explain how Amiel and the DeVeaux discovered who had taken the boys and where we were all apt to go to find some shelter."

"Of course. They gathered information on the ones they wished to be more closely allied with. Many would do the same although, kenning how they treated a daughter of the clan, one has to wonder on their motives. They also couldnae risk the Murrays kenning how the lass was being treated. Kenning what I do about that clan, and the women bred of it, I do have to wonder why Lady Arianna didnae ken the truth sooner or why she didnae just leave the mon when he showed himself to be a cold bastard."

Brian looked around to make sure that they were still alone for, while he knew he could trust Arianna's secrets to Sigimor, he did not want others to hear too much. "She was but newly turned seventeen when she married him and was determined to make it a good marriage, one as good as the others in her clan. But, from the moment she was his wife, fully separated from her kin, Claud began to break her pride and her spirit."

"Are ye sure he didnae beat her?"

"Nay. I believe she would ne'er have stood for that. That would have been an abuse she would have easily recognized. One blow from his hand and the mon wouldnae have seen her save for the dust behind her mount. Aye, and he would probably have been kept busy pulling a knife or two out of his body."

Sigimor nodded. "That sounds much akin to the Murray lasses we have kenned and heard of."

"Aye, she would have quickly acted against any physical brutality. He crushed her with words. Constant criticisms, insults, and unkindnesses. Young, innocent, and unaccustomed to such subtle cruelties, she was easy prey. She told me she could still hear him, that she still winces at the sharp cut of his words. He cut away at her pride in herself, at all that makes her a woman."

"A slow poison so that he could keep her completely under his boot."

"Aye, and so instead of wondering why he was such a poor husband, she was soon thinking herself a poor wife. He made certain that she ne'er looked too closely at him and I wonder if that is one reason he gave the care of his children into her hands, kenning that they would hold her interest and attention. I think he kenned she had the wit to uncover all of his lies. And in the end, she did, was e'en planning how to leave him and that cold place when he and his true wife were murdered."

"And all the time planning to take those two lads with her, I wager."

"Of course. 'Twas plotting how to do that without causing an uproar, which held her there even after she learned the truth about Claud." Brian shook his head. "She was hoping that she could find a way to save the boys from the shame and humiliation that would come when the truth was revealed. Aye, even thinking on how to protect the very family that had scorned her. She kens how she will be marked if the truth comes out but she thought only of the boys and the families, hers and his. All that only to discover that bastard of a husband had left a confession for his parents, one to be read if he died, one they quickly acted upon without much thought to how it could hurt her."

Sigimor cursed. "I thought the Lucettes were allies and kinsmen to the Murrays."

"Ach, weel, every family has its rotten apples."

"Aye. We always thought ours were those cursed MacFingals."

Brian laughed and tossed an uncut apple at his cousin's head. There were times when one wanted to beat Sigimor with a thick stick, but Brian had liked the man from the first moment he had met him. He had easily seen beneath that stern-faced exterior to the man who had, at a very young age, become the laird to a large number of siblings, widows, and orphans, and done his best to protect them all. The man was rough and appeared hard but just as with his own brother Ewan, Brian knew there was a big heart beneath that broad chest.

"Throwing food about?"

"Sigimor was just being his usual irritating self,"

Brian said as he and his cousin stood to greet Arianna and Jolene. "Are ye ready to leave?" he asked Arianna as he directed her to the seat on his left.

"Aye, as soon as I have eaten," Arianna said. "I am verra eager to see my lads again. I ken that your kin will protect them and have gotten them to Scarglas unharmed, but I need to see with my own eyes that Michel and Adelar are safe." She shrugged. "I need to hold them again."

"Of course you do," said Jolene as she helped herself to a large bowl of porridge. "You accepted the responsibility of their care and, no matter how much you trust in the ones who now shelter them, 'tis impossible not to fret." She exchanged an understanding smile with Arianna and then looked at her husband. "Where are our children?"

"The bairns have filled their bellies, which appear to be bottomless, and gone out to thump with their wooden swords anything that will stand still long enough. Fergus is with them."

"Your daughters are supposed to be learning how to ply their needles."

"Ye can remind them of that chore when ye are done eating. They will probably tend to their lessons a bit better after they have had a wee bit of fun thumping things."

"Ladies should not take joy in thumping things."

Arianna ate, doing her best to fill her stomach as full as she could before her journey began, and listened to Jolene and Sigimor as the pair talked about their beautiful, black-haired daughters. To some it might sound as if they argued with each other but there was no taint of anger in their words. There was, however, a great deal of teasing, and she could not help but laugh at times.

A sudden attack of envy, laden with sadness, overtook her. Here was what she had been looking for, what she had wanted to share with Claud. It was what she had seen so often among the married couples in her clan. To her it had been the normal way a marriage should be and she had been naive to think she could have one like it simply because she exchanged a few vows with a man.

She was almost relieved when Brian announced that they had to leave. Guilt pinched her heart as she truly enjoyed Jolene's company and envy was such a pitiful emotion. It was just going to take her a while to endure watching people who had what she craved, she decided as she followed Brian and Sigimor out into the bailey where the horses waited. Arianna said her good-byes to Jolene as Brian checked the packs on their horses and talked to Sigimor. From what little she overheard of the men's conversation, it was evident that Sigimor's men had been hunting for Amiel and his surviving men, reporting back only an hour ago that they had seen no sign of them. Some of the tension that had begun to tighten in her body at the prospect of more running from the enemy eased and Arianna mounted her waiting horse with no hesitation.

It was barely midday when Brian had them stop. Arianna wanted to continue and would have made no complaint if they had, but she was also pleased to dismount for a while. Aches she had thought healed by the short rest at Dubheidland were already making their lingering presence known.

"I but need to look about a wee bit," Brian said, and brushed a kiss across her mouth.

"I thought Sigimor said his men had nay found Amiel," she said, resisting the sudden urge to look around.

He smiled and tucked a strand of hair that had escaped her braid behind her ear. "He did, but it cannac hurt to see if I can find a sign that they are headed toward Scarglas. It would be good to ken if they are ahead of us."

"Ah, of course. We wouldnae want to ride into their hands."

"Nay, we wouldnae. Will ye be all right here?"

"Aye. Go. I will be fine. I will just rest here beneath the tree."

Brian hesitated and then gave her another kiss before leaving. Arianna smiled faintly as she watched him go. It was time to sit and wait again, but this time she did not mind. He needed to assure himself they were not riding into a trap and she needed to rest. It was also the middle of the day, the land around her bathed in sun, a cool, light breeze blowing, and she wanted to enjoy that for a while.

She settled herself beneath the tree. Within a short time her eyes grew heavy but she tried to fight the urge to sleep. It was not wise to sleep as if there was no danger, she sternly told herself, but her body was obviously not concerned. Just as she began to slide into a doze a faint noise snapped her awake.

Arianna slowly stood up and looked around. It was light where she stood, the trees thinner than ones surrounding her. She realized that made her very easy to see and cursed her own foolishness. She should have moved into the shadows. The faint snap of a twig drew her gaze toward where the trees thickened, the shadows they cast heavier and harder to see through. That was where she should have hidden herself. Instead, it now gave shelter to a threat. Her whole body tense as she fought a blinding panic, Arianna backed toward her horse.

Fear making her heart pound, she turned to run to her mount only to find a man between her and the horse. Now she knew why the animal had not become restless, warning her. Men did not trouble it. She spun around thinking to run in another direction only to find another man behind her. What terrified her the most, however, was the man who stepped out from behind a large tree and gave her a smile that chilled her blood.

"Greetings, *sister,*" the man drawled in French.

"Amiel, how nice for ye to slither up out of the muck to greet me," she replied in English, and briefly wondered if it was wise to be so insulting only to decide it did not matter. The man would do his best to hurt her even if she was as sweet as honey.

"I see you have sunk back into the barbaric ways of this country again, although I am rather pleased that you no longer even attempt to speak French though you still appear to understand it reasonably well." He shuddered. "It is difficult to listen to you speak it."

Did the idiot think she could forget such a skill in mere days? "Then ye will be pleased to ken that I have nay intention of ever speaking it to ye again. I shall take my barbaric ways and leave now."

Even as she bolted she knew she had little chance of avoiding capture. Amiel and his men had quietly surrounded her while she had been napping in the sun like an overfed cat. They easily kept her from getting to her horse, blocking her path no matter which direction she tried to run in. When one of the men reached for her, she kicked him in the groin and tried to run past him as he fell to his knees. A hand grabbing her braid and yanking hard sent her stumbling back into another man.

Arianna turned and pummeled him with her fists and feet in a desperate attempt to break free. She did not hesitate to use her nails and teeth as well. A punch to his nose loosened his grip and she had a brief flare of hope as she tried to run again. That hope was abruptly ended with a hard blow to the back of her head. As Arianna fell to her knees, fighting vainly against the blackness sweeping over her mind, she saw Amiel looking down at her, a thick stick in his hand and a smile on his face.

"He will rip ye into wee pieces and leave them for the carrion," she said as the blackness closed in on her, and then she fell face-first into the dirt.

"My, such a vicious little bitch," Amiel murmured as he tossed aside the stick he held and brushed off his hands.

"Should we look for the man?" asked Sir Anton as he handed the man Arianna had punched a scrap of linen to stop the blood flowing from his nose.

"No need. We have what we want. Take her up with you." He turned to the man Arianna had kicked, who was just stumbling back up on his feet. "You bring her horse."

"We are taking her to this Scarglas then?"

"Yes, but with a little stop on the way. There is no gain in trying to ride through the night. I believe we shall spend some of the evening having a conversation with this little savage."

"I doubt she was out here alone. Someone will come hunting for her."

"They cannot hunt in the dark."

Brian frowned as he reined in and looked around. He was certain this was where he had left Arianna. The fear that gripped him by the throat told him he was not wrong, that he was never wrong about such things. His sense of direction was legendary amongst his kin.

Flinging himself out of his saddle, he searched the grounds for some sign that would tell him why she was not where he had left her. Brian was just praying that she had simply wandered off even though he knew she would not be so foolish when he found the signs that told him she had been taken. Forcing himself to be calm, he carefully studied all the ground told him, moving outward from where she had so clearly tried to escape the ones who encircled her. Several yards into the shadowy area of the forest, he found the signs of several men on horseback having paused and dismounted. They had made no attempt to hide the direction they rode off in, either.

Cursing continuously under his breath, he returned to the place where Arianna had been captured. He took a deep breath and finally looked closely at the one place on the ground he had noted but fought to ignore. There was blood there and he could see that someone had fallen. He tried to comfort himself with the fact that there was not much blood but his fear for Arianna did not wish to be appeased. Brian knew he was looking at the place where she had fallen, which meant she had already been hurt.

His first instinct was to hunt her down immediately but he fought against it. That would be a mistake and he had already made one by leaving her alone and unprotected. One man against six was not good odds. And there could be more than that now if Amiel had found some more hirelings. He needed enough men to encircle Amiel and his men as they had obviously encircled Arianna. Overwhelming the men was the only way to get Arianna back alive.

Brian leapt on his horse and raced back to Dubheidland. He tried not to think of what could be happening to Arianna as the time slipped away for he knew that would drive him mad, force him into doing something reckless that could get them both killed. The certainty that Amiel did not want her dead until he had the boys in his grasp was the only thing that helped.

Sigimor was already armed and in the bailey when Brian rode in. Brian leapt from his exhausted mount and stood trying to catch his breath for a moment, certain he had never ridden so hard in his life. He accepted the water given him and gulped it down.

"He has her," he said.

"How?" Sigimor demanded as his men brought saddled horses up to them, including a strong fresh mount for Brian.

"I went out to see if the mon was between us and Scarglas. I left her alone and they found her."

"'Tis nay your fault."

"I left her alone!"

"For a good reason. Ye didnae want to ride right into the enemy's grasp and we had decided they were headed to Scarglas. Without a look round, ye could easily have ridden right into them. They obviously got farther away faster than we thought they would. How far away were ye from here when ye stopped?"

"Mayhap an hour and a half of hard riding."

"So they have already had her for a while," Sigimor muttered. "They will nay have stayed close to where ye left her, either." He glanced up at the sky. "If we are lucky we can track them to where they hold her before the sun completely sets. Dusk is a verra good time for creeping up on someone."

"I did see where they had left the horses and which direction they went off in."

"That will help. A shame we cannae ken exactly when they grabbed her as that would make it easier to judge how far they may have gone."

"I was gone nearly two hours."

"Ah, then they will have had time to get a fair distance away from where they took her. It may weel be dark ere we find her, but I have some skill in raiding in the night."

Before Brian could say another word, Sigimor was signaling his men to mount. Brian quickly swung up into the saddle of his fresh horse. No matter how hard he tried he could not stop thinking about how long Arianna would be in the hands of a man who wished her dead before they could find her. He was pulled from his dark thoughts when Sigimor gave him a hard slap on the back.

"We will find her, cousin," Sigimor said.

Staring blindly at the men preparing to go out and help him hunt for Arianna, Brian did not feel the confidence he usually felt when involved in a hunt of any kind. "What if he takes her right to De-Veaux?"

"Then we follow him until he stops long enough for us to take her back."

"Ye make it sound so simple. The mon kens we will be hunting him."

"Does he? I am nay sure the mon is as clever as ye think. It doesnae matter. He cannae ride at night unless he has a mon who kens the land weel. The dark slows us all down but he will have to stop and that is when we will have him."

As the men mounted up and started out of the bailey, Brian could only pray that his cousin was right. Fear was a hard knot in his belly and failure a sour taste in his mouth. He would not rest until he had Arianna safely back in his arms.

Chapter 12

Pain greeted Arianna as she slipped free of unconsciousness, most of it centered in her head. She decided she was growing weary of it. She had done nothing to deserve it and wanted the ones who kept inflicting her with it to suffer. It was difficult to swallow her groan of pain as she struggled to open her eyes just enough to see where she was yet not alert her captors to the fact that she was awake.

She was inside a rough cottage. Arianna immediately feared for the safety of the ones the cottage had belonged to but pushed aside that concern. She could do nothing about their fate unless she got free, although she was certain it would only be to find some justice for the killing of innocents. Amiel would not have left anyone alive to tell where he and his men were. He was the one being hunted now. Despite her pain and dire circumstances, Arianna was able to find some satisfaction in that.

Crouched by the fire in the center of the cottage was her husband's brother Amiel. There was also some petty satisfaction to be found in the fact that the ever-fastidious Amiel was mud-splattered and untidy. Beneath the dirt were clothes fit for an appearance at court and she inwardly shook her head over Amiel's idiocy. Did the fool think he could just ride into the country and bargain bloodlessly for the return of two boys he meant to kill? It did not surprise her to see the other men glaring at him with contempt when they thought he was not looking their way.

There was no doubt in her mind that the man was indeed a fool, and not only in his choice of clothing. All he had had to do was wait and he could have gotten what he craved without getting any innocent blood on his hands. Claud's family was appalled that their son and heir had married a common maid and did not wish the boys born of that union to claim anything. A little money and a few lies could make that embarrassing marriage disappear. It would just take time. Amiel, however, wanted it all now, with a ferocity that made her wonder yet again if he was in debt to someone. She wondered if some of the man's hatred for the boys was because they were Claud's. There had never been any love lost between the brothers but she had never thought the animosity would lead to murder.

The truth struck her so forcefully she nearly opened her eyes wide and had to swallow a gasp. It was something she had considered several times but now she had no doubt. Amiel owed the DeVeaux something or wanted something they could give him. He had become their pawn, although he was probably too blindly arrogant to know it. It was the only explanation for why he now rushed to kill two young boys who would undoubtedly, and unfairly, become disinherited soon. Legally made bastards by an annulment that would be bought and paid for by his parents.

Not only a traitor to his own blood but a complete, blind fool. Amiel ignored the long, bloody history of DeVeaux treachery if he actually thought they would let him live for long after he gave them what they wanted or they gave him what he sought. Every Lucette knew that the king may have forced a truce between the two families but it had not completely stopped the treachery the DeVeaux excelled at, it had merely made them more secretive. Amiel's arrogance obviously made him think he could outwit his venomous allies. She could almost feel sorry for Amiel but for the knowledge that he wanted to kill Adelar and Michel. That ended any chance of her feeling even the smallest twinge of pity for him.

"I think she wakes," said one of the DeVeaux men riding with Amiel.

Arianna silently cursed, wondering what had given her away. She had kept her breathing slow and even, was certain she had not moved any part of her body, and had kept her eyes shut enough that no one should have seen even a hint of wakefulness there. Fighting not to tense in fear and show the others the man was right, she waited.

"Nay, she still sleeps, Sir Anton," said Amiel, his irritatingly nasal voice easy to recognize.

"Are you quite certain of that?"

"She has not even groaned, has she, and that knock upon the head has to hurt."

There was the hint of pleasure in his voice and

Arianna ached to beat him with a thick stick. Her head throbbed so badly it was difficult to restrain the urge to rub her forehead. Only the knowledge that it would do little to help ease the pain kept her from doing so. What truly mattered now was neither her pain nor her injuries, but the plans of her enemy. Knowing what they had schemed could aid her in escaping them, or warning the others when she was rescued.

And she would be rescued, she told herself firmly. She had more confidence in that than in her chances of escaping, especially since she would have to flee on foot. The fact that she would be on foot if she escaped would not stop her from trying if the chance to flee came her way, however. Arianna knew she did not have Brian's skill at slipping through the shadows, or even hiding in them, but she had watched him do it enough to have learned a few things. What she had learned might be enough to help her at least stay hidden while Amiel and his men hunted for her.

"Well, I believe she is awake, or very nearly so," said Sir Anton.

"Kick her then. If she is awake that will make her cease her games."

"I will not kick a woman, especially not an unconscious woman lying on the ground."

"Such a tender heart you have, my fine knight. I must wonder what hold the DeVeaux have upon you as you are far too concerned with what is right and proper to deal weel with them. But, not to worry this time. I am not burdened by such weaknesses."

Arianna did not move fast enough to completely evade Amiel's boot. He struck her in the lower back

as she rolled away from him and struck her hard
enough to make her gasp with pain. She was still
panting from that pain when he grabbed her by the
arm and yanked her to her feet. Nausea clenched her
stomach as the pain from the blow on her head swept
over her. For a moment, she instinctively fought the
urge to empty her stomach, but then caught sight of
Amiel's boots. With a groan, she bent toward them
and allowed her stomach to have its way.

Amiel's cry of disgust and outrage gave her a
brief moment of pleasure. That was abruptly ended
when his fist hit her jaw. She sprawled on her back
on the hard dirt floor of the cottage, the force of
the blow knocking her away from him and his
soiled boots. Arianna cursed herself for provoking
the man. If she suffered more injuries she would
never be able to take advantage of any opportunity
to escape. The way she hurt now, she was surprised
she was still conscious and rather wished she was
not. A convenient swoon might save her from feeling any more pain but her body was not cooperat-
ing with her wish. Instead, she struggled to sit up.

One tall, thin man stood back from Amiel and his
lackeys. Watching everything with a frown. Arianna
was sure that was Sir Anton, the man who had been
so outraged at the suggestion that he kick an unconscious woman. She wondered if he could prove to be
a possible ally, but her head was throbbing so badly
that she could barely think straight. One needed
one's full wits sharp to turn a man against the others
he rode with, especially to make any man betray
the DeVeaux. Arianna was not sure she would be allowed any time to think clearly anyway, or be eased
from her pain, as long as she remained a captive of

Amiel. Claud had been subtly cruel. Amiel was openly vicious.

"You bitch!" Amiel cried once his boots were clean. "You did that on purpose."

Just to be contrary, Arianna refused to speak to him in French. "I did it because ye hit me on the head. Emptying one's belly after such a blow is common. Your boots were just in my way."

He slapped her and Arianna could see bursts of light behind her lids when she closed her eyes against this new pain. The fear that he was going to beat her to death rose up but she fought it. If that was his plan there was not much she could do to stop him but she did not plan to make it easy for him. She placed her hands on the ground, hung her head, and tried to breathe through the worst of the pain. When she looked at Amiel again she did nothing to hide her contempt or anger.

"You will regret that, you little bitch," Amiel said, his voice shaking with the fury he could not hide.

"Och, ye greedy swine, I have many regrets already," she said as she forced herself back on her feet. "The greatest of those is that I e'er met your thrice-cursed family. Are ye verra certain ye are Lucettes?"

"Of course we are. You, however, never were."

Arianna wondered why those words did not hurt. Amiel just spoke aloud what his whole family had felt about her. She had never been accepted, never been allowed to become a part of the family, and that had always hurt her before. Perhaps, she finally realized, she simply did not care and had not for quite a while. If she had not thought herself married to Claud the pig she would have ceased trying to please her new family a long, long time ago. She had never liked any of them save for young Paul.

"I find myself rather pleased by that," she said, and staggered when he slapped her again.

"Where are my brother's little bastards?"

The man did not give her any chance to reply before he slapped her again, catching her with a hard backhand swing for the second blow that sent her back to the floor. Through the pounding in her ears, she could hear arguing. Rolling slowly onto her side, she saw that Sir Anton now stood between her and Amiel.

"You did not allow her to answer," said Sir Anton.

"And how is that your concern?" Amiel eased his dagger from the sheath at his waist. "Too weak of stomach to do as you should, Sir Anton?"

"The DeVeaux want her alive. I also do not believe beating her to death is either right or will accomplish anything."

Arianna was just thinking that the man was brave but very foolish when Amiel stabbed Sir Anton. Amiel smiled in a way that chilled her as he yanked his dagger out of the man's side and watched Sir Anton slowly fall to his knees. Still smiling, he kicked Sir Anton aside and looked at her again. There was such a gleam of violence in his eyes that, if she could move, she would be running for her life.

Two of the men riding with Amiel moved to help Sir Anton get back on his feet. Another looked at Amiel, his hand clutching the hilt of his sword. Arianna suspected the man was a DeVeaux soldier and was wondering just how far he should go in defending a fellow DeVeaux man.

"Lord Ignace will not be pleased if you murder

the man he married his cousin off to," the man said. "It was not easy to find someone to take the woman."

"I have not killed the fool," snapped Amiel, turning toward the man.

The other men quickly joined in the resulting argument, obviously intent upon reminding Amiel just whom he owed his allegiance to. It was clear for Arianna to see that Amiel did not like to be reminded. As she began to crawl out of the cottage, she prayed the men would decide that argument was futile and just kill him.

Out of the corner of her eye she saw Sir Anton move to lean up against the wall. He was watching her but said nothing, making no attempt to draw the attention of the others to what she was doing. Arianna suspected he saw no gain in telling Amiel that his prisoner was trying to escape for they both knew she had very little chance of accomplishing it. It was going to be a while before she could even stand up without risking complete unconsciousness.

Just as she reached the middle of the cleared area in front of the cottage, the carefully tended ground already badly marred by the men's horses, she rose up on her knees. Her vision was not completely clear and the throbbing in her head made her stomach churn, but Arianna slowly forced herself to her feet.

"Where do you think you are going?"

Arianna looked toward her horse and sighed. There was no chance that she could reach it, mount, and ride away before she was caught. She simply did not have the strength. There was no doubt in her mind that, after only a few steps, if she did not fall down, she would be knocked down. She turned to face Amiel. It was not easy to keep her gaze fixed on him when she could see Sir Anton stealthily making his way to the horses.

"I confess that I grew weary of your kind hospitality and decided it was time to go home," she replied to Amiel.

"My brother never truly succeeded in showing you your place, did he?"

If only I had the strength to punch him right in that sneering mouth of his, I could die happy, Arianna thought. "My place is right here," she said, refusing to speak in French as he continued to do. "In Scotland. But dear old Claud learned his place, didnae he, Amiel? Ye taught him and his wife, didnae ye?"

"You think *I* killed my own brother?" The man sounded shocked but there was the glint of amused satisfaction in his eyes.

"Aye, I do. Mayhap ye didnae dirty your own hands, but ye hired the ones who did. Grew tired of waiting for him to die, did ye? Did ye think no one would learn that he was truly married to Marie Anne? That no one would ken that Michel and Adelar are Claud's legal heirs?"

"They will never be accepted as the heirs. My family will see them marked as the common-born little bastards they are."

"Aye, they probably will, so why dinnae ye just wait for that to happen? Why this hunt for them? I was taking them far away so ye wouldnae e'en have seen them about while your parents worked to annul Claud's marriage to Marie Anne. And to ally yourself with the DeVeaux? Ye will have your whole clan wanting to kill ye and spit upon your grave."

"Foolish woman. Claud was right. You are not very clever. I could have waited but then I would have been no more than another Lucette, another titled, landed Lucette among dozens of titled, landed Lucettes. But, with only the gifting of a small piece of land to the DeVeaux, I have an ally all the other Lucettes fear." He shrugged. "And the very full purse they plan to give me as well."

"All that still doesnae explain why ye hunt the boys. It only tells me that ye have no loyalty to your own blood."

She tensed when he clenched his hands into fists, but he did not hit her. It was clear that he suddenly wanted to boast of his cleverness. Arianna could not understand how the man could betray his whole family as he had done and she made no secret of the disgust she felt for him. She knew it was revealed on her face if only because of the way Amiel grew more furious the longer she looked at him.

"Ah, I forgot that you paid little heed to the reading of the will."

"Hard to pay attention when one isnae e'en told about it."

"Claud left the land the DeVeaux want to the boys. There is no way of changing that unless the boys die, for it was Claud's land alone, to do with as he pleased. I was there when he wrote the will and convinced him to name me as heir should anything happen and the boys did not live into manhood." He scowled. "I could not stop him from naming you their guardian, however. That was a disappointment."

"For which ye slaughtered him and Marie Anne."

"One of but many reasons."

Arianna found it all hard to believe. Claud had

finally done something worthy for his children and it had put a knife at their throats. It also surprised her that he had officially made her their guardian for it was unusual to name a woman one and Claud had never shown any faith in her ability to do much of anything right.

"And for that wee piece of land and a few coins, ye killed your own brother and Marie Anne, and now mean to kill two bairns who have ne'er done ye harm, your own nephews."

"I told you that I did not kill my brother and his sow."

"Nay, I believe ye. I believe that ye didnae bloody your own soft hands with the black deed of killing your own brother, but I do believe that ye put the sword in the hands of the ones who did."

"The DeVeaux . . ."

"Have kenned that Claud held that land for years and either didnae, or couldnae, do anything about it. Ye found a way to have it done or conspired with them to do it. Aye, I suspicion ye could stand before the king himself and claim innocence because ye didnae actually do the killing, but ye are guilty right enough. I am nay sure how ye think ye can do the same once ye kill the boys, though, since ye are hunting them down like dogs."

"We are merely trying to retrieve my brother's heirs, who were taken from their rightful place by the woman my brother betrayed. We feared for the safety of the children in the hands of that woman and it appears we were right to do so. Sadly, the children were murdered before we could save them."

The smug tone of his voice, his obvious delight in the plan for how to explain the deaths of Michel and Adelar, chilled Arianna. Amiel did not care about blood at all. All he was concerned with was gaining riches and power, and if he had to start gaining that wealth by stepping over the bodies of two murdered children, he would do so without hesitation.

And, after the murder of the two boys, the rest of the Lucettes who had something Amiel wanted would begin to suffer. Arianna was certain that Amiel intended to reduce the number of landed, titled Lucettes until he was weighted down with their honors. The heirs would be the first to go for he would need to clear the path for himself. He apparently had the intention of being the last Lucette standing. It was a mad plan and one she doubted would work for a rapid decline in heirs to the various Lucette properties would soon draw a lot of attention. Unfortunately, a great many innocent Lucettes could die first.

"And do ye truly believe that the DeVeaux will sit back and allow ye to slowly grow more powerful than they are, to watch ye reap titles and lands until ye are a threat to them?"

"I but seek what Claud would have gained in time, and retrieve those riches which he would have foolishly handed over to ones not worthy of them."

"Nay, I think ye want more. Much more. After all, ye just said ye were but one of far too many titled Lucettes and ye ally yourself with the deadliest of your kinmen's enemies. Nay, ye have some mad plan to try and get it all." She shook her head, forgetting how badly it would hurt to do so, and had to stiffen her stance to remain upright. "It is a plan that can only fail, Amiel. E'en if the king or your own kin dinnae guess the deadly game ye mean to play and stop you, the DeVeaux will."

"As they all guessed how dear old Claud died?"

"Claud was but one mon. Now ye think to add two wee lads and follow their deaths with many others."

"At this moment my only concern is for those boys. Where are they?"

"Somewhere where ye will ne'er get your filthy hands on them."

The blow he struck against her face snapped her head sideways with such force pain shot through her neck. Arianna again steadied herself, holding her legs so taut and straight that they ached, too. She knew Amiel could not allow her to live no matter what the DeVeaux wanted. He had let her see the truth of all his plans. She knew too much now.

"You will tell me where Claud's whelps are, bitch, or you will suffer."

Arianna touched her mouth and then looked at the blood on her fingers. She could already feel the swelling in her face, her skin tightening with it. There were very few places on her body that did not already throb with pain from Amiel's fists and booted feet. She knew it would only get worse because she had no intention of telling him anything. What she wished she could do was fight back, to knock him down and kick him a few times.

Still staring at the blood on her fingers, she suddenly wondered where that spine had been when Claud had battered her with his cruel words. If he had backhanded her even once, she would not have hesitated to leave, undoubtedly making sure that Claud tasted a little pain himself before she walked away. Yet she had allowed him to cut her with words. Claud had found a weakness in her that she had not seen and used it to turn her into a quiet little shadow, one who never fought back, never questioned. She looked at Amiel and saw that same cruelty in him, only Amiel preferred to be more direct in his abuse. *I should have seen it,* Arianna thought.

"And 'tis a strange time to have an epiphany," she muttered, knowing there was a very good chance she would not be alive long enough to shake free of the chains Claud had bound her with.

"What did you say?" demanded Amiel.

"Naught that concerns you," she replied, idly wondering if she had the strength to kick him right in his precious manparts.

"Where are the boys?"

"Why are ye even troubling yourself to ask? Ye ken where they are already, or think ye do. The De-Veaux have sent ye word several times, have they nay?" She almost smiled at the surprise on his face, something he tried to quickly hide from her.

"They have only surmised where they might be. I think you know exactly where they are."

"And I think ye just wish to pretend that ye have a good reason to beat a lass half your size."

Even as he moved to strike her, she kicked out, slamming the toe of her booted foot right between his legs. She stumbled back a few steps as she struggled to right herself. Amiel gave a strangled scream, clutched himself, and fell to his knees. Arianna knew she was going to pay dearly for that. All that troubled her was that it had not even given her a chance to try and get to her horse because two of Amiel's men immediately moved to guard her.

The way Amiel retched and muttered vile curses against her under his breath should have terrified her, Arianna thought. Instead, she moved to kick him again, trying to strike a blow to his head. The men flanking her put a stop to that and she sighed. As Amiel stumbled to his feet, his expression a twisted grimace of pain and fury, she knew that even threatening him with the anger of the DeVeaux would not stop him from beating her to death now.

When Amiel swung his fist at her it hit her hard enough to send her staggering into one of the men guarding her. She cursed the man for that as it kept her upright and made it easier for Amiel to keep pummeling her. When the man finally moved, if only to get out of the way of Amiel's flailing fists, she fell to the ground and braced herself for the hard kicks she knew would come next.

Instead, a heated argument ensued. She was fighting unconsciousness so fiercely that she caught only a few words, but Lord Ignace DeVeaux was mentioned several times. It was strange that the man's name was not enough to terrify Amiel out of his rage, and she had to wonder if they were being chased by the winemaker and not the torturer. The men were still trying to remind Amiel yet again of his obligations, but she knew they would fail. She had seen her death in Amiel's eyes.

She struggled up onto her hands and knees, and she prayed that Brian had returned for her and was, even now, coming to rescue her. It was the only hope she had of surviving.

Chapter 13

"Easy, lad. Ye cannae just ride o'er them," Sigimor said as he grabbed the reins of Brian's mount to halt his cousin's attempt to gallop off.

Brian nearly yanked the reins back but good sense pierced his fury. Sigimor was right, although he would prefer to cut out his own tongue before telling his cousin that. Fergus's report of what was happening to Arianna but a short ride away had blinded him with fury. He was also angry with himself for attempting to charge over the land with nothing but his fear for Arianna to lead him. It was only Sigimor's calm leadership that had kept him on the right trail.

From the moment she had been taken, he had had to struggle fiercely against the fear for her and the fury against himself for not keeping her safe. Worse, there had been no sign that it had been a carefully planned attack. Lucette and his men had simply stumbled upon the prize they had been scouring Scotland for. Brian could not help but take the blame for that upon his shoulders. He had known Lucette was out there somewhere, that the man had too much knowledge about the places Arianna might go to seek safety, and he should have taken more care with her.

"How long do ye intend to wear that hair shirt?" asked Sigimor even as he signaled his men to dismount and secure the horses.

"I should have stayed with her," Brian said as he dismounted and tugged his mount deeper into the shadows of the trees, securing the reins to a low-hanging branch. "I kenned that Lucette was aware of where Arianna might run to yet I left her to try to see exactly where the fool was. I kenned he was on the same trail. I didnae need to see that with my own eyes."

"Nay, ye did. He might ken where she will go but he doesnae ken the exact path or even have to take it."

"Nay, it didnae matter. Since they were nay anywhere in sight or riding up our arses, I could have let it be."

"Nay, ye couldnae have and ye will ken it when ye clear your wee head. Hold," he snapped when Brian opened his mouth to continue the argument. "Someone approaches," Sigimor said, and drew his sword. "One. Coming slowly. Hide."

Brian joined the others in slipping silently into the shadows. A man rode into the small clearing where they had all stood but a heartbeat before and Brian immediately recognized him as Sir Anton, one of Lucette's men. Staying close to his cousin, he stepped out into the clearing while Sigimor swiftly snatched the reins from the surprised man's hands and held a sword on him.

Sir Anton slowly raised his arms. "I am not your enemy," he said.

"Nay? I saw ye with Lucette," said Brian. "Ye ride with the pig. Has he sent ye to watch for us?"

"No. The fool, he does not think to look for anyone to follow or hunt for the Lady Arianna. He holds the same blind contempt for the lady as his brother did, and for all who live in this country. I but try to make my way home."

"Ye are leaving his service?"

"I was never in his service. I was asked by the Lady DeVeau to join them on this journey and one does not refuse the DeVeaux, not if one is married to one of their women. I intend to get home now. I will collect my family and retire to the lands my father holds. I am nay sure I will be in danger but I am thinking the Lady DeVeau is as bad as so many others in that family."

"It might help if ye stop bleeding first," said Sigimor. "Anger your fool of a laird, did ye?"

Sir Anton frowned at Sigimor for a moment and then said, "Ah, you speak of Lucette. *Oui,* I angered him. I did not like what was being done to the woman, to the Lady Arianna. I had not understood all that was planned when I began this journey. I was standing on the shore of this land before I knew the truth." He shrugged and then winced. "I was believing I was trapped but I change my mind. I think they will all die here and that means I can leave."

"Get down. We will bind that wound and I will tell ye how to get to a ship."

"This is most kind of you." Sir Anton started to dismount and faltered, requiring Sigimor's aid.

"You are most kind, sir. I am thinking I chose the right time to leave this place. I am right, *oui*? You will kill them all?"

As Sigimor tended to the dagger slash on the man's side, he said, "I believe my cousin here wants Lucette dead but, if the others fight, they will die, too."

"Lucette is not a man any will grieve for. Not even his mother, I think."

"What were they doing to the Lady Arianna?" demanded Brian, praying the man would say something to prove Fergus was mistaken in what he had seen.

"Beating the truth out of her."

"Stand back, Brian," ordered Sigimor. "Ye are scaring the mon."

Brian abruptly noticed that he was looming over the man, his sword pointing at Sir Anton's throat. He slowly stepped back and sheathed his sword. There was no question in his mind that the man spoke the truth, that Sir Anton was no more than a man who found himself caught up in something he did not approve of and was trying to get out of it.

"Tell me what made ye risk your life and stand against Lucette and the DeVeaux," he demanded.

"First I am refusing to kick the Lady Arianna when she is unconscious on the floor," Sir Anton replied. "Then I make a complaint when Lucette keeps slapping her even when she had no chance to answer the question he asked. I see that he likes it, *oui*? He is much liking the causing of her pain. He stabbed me. Then I begin to realize he means to kill the two boys when he gets them and I did not come here to slaughter children. He means to kill the woman, too. I walked away for I now understand and will have no more part of this. I will go home now. I will pray that this ends it and none return to tell of how I walked away. I do not wish to die for this travesty." He moved to remount, his movement somewhat more graceful now that his wound had been tended to. "They are not far ahead of you."

"We ken it," said Sigimor, and then told the man how to reach a port and a ship home. "Get your wife and bairns and get as far from the DeVeaux as ye can. The ones here willnae be going home and that might irritate their kin. Ye dinnae want to be close at hand when they hear the news. And there is also the chance that Lady Arianna's kinsmen will nay be pleased with how she has been treated and look for some revenge. Ye truly dinnae want to get caught in that."

Brian watched Sir Anton ride away and then looked at Sigimor. "Why did ye help him?"

"Mon needed it," replied Sigimor. "'Tis easy for the ones with nay power to get pulled into things they dinnae want to do by the ones who hold the power. Sir Anton finally found the spine to risk his life to say nay and then to walk away. Didnae seem right to cut his throat. Now, let us go and get your lady."

"They are beating her, Sigimor," Brian whispered, fighting the urge to run to where they held Arianna. Only the knowledge that such a rash act could get her killed held him back.

"Aye. Fergus told us that but, mayhap, ye needed it said again, aye?" Sigimor slapped him on the back. "Rein yourself in, lad. Now ye have had two people tell ye she is still alive and verra close at hand."

As his cousin silently directed his men toward

where Lucette and his men were holding Arianna, Brian wondered why he had no urge to lead. This was his battle. He had taken on the duty of protecting her. She had been taken while in his care. The lead in any attempt to rescue should be his place

He immediately told himself not to be a fool. Sigimor was good, as good as anyone in the MacFingal clan. It was a wise choice for Sigimor to lead them because he could keep calm no matter what they saw, no matter what they found. The emotions churning inside him told Brian that he was not fit to lead anyone anywhere at the moment. It would take but one look at an injured Arianna to make him act recklessly, to have him thinking of nothing else but the need to get to her and cut down any man hurting her.

Slipping through the trees and shadows as silently as his cousins, Brian struggled to firmly leash his fear for Arianna. Cold blood and a clear head were needed to successfully rout an enemy. It was even more important when rescuing someone, for unthinking, blind rage could easily get the captive one was trying to rescue killed instead of freed. Brian silently swore to himself that, even if they did not get Lucette and all his men this time, he would be satisfied by simply freeing Arianna. He could make the ones who hurt her pay dearly later.

Sigimor halted and grabbed Brian by the arm when he stepped up next to him. A heartbeat later Brian understood why his cousin felt there was a need to restrain him. Arianna was on her hands and knees, struggling to stand up. Lucette stood over her, his hands clenched into fists as his men argued with him. Brian did not need to see bruises or blood to know that Arianna was hurt. It was clear in the way she moved. He clutched his sword so tightly the carvings on the hilt dug into his hand as he fought to maintain the cold calm he needed now.

"The lass ought to just stay down," whispered Sigimor as he signaled his men to begin encircling Lucette and his men. "I think it best if ye and I run straight for her as all the others are verra close to the horses. They see us coming for them and they will try to run. We want to be verra sure that they dinnae take your lass with them."

Brian forced himself to study Lucette's men. They were all close to the horses. He wondered if they were thinking of deserting Lucette as Sir Anton had done.

Looking at Arianna again, Brian trembled from the strain of fighting the urge to immediately race toward Lucette and cut the man down. She was conscious. If she knew they were about to rescue her she might be able to do something to help them keep her out of Lucette's hands until they could free her. Watching her struggle, knowing she was hurting, made waiting to act a pure torture for him.

"If she turns to face us," Brian whispered to Sigimor, "I will show myself. I believe all eyes will be on her then, too."

"Ah, and then she might be able to keep herself from being grabbed." Sigimor nodded and pulled a dagger from the sheath at his hip. "Then we only need to be close enough to hurl one of these at anyone who tries to take her when they all bolt for their horses."

"Aye, which they will do the moment they see us, curse their eyes. I doubt they will stand and fight."

"Getting your lass away from them is all that is important now."

"I ken it. Your men are ready?"

"Aye, they but await my signal."

Recalling that Sigimor's signal was a battle cry that could shake the walls of any keep, Brian almost smiled. He crouched beside Sigimor watching Arianna struggle and trying to will her to her feet facing his way. If she did not see him when he stood up, he would not hesitate to yell at her to run. His heart broke when she finally got to her feet and lifted her head. Her pretty face was battered and bleeding.

He stood up, Sigimor rising to his feet at his side. Arianna's eyes looked swollen and he feared she could not see him. Brian glanced at Sigimor and his cousin nodded.

"Run, Arianna!" he yelled, and a heartbeat later Sigimor bellowed out his war cry.

To Brian's relief Arianna lurched away from Lucette. Lucette started to go after her but then jerked to a halt when Sigimor's cry tore through the air. The man stared at Brian and Sigimor in horror and then bolted for the horses his men were already scrambling to mount. Brian started after Lucette but knew he would never catch the man. He drew his knife and hurled it. A scream erupted from Lucette as the blade buried itself deep into the man's shoulder, but fear gave the man the strength to still mount his horse and gallop away.

Brian turned away from the confusing melee and hurried toward Arianna. She had not gone far before collapsing on the ground. She was just struggling to get up again when he reached her side.

Arianna cursed her weakness as she fought to get back on her feet. All around her she could hear the sound of running feet and then the pounding of horses galloping away. There were only a few cries of pain and a brief moment of the ringing of steel upon steel. The sound of Brian's voice telling her to run had been the sweetest sound she had ever heard, but that had not been enough to give her the strength to go very far. She could only hope that she had gotten herself far enough not to hinder what sounded like the rescue she had been praying for.

Out of the corner of her swollen eyes she saw hands reaching for her and tried to crawl away.

"Arianna, 'tis I. Brian."

She stopped and clumsily sat down. "Brian?"

"Aye, love."

"Are they gone? Did ye kill him?"

"Nay, I fear Lucette escaped but he rode away with my dagger buried deep in his shoulder. Unless he suffers a putrefaction of the wound, however, it wasnae a mortal blow."

"Ah, weel, at least it will hurt him."

Brian blinked away the tears that stung his eyes as he looked her over. Her eyes were nearly swollen shut, her lips also swollen and cut, and blood dripped slowly from a wound on her forehead. The way she swayed and trembled told him that she was very close to unconsciousness. He did not know where or how to touch her, afraid to add to the pain she was in.

"What was that terrifying bellow that came right after ye told me to run?" she asked, reaching out to him in the need to know that he was truly there. Since she could see very little, she needed to touch him.

"Sigimor." He gently took her hand in his, careful not to touch the cuts and scrapes on her palm. "Ah, lass, he beat ye sorely. I should ne'er have left ye alone."

"Ye needed to be certain the path to Scarglas was clear and safe. I should have hidden myself better and nay closed my eyes. Took a wee nap. Foolish." She licked her lips and tasted blood. "Do ye have anything to drink? Cider? Water?"

Brian carefully put his arm around her shoulder and, seeing Fergus, signaled to the youth to bring him something to drink. There were two bodies before the little cottage, both of them Lucette's men, and none of Sigimor's men looked to be hurt. A quick count told Brian that Sigimor had sent a few of his men to follow Lucette even though they were all certain of where the man was going. Brian was not too furious over Lucette's escape. Unless Lucette and his allies had the sense to see that there was no way to get the boys out of Scarglas, there would still be a battle to be fought, so there would be another chance to kill the man.

Sigimor crouched beside them. "I think we may need to wrap those ribs of hers tightly before we ride back to Dubheidland."

The way Arianna had her arms wrapped around her ribs told Brian that Sigimor was probably right about that. "Do ye think anything is broken, lass?" he asked her.

"Nay, just verra badly bruised," she replied, and attempted a smile although she was certain it was a ghastly sight. "Mayhap a wee bit rattled. He kicked me, hard, several times, but I kicked him, too. Once."

"Good lass. I hoped ye kicked him hard."

"I did. I am surprised he could ride a horse. I kicked him right between the legs. Suspicion he was a wee bit sore."

Brian exchanged a grin with Sigimor and then began to unlace Arianna's gown. Sigimor moved quickly to find something to use to wrap her ribs. It was hard to ignore her soft gasps of pain as he tugged her gown down to her waist and pulled her shift up to just under her breasts. Brian was pleased to see that all of Sigimor's men kept their gazes averted, but it was all he could be pleased about. The massive bruises on Arianna's rib cage made him wish he could get his hands on Lucette. Brian would make very certain that the man suffered in agony before he killed him.

Sigimor returned with several long strips of blanket. Brian clenched his teeth to hold back a demand that Sigimor get his hands off Arianna when his cousin gently explored all along her ribs, searching for signs of a break. Her hiss of pain only added to that urge.

"Naught is broken, but, as ye said, lass, they are a wee bit rattled," said Sigimor as he began to wrap the strips of blanket around her ribs. "This will help and give them some protection from the ride back to Dubheidland."

"But we were going to Scarglas," Arianna said, her voice a hoarse whisper rife with pain.

"Nay, not until ye heal," said Brian. "Ye cannae ride that far as battered and bruised as ye are."

"That is where Amiel is going. Where they are all going."

"If they are fools enough to try and attack Scarglas

they will need more men than they have and that will take time. I am hoping that land ye think the De-Veaux want from Lucette and their need to use ye for some old and should be forgotten vengeance on your clan willnae seem so verra important once they get a good look at Scarglas."

"'Tis more than the land. Amiel will let them have his kin, too."

"What do ye mean?"

"Amiel said he didnae like the idea of being but one of many landed and titled Lucettes. He intends to use the DeVeaux to help him thin out the crowd."

"Jesu." Sigimor sat back on his heels as Brian got Arianna fully dressed again. "He means to turn the Lucettes' worst enemy on them? To kill off his own family?"

"Aye, little by little until he is heir to it all, or most of it," Arianna replied. "And the DeVeaux cannae get the land they want until my laddies are dead. Claud held that land himself, nay as part of an inheritance or entailment. He could dispose of it as he wished and he left it to the boys in his will, something I wasnae invited to hear read so I didnae ken it all. My bonnie wee laddies now hold what the DeVeaux want." She panted softly in a vain attempt to overcome the pain washing over her as Brian urged her up into a seated position. "Claud made me their guardian."

"He hung a target on all your backs."

"He did. Aye, the DeVeaux might want to use me to avenge themselves upon my family but they also need me dead. As guardian I nay only control the lads but the land." After pushing the last few words out, Arianna gave in to the darkness flooding her mind and escaped the pain wracking her body.

Brian felt her go limp in his arms and panicked. He pressed his fingers against her throat and used the steady throb of her pulse to push the fear away. She was better off being unconscious. The ride back to Dubheidland would prove to be a long time in agony for her otherwise.

"She will heal," Sigimor said as he stood up.

"Ye sound verra sure of that." Brian got to his feet, holding Arianna in his arms and trying not to jostle her too much.

"Bones are nay broken, there isnae any bad bleeding from open wounds and, although verra colorful, the bruising didnae have the look of the ones caused by something bleeding inside her." He started toward the others who had brought the horses to them. "Jolene and the women can give her a closer look but I think we reached her in time."

"She shouldnae have fallen into the bastard's hands at all," said Brian, fury at himself a bitter taste on his tongue. "If I hadnae left her . . ."

"Then they would have found ye, too, and there wouldnae have been anyone to come and get help for her. Aye, ye are a good fighter, but I think e'en ye would have had a wee bit of trouble fighting off so many men. Ye had to be certain the path was clear, that ye wouldnae be riding into a trap. Ye are a clever lad. I suspicion ye will understand that soon enough if ye think on it a while."

Brian doubted his guilt would ease much until he was certain that Arianna would heal. "What do ye think happened to the people who lived in this wee cottage?"

"They ran when they saw armed men coming,"

replied Sigimor, holding his arms out for Arianna when they reached the horses.

"Ye are certain of that?" Brian asked as he mounted his horse and then took Arianna back into his arms.

"Aye. Brice found their trail. They will return as soon as they ken that the men are gone."

A quick glance around was proof enough that Sigimor had reason to be confident of that. The two bodies were gone, taken away from the little home and left for the carrion. Since Brian saw no sign of any livestock, he knew the family had undoubtedly had some warning of the men's approach. Isolated as the little house was, it was no surprise that the people living in it would always be alert for any sign of danger.

They started back to Dubheidland, and Brian adjusted his hold on Arianna. He hoped to save her from as much movement as possible. Since galloping all the way back to Dubheidland was out of the question, he prayed she stayed unconscious for a very long time. She would face enough suffering when they reached Sigimor's keep and her wounds would be tended to.

"I sincerely hope you intend to kill that man," said Jolene when she stepped out of the bedchamber where Brian had placed the wounded Arianna. "Slowly."

"I intend to," answered Brian. He straightened up from where he had been leaning against the wall and staring at the door to that bedchamber for the last two hours. "How is she?"

"She will heal. I think many of the bruises look far worse than they truly are. Her skin is much akin to mine. I have occasionally noticed a very vivid bruise yet have no memory of any serious injury. Cool cloths and some of the salve I left by the bed will quickly bring those bruises down. She is sleeping now. She will also need a few days of rest."

"She will have it."

"You are dealing with a madman, you know. She told me of his plots. To unleash your family's worst enemy upon them? To murder two innocent boys and an equally innocent woman? To kill your own brother? To plot the deaths of what might be every male Lucette who could possibly inherit something? Aye, he is definitely a madman."

"I ken it. I also intend to make certain the Lucettes realize how fortunate they are that Amiel and his allies didnae leave this land alive." He watched as Jolene rubbed her lower back. "Go rest, lass. I can care for Arianna now. Salve and cool cloths." He winked at her. "Have something to eat and then go rest ere that large husband of yours comes stomping up here looking for you."

He watched until she made it safely down the steps before he went into the room where Arianna slept. His first sight of Arianna since giving her over into Jolene's care made his heart clench with sorrow. She looked so small in the large bed, the bruises on her face and her bandaged hands an abomination in his eyes. After changing the wet cloth draped over her eyes for a cooler one, Brian sat in the chair that had been pulled up to her bedside.

Brian knew he loved her. The emotions that had

torn through him when he had thought her lost to
him had made that clear, too clear for him to continue to try and deny it. It changed nothing, however, if only because he did not have any idea of how
she felt about him. Worse, the fact that he had given
her her first taste of passion could easily confuse
her. He had thought himself in love with the first
woman he had bedded down with. It was far too
easy to think passion was born of something deeper,
richer, and longer lasting, especially if it burned as
hot as what he and Arianna shared.

Neither did his love for her change the fact that
she was far above his reach. She deserved more than
he could give her. He had seen enough mismatched
marriages to know how discontent and bitterness
could grow to turn the union into a living hell. Lady
Arianna deserved a man equal to her in birth, wealth,
and breeding, a man who could make her happy and
content in all ways. Brian doubted she would stay
unwed for long after he let her go and was sure that
her family would be far more cautious in choosing
her a husband this time. She would soon have all a
lady like her deserved. It was only honorable to let
her go, to not try to bind her to him with passion.
Brian just wished he could be happier about doing
the honorable thing.

Chapter 14

Arianna sat on the stone bench beneath a tree and smiled faintly as she watched the Cameron children playing in the garden. Her pleasure in the sight was mingled with sadness for she desperately missed Michel and Adelar. Although she had enjoyed, and badly needed, the four days of rest she had taken at Dubheidland, she was anxious to resume the journey to Scarglas. It was time to put an end to Amiel's game.

"Are ye certain ye are healed enough to be out of bed?"

Startled out of her thoughts by Brian's voice, Arianna turned to look up at him scowling down at her. "Aye, I am verra certain. As Jolene told you when she first viewed my injuries, naught was broken and naught was bleeding inside me. There remain a lot of bruises but they will continue to fade." She had no intention of telling him that she still ached a little or how tender a few of those bruises still were in certain places.

Brian grunted and sat down beside her. "Ye are

nay completely healed, lass, and ye dinnae fool me. That mongrel was intent upon beating ye to death from what little I saw."

She shivered as the memory of Amiel's brutality flooded her mind. "I wasnae doing as he wanted me to, wasnae telling him exactly where the lads were, and I refused very crudely to help him use me to get them. His temper rose beyond reasoning, beyond even recalling that the DeVeaux wanted me alive. The fact that I kenned his plans, kenned that he was already certain of where the boys were, only made him angrier. The odd thing is, when the men reminded him of what Lord Ignace wanted, Amiel should have been terrified. Any sane person would be. But he wasnae deterred from beating me at all." Arianna took a deep breath and let it out slowly, pushing away the fear and the helplessness of that time when it threatened to return. "I was just thinking that 'tis past time we continued our journey to Scarglas."

"I dinnae think ye are healed enough for that."

"How long a journey is it?"

"It depends upon how fast a pace we can keep. Three days. Mayhap more. Mayhap less."

"As long as we are nay taking the whole journey at a full gallop, I will be fine." When his scowl did not lighten at all at her assurances, she said, "We ken that Lucette and his men are joining the others. We need to be inside Scarglas when they come to its walls."

"They will have little chance of breeching those walls."

"And I would prefer to be inside those walls when they try, nay outside trying to find a way in without being killed."

As would he, Brian decided. The number of men

Lucette and the DeVeaux had brought had been reduced but they could hire more. Word was drifting their way that they were doing just that. There was no telling if they would give up and flee back to France when finally faced with the high, impregnable walls of Scarglas, or if, with an army of hirelings at their backs, they would risk attacking. They could easily decide that what they would gain if they won was worth the risk.

"We will leave on the morrow," he said, and sighed when she hugged him. "I dinnae think ye will be so verra pleased to have resumed the journey after ye have been in the saddle for a wee while."

"I suspicion ye are right about my nay liking to be back on a horse, but I will be verra pleased to be traveling to where my boys are. I need to see them, Brian. They are all I have and I need to be with them if there is to be a battle for their lives." She rubbed her cheek against the linen of his shirt, a little surprised at how openly affectionate she had become, and added softly, "They are all I might ever have."

Brian leaned back and, placing his hands on her cheeks, turned her face up to his. He could tell she was realizing what she had just said and wanting him to ignore it. That was not something he could do.

"What do ye mean?" he asked.

"Naught. 'Twas naught," she muttered, but knew she was blushing, signaling the lie she had just told him.

"Arianna, what did ye mean? Aside from having a verra large army of kinsmen, ye are still young. Ye can wed again and have a few bairns of your own."

The mere thought of her with another man made Brian's insides clench with jealousy and denial. He knew that was unreasonable. He could not have her, was not good enough for her, but he obviously wanted to deny her all chance of making a home and a family with some other man. It was hard to accept that he could be so selfish, but he was.

"Nay, I cannae." Arianna hated to reveal her fear yet was compelled to let Brian know just how poor a choice of wife she would be for a man, even if he had never once indicated that he wanted her in that way.

"I am certain there are many weel-born lads with fat, full purses who will rush to woo you once 'tis kenned that ye are free."

She was not sure what a man's birth or the weight of his purse had to do with it all, but she shrugged aside the urge to question his words. It would be too easy to use such questions to turn him away from the truth she had been hiding. He was owed the truth.

"A mon wants children, Brian. I failed to give Claud one despite five years of marriage. The one time I conceived a child, I lost the bairn verra quickly."

There was such sorrow weighting her words and darkening her eyes that Brian pulled her back into his arms. He stroked her back, resting his chin upon her head, as he struggled to think of what to say to ease that sorrow. Unfortunately, he knew very little about women's ills, childbirth, or the how and why of losing a baby before it was even born.

"The trouble could have been with Claud," he said, and inwardly grimaced at the weakness of that assurance.

It struck Arianna a little odd that that would be

the first thought in his mind but she just said, "Claud gave Marie Anne two fine lads, didnae he? He gave me but the one bairn who couldnae cling to life and ne'er another after that. Nay, I fear I am not fated to bear a child."

"I dinnae believe it but I ken naught about such matters. Dinnae want to." He smiled when she laughed softly. "Ye need to speak to women who ken about such things. Jolene has been wed seven years with three children and another to come soon. She will ken a few things, aye? Fiona was trained by your clan in the healing arts. She, too, has knowledge both from having her own bairns and all she learned from the healing women in your clan."

Arianna nodded but knew she would not follow his advice. It had been hard enough to talk to Jolene before and to confess her lack to him now. To face another woman, especially one who had a bairn to love, and try to get even more assurance that she might not be barren could prove an impossible task. She could not bear to see the pity that would surely appear in Fiona's eyes. Yet there was no denying that it would be wise to continue to talk to someone with knowledge, even if it confirmed what she feared and what Claud had told her the physician had said—that she was probably barren, unable to get with child, and unable to hold a bairn in her belly if she was lucky enough to get with child. Fiona would have had training Jolene had not had.

Brian stood up, took her by the hand, and pulled her to her feet. "Come. Since we have decided to resume our journey, we had best go and prepare for it."

* * *

It was not until Arianna was packing up the clothing Jolene had so generously given her that she really thought over what she had confessed to Brian. She suddenly knew why she had felt compelled to tell him such a private, painful truth. It was to see what he would say. He had been encouraging and sympathetic but he had not said the one thing she had ached to hear. He had not told her that it did not matter to him.

"Foolish, foolish woman," she said, and sat down on the bed, staring blindly at the fine linen shift Jolene had given her.

"Why do you call yourself foolish?"

Arianna jumped a little in surprise and stared at Jolene, idly wondering how people kept managing to sneak up on her. She began to think nearly drowning had damaged her ears. After five years of misery with Claud it was not easy to recall much from the years that had gone before, but she was certain she had not always been so completely unaware of what was happening around her or of who was approaching her.

"Why are you frowning at me?" asked Jolene. "Have I offended you in some way?"

"Och, nay! I was just wondering why I seem to be unable to sense anyone sneaking up on me. Weel, mayhap sneaking is too harsh a word to use. 'Tis just that Brian often comes up to me and I ne'er hear him approach. I didnae have any idea that Lucette was slipping up behind me until it was too late. Now ye are just, weel, just here, and I ne'er heard a sound. I am beginning to think I damaged my ears in that cursed water when we had to leap off the ship to save ourselves."

Jolene laughed as she sat down on the bed. "I doubt that happened. I suspect you simply have so much on your mind, so much to worry about, that your own thoughts often hold you captive."

Arianna nodded and smiled, all the while fighting hard not to stare at Jolene's very rounded belly with all the envy she felt. She was happy for Jolene, whom she had liked almost immediately, but her arms ached to hold a child of her own. Although she clearly recalled all Jolene had said in response to her fear of being barren, she wanted to discuss the matter some more but hesitated. Then she decided that Jolene would understand her need to hear such assurances again.

"Jolene, are ye quite certain of the truth of all ye said about how I may nay be barren or were ye just trying to ease my fears?" she asked, and then winced, realizing that she was almost accusing the woman of lying.

"It ne'er hurts to allay a woman's fears about such a thing, but I was indeed very certain of all I said. I still am, even after thinking over the matter for a while," replied Jolene. "People always look at the woman first when no child is born. If it takes two to make a babe then 'tis only reasonable to look at both people when no child is born. If a fever or a wound can leave a man as limp as an unwatered flower, then it seems to me such things could also affect the potency of his seed."

Arianna sat down next to her and nodded. "Verra true. And, as I thought on all ye said, it did seem verra odd to me that Claud ne'er gave me or Marie

Anne a child after he and I were married and I quickened that first time. For a mon to be bedding two women for about four years yet never produce a child is something worthy of a few questions."

"There is a very good chance your body did not hold fast to the babe because there was already a fault in Claud's seed."

"Weel, if something happened to him it did so before we were wed and I cannae ask his family about it now."

"You wish to stay with Brian?"

"Och, aye, but e'en if he wants me, I willnae condemn him to a childless marriage."

"Then it comes back to ye needing to get with child first."

"I think I would like to ken for certain that he wants to keep me ere I try to tie him to me with a bairn." The glimmer of hope Jolene's assurances stirred within her was almost painful and Arianna had to struggle to keep it from possessing her heart and mind.

"I still say that he does but I understand that you need more than my opinion on that. I think you also need to consider the possibility that he does not think himself worthy of you."

"Brian has great confidence in himself, can be almost arrogant at times. Why would he think such a thing?"

"His notorious father, his equally notorious family, and the fact that he is a younger son with little coin and no land. No prospect of inheriting anything, either. Men find it difficult to believe that a woman values love over such things. I think they see it all as their responsibility to provide such largesse, not realizing that many of us can be happy with naught but a roof o'er our heads, food enough to stave off starvation, someone strong enough to protect us and whatever children we may be blessed with, and mayhap a new gown now and then so that we are not always wearing rags. And"—she grinned and rubbed her belly—"fat, pretty babes."

Arianna smiled but then frowned in thought. "'Tis odd to think that Brian, who truly can be arrogant, would worry that he was not worthy of me. 'Tis a shame that I cannae just ask him if that is what is rattling about in his wee monly brain." She grinned again when Jolene laughed. "I will have to think upon this, to see if there is some way to ken his true feelings without him actually saying anything. I am too much the coward to open my heart to the mon without some hint that he cares, that we share more than desire."

Jolene stood up and started for the door. "You could start by thinking on how he acted when you were hurt." She stepped out the door and glanced back at Arianna. "He ne'er left your side."

It was impossible not to think about it. Arianna could not stop the constant spin of thought in her mind. She could not ignore the signs of caring Brian had shown when she had been injured. The question that had to be answered was whether or not that caring went deep enough. She wanted it to, with all her heart she wanted it to, but she could not be certain.

She had considered Jolene's suggestion that she simply get with child by Brian but her conscience troubled her over that plan. It was true that what they were doing together made children and he was taking no care to keep from seeding her. However, it was quite another matter to actually consider trying to bind him to her with a child or, worse, hold a child from him if he could not give her what she needed. Her mother would be ashamed of her for even thinking of such a thing.

Arianna rubbed her temples in an effort to push back a slowly forming headache. Her mind had latched onto the possibility that she was not barren and would not let go. In the end it did not matter if she was or was not. All that mattered was trying to decide if she wanted to fight to hold fast to the man she wanted, if she dared. In the end, he could crush her spirit with the simplest rejection far more than Claud had ever done with five long years of constant belittlement.

"Ye are certain they havenae gathered near Scarglas yet?" Brian asked as he paced before Sigimor's large ledger table.

Sigimor put his feet up on the table and watched his cousin pace his ledger room like a caged beast. "Ye doubt the word of my mon? My mon who also happens to be my cousin?"

Brian cursed and then flung himself into the heavy oak chair to face his cousin over the wide table. "Your men are mostly your brothers or your cousins," he grumbled. "And, nay, I dinnae doubt his word and weel ye ken it. I just need to be verra sure ere I take Arianna away from the safety of these walls." He frowned. "Mayhap I should make her stay here until this is done."

"Ye will fail at that. The lass needs to see those lads. Dinnae forget that I had a lot of trouble with my Jo because she was protecting her nephew. Those wee lads of Arianna's might be safely tucked behind the walls of Scarglas but someone still means them harm. That lass will nay stop trying to get to them. Ye try to leave her behind and she will find a way to follow ye."

"Nay if I chain her to the bed." He exchanged a grin with Sigimor but quickly grew serious again. "She is under as great a threat. I took on the responsibility for her and those lads. It wouldnae be right to leave the guarding of her to ye anyway."

"Ye can if ye want and ye ken that she will be weel guarded."

"Och, aye, I ken it, but 'tis best if she goes with me. If I leave her here I risk her doing something foolish. She would ken it wasnae wise to leave here on her own as she isnae a dim-witted lass, but her need to be with those two boys would have her doing it anyway."

"Still hoping that one good look at Scarglas will be enough to send the bastards back to France?"

"Aye, but, if Lucette's arrogance and disdain for us is aught to go by, they may still try. Sad to say, despite the peace Ewan has brought us, there are a lot of men about who wouldnae mind raising a sword against us. And to be offered coin to do so? They would grasp that chance with both hands."

"Men who only fight for the coin offered are quick to retreat," said Sigimor. "Any those Frenchmen find near to Scarglas will also ken the reputation of the

MacFingals as being excellent fighters. A reputation ye earned."

Brian nodded in acknowledgment of that compliment. "I dinnae anticipate a long battle."

"But ye do anticipate a fight, aye?"

"I cannae rid myself of the conviction that they will try at least once."

"Mayhap a few of my lads will ride over and lend a hand."

"Ye mean they will follow us."

Sigimor shrugged. "Nay too close. If naught else, a few of my lads riding toward Scarglas will draw the eye more than two people riding in that direction."

"That could put them in danger, Sigimor," Brian said in protest, even though the thought of a diversion like that intrigued him and he could easily see its value.

"'Tis nay only the MacFingals who can be as elusive as smoke."

"'Tis in the blood," Brian agreed, and then he stood up. "Best I seek my bed now. I intend to ride as long and as hard as I can without causing Arianna any further injury." He grimaced. "And what Lucette did to her when he held her is still too fresh in my mind for me to be able to sleep until we reach the safety of Scarglas."

"Rest weel this night then."

Brian paused in the doorway and looked at Sigimor. "No word from the Murrays yet, aye?"

"Nay. I wouldnae be surprised if ye find a few at Scarglas when ye get there, though."

"Ah, weel, I am certain Arianna will be pleased to see some of her kinsmen."

He shut the door on Sigimor's laughter and headed

for the bedchamber he shared with Arianna. Brian
hoped she had been telling the truth when she had
claimed to be healing nicely. He did not care if he
had to be as gentle with her as if she were made of
glass; he intended to make love to her tonight.
There could be no chance to do so on the journey
to Scarglas and, if some of her family were already
there, there would be no chance for lovemaking
once he and Arianna arrived.

The sight of her sitting before the fire brushing
out her hair made his gut clench with hunger as he
entered the bedchamber and shut the door behind
him. She wore only her shift and her strong, slim
arms were bared to view, a few fading bruises still
marring her fair skin. Brian looked at her small
bare feet peeking out from beneath the hem of her
shift and shook his head. He even found the sight
of those delicate feet enough to rouse his interest.

"I see ye are ready to leave in the morning," he
said, and nodded toward her pack.

"Aye." She watched him warily as she began to braid
her hair. "I thought that was what we had decided."

"It was. Cannae say I like it but, aye, it was decided. There is nay avoiding it, is there? The need
for rest, the need to heal, cannae be allowed to stop
us. There is a battle coming."

"Why?" She stood up to face him. "Ye tell me Scarglas is strong, Brian. Sigimor says the same. So why
would Amiel and the DeVeaux attempt to knock
down a keep that is so strong? Especially when they
dinnae have many of their own men and will need to
rely upon hirelings. Why would they attack?"

Brian wrapped his arms around her and rested
his chin upon her head. "I have no idea." He smiled

when she laughed softly. "I may be wrong. There may be no battle. E'en if Lucette is mad enough to attempt an attack upon Scarglas, the DeVeaux may have the wit to decide that no wee scrap of land is worth it."

Arianna put her arms around his waist. "Weel, I shall put the whole mad puzzle out of my mind and just wait until we reach Scarglas and I can see what is happening for myself."

He picked her up and took her to the bed, setting her down gently. The way she watched him as he shed his clothes had his desire for her running hot in his veins. There was a light flush upon her cheeks and her eyes had darkened with a desire to match his own. They might have to make love very carefully in deference to her wounds, but her welcome was all he needed.

It puzzled Arianna that the sight of Brian naked could affect her so. He was, without question, a very fine specimen of manhood. Tall, lean, and muscular, his skin a light tan as if he bathed naked in the sun. His legs were long, well shaped, and strong. He was not as hairy as some men were, having only a small patch of hair on his broad chest, a thin line of hair from his navel to his groin where black curls cushioned his manhood when it was not standing long and proud as it was at the moment. There was enough hair on his forearms and legs to be manly. She decided he was the kind of man any woman would like to look at, one who could easily stir any woman's interest.

Claud had also been a fine-looking man, however, she reminded herself. Yet, she had never once felt her heart race at the sight of him. Neither had her hands itched to touch Claud's skin as they did to touch Brian's. She certainly had not found Claud's manhood of any great interest. The sight of a naked Brian, however, caused her to react in all of those ways. It also caused her to think on all the things she would like to do to that beautiful, strong body.

She made no protest when he joined her in the bed and quickly removed her shift, tossing it far out of her reach. Arianna liked to be flesh to flesh with him. He kissed her and she began to stroke that body she so admired. The soft growl of appreciation that escaped him told her he liked her daring.

Arianna shivered with pleasure when he kissed her breasts, enjoying the slow rise of her desire. She suddenly recalled something that Claud had demanded she do for him several times. He had told her it was the only way he could be aroused enough to perform his husbandly duties with her. Arianna still hesitated to believe all of Brian's flatteries, but she had no more doubt about his desire for her. She had to wonder if, when a man who did not desire her liked her to do what Claud demanded of her, how much would a man who did desire her like it?

Before she could think about it for too long and lose both her courage and her desire, she pushed Brian onto his back and straddled him. Arianna ignored his questioning look and began to kiss her way down his strong body. She felt him tense when she nipped his taut stomach but the way he clenched his hands in her hair told her that it was not a sign of rejection. The groan that rumbled in his chest when she settled between his long legs and ran her tongue up the hard length of him was all the encouragement she needed.

Brian closed his eyes and then quickly opened them again, wanting to watch Arianna as she made love to him with her mouth. When she took him into her mouth he knew he would not be able to enjoy the pleasure she gave him for too long. It was too intense. Gritting his teeth when the need for release built to the point of pain, he grabbed her under her arms and pulled her up his body. He had to hold on to her firmly when she tried to move off him to lie on her back.

"Nay, lass, ye will ride me tonight," he said.

"Ye want me on top?"

She sounded so stunned he knew that Claud had never had her do more than lie beneath him. "Och, aye, love. I want ye on top and I want to be seated deep inside ye. Now."

He had to help her in the beginning but he did not mind, despite his desperate need. It was just more proof that she had no experience in such things, her surprised wonder as clear to see as it was when he had shown her they could make love standing up, as well as when he had made love to her with his mouth. The fact that he was sharing things with her that she had never shared with that thrice-cursed Claud pleased him beyond words. Before he could worry about why that should be, however, Arianna began to reveal a true skill at riding her man. Brian rapidly lost all ability to think about anything save for the pleasure she gave him.

* * *

Arianna was drowsy, so pleasantly sated she did not even flinch when Brian cleaned her of the remnants of their lovemaking. The moment he got back beneath the bedcovers and took her into his arms, she curled up against his warmth with a happy sigh. There was a chance she would be embarrassed by her behavior in the morning but she promised herself that she would do her best to fight it. She was a grown woman, a widow, enjoying her lover, and she should not be blushing like a virgin over any pleasure they shared.

"Ye didnae aggravate any of your wounds, did ye?" asked Brian as he idly stroked her back.

"Nary a one," she replied.

"Thank ye, love."

"For nay aggravating my wounds?"

He laughed. "Nay, for the pleasure ye gave me."

"Ah. I think it was my pleasure, too," she whispered.

"Good. Ye shouldnae do anything unless the pleasure of it can be shared." He kissed the top of her head. "Sleep, love. Ye need your rest now."

It was not long before she was asleep, her body going limp against his. Brian stared up at the ceiling and tried very hard not to think about how soon she would be gone from his life.

Chapter 15

Brian eased the bedcovers down and looked at a soundly sleeping Arianna from head to toe. She was beautiful but he knew it might be a long time before she believed anyone who told her so. Passion eased her shyness and stilled the worry in her mind that her body was flawed, but he wanted her to revel in the fact that she was a passionate woman. He wanted her completely free of the chains of doubt Claud had wrapped her in. The sudden thought that he would be freeing that passionate woman only to send her to another man was one he ruthlessly banished.

From her plump breasts crested with pink nipples to her tiny waist, rounded hips, and long, slender legs, she was a delight to his eyes. He almost grinned for he truly did find her small feet attractive with those long toes. The tidy patch of red curls between her slim thighs drew his attention and he slid down her body to kiss her there.

Arianna woke to hear herself panting, her stomach knotted tight with desire. Brian was kissing her down there again, she thought, but passion had already banished her shock over such intimacy. Instead, she reached down to curl her fingers in his thick, black hair and a heartbeat later cried out his name as that knot of desire broke, sending pure fire through her body. She was still reeling from the force of her release when he joined their bodies with one hard thrust. Arianna clung to him as he sent her soaring again and, this time, shattered with her.

The pleasant lethargy of satiation was just beginning to fade when Brian eased out of her arms. "Ah, time to leave?"

"Aye, love, I fear so." He brushed a kiss over her lips, slipped out of bed, and disappeared behind the privacy screen.

The moment Brian came back out from behind the screen, Arianna tugged the bedcovers up over her breasts and sat up to watch him dress with a swift efficiency she could only envy. "We could try riding hard to begin with so that we make better time on the journey."

He glanced over his shoulder at her as he laced on his boots. "I am nay sure ye are healed enough for that."

"I promise to tell ye the verra moment I suffer any discomfort from the pace we set."

"Fair enough." He stood up and kissed her again before striding to the door. "I will see that ye have some hot water to wash with. Dinnae linger too long, love, or Sigimor will eat all the food."

Arianna laughed softly as she got out of bed, desperate to relieve herself. Sigimor was a blunt-speaking rough man, and a little odd, but one could not doubt his love for his wife, his children, or his family. She could only hope that the MacFingals were the same.

"Are ye certain ye dinnae want me to send any of my men with ye this time?"

"Verra certain," said Brian as he grabbed the plate of oatcakes before Sigimor could eat them all. "We talked this to death yestereve. 'Tis still true that two people can slip about unseen a lot easier than six or more nay matter how skilled they are at sneaking about."

"Aye, and the whole lot of ye MacFingals are verra skilled at creeping about."

Brian grinned at the note of respect in Sigimor's voice. His cousin was one of the few who would find the MacFingals' skill at stealth one to admire. Sigimor and his brothers were very good at it as well.

For a moment he wondered if he was letting foolish pride lead him. After what had happened the last time he had ridden away from Dubheidland with no escort, he feared he could be risking Arianna's life. Then he inwardly shook his head. He would leave Sigimor and his men to keep an eye on their backs until they were out of Cameron territory. After having been beaten twice he was certain that Amiel and what few men he had left had headed for Scarglas and the others, needing the aid of the other men now more than ever. He would work to get Arianna to Scarglas and her boys as quickly as he could and this time he would never let her out of his sight.

"We are verra good at it, aye," he agreed, and laughed softly when Sigimor tossed a piece of bread at him. "Arianna begins to show a true skill at it as weel." He poured himself some cider. "We will leave as soon as she packs the things your wife gave her. Every instinct I have tells me the DeVeaux ken exactly where the lads are and that is where this will end."

"So ye really do think they will all gather at Scarglas?"

"From what Arianna heard while that bastard held her, aye, that is their plan. He was headed there when he stumbled across her. She is certain that Lucette's plan was still to try and use her to bargain for the boys, despite what the DeVeaux want to do with her. Unfortunately she was nay fully conscious when he and his men argued over what the DeVeaux had planned."

He took a deep drink of cider to try and cool the rage that still burned hot in him when he thought of what had been done to Arianna. Brian doubted he would ever forget how she had looked, bruised and bloody as she struggled to rise up off the ground. It galled him that Lucette had escaped punishment for the blows he had struck, a punishment that would have had the man dangling from the end of Brian's sword.

"We will do our best to keep them running for their lives and hiding from us as ye get that lass to Scarglas," Sigimor said. "My lads are eager for the work."

"That is what I am hoping for, that they will be more concerned about ye and yours and nay take time to try and find us. Although, they may have already reached Scarglas. They have certainly had enough time. But, if ye do happen to stumble upon them because they stopped to lick their wounds, or have been so busy trying to avoid ye and your men they have done naught but run around in circles, I would appreciate if ye gave me the courtesy of leaving Amiel alive. I dearly want to be the one to end that bastard's life."

"Aye, that is how it should be. And, I ask again ere ye leave for ye may have given my words of wisdom a wee bit of thought by now. What do ye plan to do with the lass when ye have ended the threat to her life?"

That was not really a question Brian wanted to answer. He attempted to keep his attention firmly on the simple chore of finishing his morning meal. It was a ridiculous ploy to ignore his cousin. Brian often wondered if Sigimor ever noticed when someone ignored him and then sighed. His cousin had a too sharp wit so of course he noticed. Sigimor just refused to be ignored.

"I can wait longer than ye can pretend ye dinnae hear me."

Brian glared at his cousin, but Sigimor just crossed his arms over his chest and cocked one ruddy brow. "I dinnae ken yet what I will do save to reunite her with her family, which has been what she has sought from the verra beginning."

"It pains me to have to lay claim to such an idiot of a cousin."

"I begin to think 'tis ye who doesnae listen. Why cannae ye see that she is better born than I am?"

"Because I didnae ken that the Murrays had their bairns differently than we do. Do they use special herbs? Mayhap only birth their bairns on a particular sort of linen. Mayhap the women dinnae sweat or groan or curse the mon who set them on the birthing bed."

"I often wonder how it is that ye have lived so long. There must be hundreds who have dreamt of killing you."

"Nay, I dinnae ken that many people."

It annoyed Brian that he wanted to laugh. "Sigimor, ye cannae ignore the simple truth that she is higher born, richer, and from a clan that continues to gain power and honors. I am a MacFingal, a son of Fingal MacFingal who, whilst apart from his clan because he had a feud with his brother, decided to breed his verra own clan. He bred so many bastards it makes even the greatest of lecherous goats gasp in shock."

"Might be envy."

Brian ignored him. "He thinks an argument is polite conversation, says whate'er is in his mind without one thought to the consequences, and he paints himself blue and dances naked round a stone circle when the moon is full." He narrowed his eyes when Sigimor chuckled. "Aye, laugh. Ye dinnae have to claim the old fool as your fither. Ye also dinnae have to have people looking at ye as if they fear the madness they are certain inflicts the old mon might be running in your veins."

"Nay, I just have to claim him as my uncle, something I worked verra hard to do despite his refusals, if ye recall. So, if your wee lass doesnae grab those lads and run screaming from the place once she kens whose seed ye sprung from, I ask again—what will ye do?"

Brian dragged his hands through his hair. "Cousin, talking to ye is much akin to slamming my head into a wall. I repeat, no land, no house, and little coin. A bonnie Murray lass such as she is can do far better than me."

"As could the daughter of an English earl do far better than a laird with more kin depending on him than most would tolerate, but that didnae stop me. I won her."

"Naught can stop ye. Ye are like some thick-horned bullock," Brian muttered.

"And it should nay stop ye, either. She already wed as her family bid her to once, didnae she? And just where has that gotten the poor lass? A puling coward of a husband who wasnae really her husband, who betrayed her and scorned her, and now a hard run to save her life and her husband's sons from the greed of the bastard's brother. The family that should have welcomed her as a new bride, as a new daughter, that spat on her and still took all her dowry. Are ye telling me that, even with that old fool we must both claim as blood, ye cannae give her better than that?"

"Oh, aye, I could, but I doubt her clan would want a mon like me to have her. If naught else, once they met my fither, they would fear madness ran in the blood."

"Ye mean that clan that let a daughter marry an Armstrong? Another marry that mad MacEnroy? And another wed your brother Gregor? And let us nay forget that some fool of a Murray let one of their lasses wed my cousin Liam. That clan?"

"All those lasses didnae have much choice as they were maids who spent far too long alone with an unwed mon. It doesnae matter that they wanted to marry the men. E'en if they hadnae someone would have demanded it. Arianna is a widow. We both ken that the rules are a wee bit different for such women."

"I believe Liam's wife Keira was a widow."

"Sigimor . . ." Brian struggled to think of what else he could possibly say to shut the man up.

Sigimor cocked his head to the side and studied Brian for a moment before saying, "I think 'tis your own pride choking ye, cousin. Ye just dinnae want to wed a lass who might have more than ye do. I was mistaken. I had thought that ye cared for her."

Before Brian could respond to that Arianna and Jolene joined them. Arianna smiled at him as she took the seat beside him and Brian felt his heart clench. Perhaps Sigimor was right, although it galled him to even consider the possibility. Maybe it was his own cursed pride holding him back from just grabbing hold of what he wanted and not letting go.

He wanted to soundly deny that but was unable to. Brian also knew that it was not as simple as Sigimor thought it was. Arianna had already suffered through a bad marriage, one that had hurt her in ways many would never see or truly understand. She had earned the right to have all any woman could want from a husband who cherished her with rich gowns and fine jewels. He could give her the former but the comforts she deserved would be beyond his reach for a long time yet. Yet, he began to think he needed to try and find out what she wanted. His own opinions of what needed to be done began to taste a little too much like a condescending male deciding what was best for a poor, weak woman.

"Will we need to worry about Amiel as we journey to Scarglas?" Arianna asked as she helped herself to some porridge and sweetened it with honey and cream, struggling not to let the fear she felt reveal itself.

"Nay, I dinnae believe we will and I willnae leave ye alone again," he replied, glad of the diversion from his increasingly confused thoughts. "Two days, three at the most, and we will be safe behind the walls of Scarglas."

"And then I shall see Michel and Adelar again. I hope they are nay causing trouble for your kin."

"Nay, and e'en if they do get into mischief, there are plenty about to get them out of it. They cannae do anything worse than what we have all done at least once."

Arianna smiled and ate her food with as much delicacy as she could when what she really wanted to do was shovel it into her mouth as fast as possible. She was eager to begin the journey to Scarglas. She felt a pang of guilt for being so eager to leave the Camerons for they had been kind to her, welcoming her into their keep despite the trouble she had brought to their door. Her need to see Michel and Adelar could not be subdued, however. Not even her fear of riding away from the safety of Dubheidland could dim it. It had been much too long and she needed to see that Adelar and Michel were safe with her own eyes.

It troubled her that fear crept into her heart and mind every time she thought of continuing their journey. She did not like to think she was such a coward. Reminding herself that Amiel had lost another two men and was wounded only helped to ease her fear a little. If she did not have such a need to see her boys again she doubted she would get back on a horse and ride away from the safety of these walls.

"I *will* get ye safely to Scarglas," Brian said quietly, and patted her hand. "Ye dinnae need to be afraid."

"I ken it. That fear ye glimpse has no logic to it." She shrugged. "It willnae stop me, either."

"Aye, I ken it. 'Tis why I decided it would be a waste of time to chain you to that fine bed we have been sharing." He patted her on the back when she choked on the cider she had been drinking. "There is something I should warn ye about. My fither is a wee bit odd." He ignored Sigimor's laughter.

"Ye already warned me some. Dinnae worry. A wee bit touch of oddness doesnae frighten me."

Brian prayed that was the truth. His family, especially his father, was a little more than *odd*. He said nothing, however. He did not wish to worry her too much about what she might find at Scarglas. Telling her any more might have her wanting to grab the boys and flee before they even rode through the gates of his home.

His mind was still fixed on how much to tell her about his family and Scarglas when they stopped to camp for the night. They had traveled a lot farther than he had thought they would be able to and with no sign of trouble. If they did as well the next day they could reach Scarglas before nightfall. Arianna looked a little pale but did not move as if she was in a lot of pain.

After she had walked around for a few minutes to ease any stiffness from the long ride, he made her sit down and tended to the horses himself. Brian then brought the blankets to her, urging her to sit on them to keep away the chill of the ground. He watched her closely as he unpacked some of the food they had brought with them from Dubheidland.

"Ye are coddling me," she said with a smile as he handed her some bread, cheese, and cold venison.

"A wee bit," he admitted as he built a fire to warm them. "We traveled a goodly number of miles today."

"Aye, we did, but I dinnae ache much. Weel, nay much more than I would have anyway after such a long day in the saddle."

"Good. If we can do as weel on the morrow, we should be riding into Scarglas ere night falls or early the verra next morning at the latest."

She nodded, fixing her attention on her food to hide how relieved she was to hear that. Her body was one huge throb of pain, not so severe that she could not hide it, but bad enough that she wished she could soak in a hot bath for a few hours and then curl up in a soft bed. Arianna was not looking forward to sleeping on the ground and then spending another full day riding.

"There has been no sign of Amiel and his men," she said, hoping that talking would keep her mind off her own misery.

"Sigimor and his men will keep them too busy to trouble us. May e'en cull their number a wee bit more."

"So much death." Arianna shook her head. "For what?"

"Greed. It can drive a mon to madness, love. Unless one of our enemies decides to tell us every wee, twisted plot he has hatched in his mind ere he dies, I doubt we will e'er understand." He took a deep drink of cider from his wineskin and then handed it to her. "Does it matter?" he asked as she drank.

"Nay." She handed the wineskin back to him. "'Tis just curiosity. There is something I dinnae ken about it all and it picks at me. Claud's death can be easily explained. He was the heir and Amiel wanted to be the heir. Simple. Clear. Yet why kill Marie Anne? Why kill the boys?"

"Why kill you?"

She waved aside that question with a flick of her hand. "I am fair certain that has to do with the De-Veaux's hatred of all Murrays. Wheesht, Amiel's own family could want me dead ere I can get home and tell my kin all they kept hidden from them. That truth could certainly cause Claud's family more trouble than they wish to deal with."

"There is naught I can tell ye, especially as I dinnae ken what *picks* at you."

"Marie Anne."

"Ah, your false husband's true wife."

Arianna nodded. "I have ignored how my thoughts kept turning to her. Feared it might be jealousy, but, nay, it isnae. It was rumored that she was the bastard get of some highborn lordling. I confess, I thought Marie Anne the one who started that rumor just to give herself some prestige, but now I begin to wonder. What if she was blood kin to someone verra highborn, mayhap verra powerful?"

"Someone who could make certain the marriage of Claud and Marie Anne stood firm."

"Exactly. When I start wandering down that path I dinnae find so many answers but I do find more reasons for this hunt, e'en for the alliance between Amiel and the DeVeaux. Lord Ignace is no minor DeVeau lordling yet he also hunts the boys. At least the one I fear may be here isnae. There is something behind his presence here that I just cannae see, but ken 'tis important. If we could learn what that was then all our questions would be answered."

"And that would be good but, in the end, it still doesnae matter." Brian put his arm around her shoulders and tugged her close to his side.

"Nay, ye are right. In the end it doesnae matter at all. All that truly matters is that Michel and Adelar are nay hurt." She rested her head against his shoulder and stared up at the night sky. "They deserve a life in which they are nay surrounded by scorn or in constant danger. It was why I was taking them home with me. I kenned that they could find that with my kin."

"Ye will be able to give them that soon," said Brian, hoping his reluctance to grant her wish to go home did not reveal itself in his voice.

Arianna forced herself not to wince. It hurt to hear him speak of sending her home once the threat from Amiel and the DeVeaux was gone. She had hoped he had begun to change his mind about that. Although she had little confidence in her judgments about people, especially considering what the man she had thought would make a good husband turned out to be, she had thought Brian showed a caring for her that went beyond that of just a satisfied lover. Now she was not so certain. If he did care for her as more than a woman who gave him pleasure, surely he would have begun to hint at some change in his original plan to send her home. She was not sure what else she could do to make him want to keep her.

"Did ye love him?" Brian nearly cursed as he heard himself ask the question, if only because he really did not wish to hear her talk about that thrice-cursed Claud.

"Love Claud? Nay, although I thought our marriage could become one of love." She sighed and shook her head. "I was such a young, blind lass. Claud was handsome, charming, and always dressed so prettily. I thought he was treating me with great respect when he did nay more than gently kiss me from time to time. Now I see that what I thought was a gentlemon's respect for a maid was really just distaste. He was doing what he had to, nay what he wanted to."

"So when he courted ye he was weel spoken and ye thought ye could make a good marriage with him."

"Aye. My kin tend to marry for love, ye ken. I wished to, too, but it was verra clear that many of my clan wanted there to be a marriage between Claud and me. They wanted to strengthen the old bonds between the two families. I could have refused for they ne'er would have forced me to do it, but I didnae. None of my kin who have a gift for seeing the truth of a mon were there at that time so I got no warnings to make me look closer at the mon I was to marry. I e'en saw it all as an adventure.

"It wasnae until we were wed and the marriage duly consummated that Claud began to shed his disguise. At first I tried verra hard to please him, thinking that he was but trying to turn me into a good wife. 'Twas the same with his parents. When they revealed their scorn, I tried harder to win their approval. I am nay quite certain when I ceased to try, when I began to think myself too full of faults to e'er be able to succeed in pleasing any of them."

"Ye were nay full of faults."

"Weel, I wouldnae be so vain as to say I had none." She chuckled and patted his thigh, deeply touched by how angry her tale was making him. "Howbeit, I had begun to think that I was just a miserable failure, ne'er meant to be a wife any mon wanted, but I kenned that I was a verra good mother to Michel and Adelar. I kenned that deep in my heart and none could tell me different. I had also begun to think that I wasnae as bad at the running of the keep as they all implied for, if I was so abysmal a chatelaine, why did they keep giving me e'en more to do? It wasnae easy, either, for many of their people followed the lead of Claud and his family, treating me nay better than they would some unwanted guest."

She quickly covered a yawn with her hand and cuddled closer to Brian. "When I was held by Amiel and he began to hit me, I kenned that I would ne'er have accepted such treatment from Claud, from anyone in that family. One strike and I would have left. In a strange way, I found that knowledge a comfort. I e'en wondered where that cursed spine of mine had been when accepting all those cruel words, all that utter disdain."

"Ye were just a young lass."

"True, but I think it was more than youth. What Claud and his kin did was, weel, insidious, subtle . . ."

"Sneaky."

"Aye. I obviously wasnae as sure of myself as I thought I was. Claud found that wee weakness and fed it until it grew strong enough to conquer me. A part of me truly believed that I was an utter failure as a wife and a woman as he so often claimed I was. Believing my kin didnae care, or didnae see what I suffered was wrong or a problem, I felt I had nowhere else to go, either. So, I stayed far, far longer than I e'er would have if Claud had just once hit me or slapped me or kicked me as Amiel did. And every day I was there Claud, his family, and e'en many of the people on their lands kept picking away at whatever pride, vanity, or confidence I had. Ye hear something said often enough and ye believe it. I should have seen what he was doing to me."

"Love, ye were so young . . ."

"Old enough to be a wife."

"But still young and ye came from a loving family, aye?" She nodded and he continued, "Then why should ye have questioned anything the mon ye believed was your husband said to ye? And, as ye said, your family had seen naught wrong with the mon when he courted ye. As far as ye kenned, they also didnae think your complaints about what was happening to ye were even worth replying to."

"I should have left when I thought he had a mistress."

"Ye probably kenned that few would think that a good reason to leave your husband."

"Aye, true enough, though I did think it verra strange that there was no outrage from my family when I wrote them about that. Of course, they didnae get that missive, did they? I ken that now." She hastily covered her mouth as another yawn overtook her.

"Time to rest, love. We have a long day ahead of us on the morrow."

Brian took her by the hand, stood up, and tugged her to her feet. She blushed faintly and disappeared into the shadows of the trees to tend to her personal needs. He spread out the blankets for the bed as he waited for her. It made him think of making love to her but he tamped down the desire rising inside him. She had endured the journey with far more ease than he had anticipated, but he knew she was exhausted and undoubtedly ached all over. Sleep was what she needed.

The moment she returned, he strode away to tend to his own needs. By the time he returned, Arianna was sound asleep. Brian doubted she had been prone for a moment or two before exhaustion had claimed her.

He sat down and removed his boots. There would be little sleep for him tonight. Brian trusted Sigimor's men to keep Lucette and his men too busy to bother hunting for him and Arianna, but the memory of how badly she had been beaten by Lucette was still a stark, taunting scar on his mind. He could not leave her unguarded. There would be no sleep for him until he had her tucked safely behind the high walls of Scarglas.

Sigimor sipped his ale and studied his brothers Tait and Ranulph. "Ye didnae kill Lucette, did ye?"

"Nay, just relieved him of the burden of two more men," said Tait. "Followed him for a wee while and he is headed to Scarglas. Nay doubt about it."

"Also heard that a certain Lord Ignace is gathering himself an army about a day's ride from Scarglas," said Ranulph.

"Is he now. A big one?" asked Sigimor.

"Could be. Talk of coin being tossed about freely

is drawing the attention of a lot of men who havenae seen much coin for a while."

"We left Brice and Bronan, as weel as two other lads, to follow them just to make certain they did-nae try to find Brian and the lass," said Tait.

"Good. I am thinking I might wander to Scarglas myself with a few of ye lads for company," said Sigi-mor.

"There are already six of ours following Brian and the lass."

"Aye, but it ne'er hurts to have more. Be ready to ride in the morning."

"Do ye really think those Frenchmen will be mad enough to try and attack Scarglas?"

"They have hunted the lass and those lads of hers since she took them from her fool husband's keep, e'en sank a ship to try and kill them. Aye, I think they just might be mad enough." He grinned. "We will do our old ally France a fine favor and make certain that insanity gets buried deep here."

Chapter 16

Intimidating. Formidable. Threatening. Arianna stared at Scarglas as those words rolled through her mind. She desperately tried to think of a flattering word for the dark keep they were about to enter. Not one came to mind. Scarglas was built for defense, for keeping the people within it safe and making it easier to slaughter any enemy that approached its walls. It did not say *welcome* to any traveler brave enough to approach. It said *beware*. Brian's soft laughter distracted her and she looked at him, a little afraid that the expression on her face might have revealed her less than flattering thoughts about his home.

"Ye seem much akin to the others who catch their first look at this place," he said. "It isnae pretty."

"Nay, it isnae." She glanced to either side of them as they rode through an opening in a berm that rose as high as their horses. "I was just thinking that it doesnae appear to offer shelter as much as it offers a tomb for anyone foolish enough to attack it."

Brian nodded. "'Twas just that message that my

fither wished to send. I am thinking the mon who left it to him had a verra similar plan in mind but ne'er finished it. Your lads are safe in there."

She looked at the keep, which grew even more imposing as they drew nearer, and then smiled. "Oh, aye, I am sure they are." She glanced at him. "As were ye and all your brothers."

"True enough, although, if my fither hadnae been so skilled at making enemies, it all wouldnae have been so dearly needed. But Ewan has been the laird now for o'er a dozen years and we arenae surrounded by enemies any longer. I willnae call them all friends or true allies, but they dinnae wish to see us all dead and this place razed to the ground any longer."

"Ah, weel, that is certainly a good thing."

The dry tone to her voice made him laugh. "Aye, a verra good thing indeed. I warn ye that 'tis a strange lot ye are about to meet. My fither has calmed some since he wed Mab, but only in that he doesnae try to lift the skirts of every female twixt here and Berwick. He is also verra fond of arguing."

"Oh, I have kenned a few men like that. A few women, too. Dinnae worry, Brian. I am certain I shall like your family."

Brian was not as certain of that but said nothing. The one thing he was most concerned about was how sharp his father's tongue could be. He could all too easily recall some of the things his father had said to Fiona, but she was a strong, confident woman. He was sure that Arianna would be, too, once she had shed the rest of old Claud's poison, but for now she was still bleeding a little from the wounds he had inflicted.

He shook aside his concern as they rode through the gates of Scarglas. All he could do was make certain that his father did not verbally bludgeon Arianna. Aside from that, she would have to stand on her own. He inwardly grimaced, doubting he could hold fast to that decision. He was more likely to lurk around her like some fretful nursemaid, ready to shield her from any harsh words.

Arianna edged her mount a little closer to Brian's as they entered the bailey. It was crowded with a lot of tall, dark-haired men. A closer look revealed that many of those men bore a strong resemblance to Brian. She had heard all the tales of how old Fingal had been trying to breed his own army. Brian made no attempt to hide the truth about his father's profligacy. To see so many gathering in the bailey and knowing with but a look that most were Brian's bastard brothers drove that truth home with a vengeance.

Then she caught sight of Ned and Simon nudging their way through the growing crowd. The moment they made an opening in the large group of men, Michel and Adelar rushed through, stumbling to a halt mere feet from her mount. Their smiles were bright and wide, the smiles of boys who felt they were safe. Arianna dismounted with more speed than grace and rushed to embrace them, falling to her knees in the dirt to hug them tightly to her.

When the boys began to squirm in her arms, she eased her hold on them and leaned back a little. "Ye both look verra hale, my bonnie lads. No hurts, aye?"

"Nay, we are hale," said Adelar, still clutching

her braid with one hand. "It was a verra hard ride, though."

"I am sure it was, but ye are safe now."

"Aye, we are," said Michel, resting his cheek against her arm. "Ned and Simon are stout warriors."

Arianna hid a grin by pressing a kiss to his dark curls. "I could see that when I first looked at them, which is why I was able to leave ye in their care."

"Ned's *père* says that his laddies can steal the coins off a dead mon's eyes e'en as the widow is crying o'er the corpse. So, that is why they could bring two wee laddies safely here with ease."

Sensing someone by her side, she looked up in time to see Brian grimace at Michel's words. It was not easy to hide her shock over a man saying such a thing to a small boy, but she did so. Brian did not choose his father, and her clan was hardly free of the sort of men and women others found shocking. Sir Fingal might have mightily sinned but she glanced around at the vast number of his progeny, who all looked hale, well fed, and happy, and could see that he took care of what children he bred. It was a strong point in the man's favor for too few men supported their bastard children. He had also taken in her boys despite the trouble nipping at their heels. For that she would always be grateful.

"Best we go and greet the boastful old fool," Brian said as he grasped Arianna by the arm and helped her to her feet. "He would have been here to greet us but one of the lads told me he turned his ankle last eve."

"Aye," said Adelar as he pushed himself between Brian and Arianna to take her by the arm. "He was practicing his dancing for the next full moon."

Arianna thought that sounded like very odd behavior, but not odd enough to make Brian blush as
fiercely as he was doing now. She was just about to
ask him what dancing his father needed to practice
when they stopped before a tall, dark man standing
in front of the doors leading into the keep. The
man was scarred, his harsh features made all the
harsher because of the deeply serious look he wore.
But the ice in his blue-gray eyes softened briefly
when he looked at Brian and his thumb brushed
lightly over the knuckles of the hand of the woman
at his side, a hand he made no move to release.

One look at the woman stirred a lot of memories
for Arianna. It had been almost ten years but she
recognized that face, despite the small scars now
decorating each delicate cheek. Those violet eyes
were hard to forget. There had been several times
when she and Fiona had shared in learning the lessons of healing from her grandmother, Maldie
Murray.

"M'lady, this is my brother, laird of Scarglas, Sir
Ewan MacFingal," Brian said. "Ewan, this is the
Lady Arianna Murray." Since Arianna had seen fit
to drop her false husband's name when she had
reached Dubheidland, Brian was more than willing
to do so as well.

Arianna curtsied to the man despite the difficulty
in doing so with Michel and Adelar pressing so close
to her. "I thank ye for helping us, sir."

"No thanks are needed. This is my wife, Lady Fiona
MacFingal," Sir Ewan said in a deep gruff voice.

"I recognize ye," said Fiona, moving to kiss Arianna
on the cheek.

Returning the kiss, Arianna smiled. "I just recalled ye as weel. We shared a few rounds of my grand-mother's teachings. Ye were so verra much better at it than I was."

"Come in," said Ewan. "I am certain ye wish to wash up and then we can talk o'er some drink and food." He looked at Brian and cocked one dark brow, then looked at his wife when Brian responded to the silent question with a curt nod. "Fiona, can ye get one of the lassies to show them to a room?"

A room? Arianna opened her mouth to ask what that meant, and then shut it again. She did not wish to discuss sleeping arrangements before such a huge crowd of men, all of whom seemed to be eyeing her and Brian with undisguised curiosity. When the maids arrived, Arianna reluctantly let go of Michel and Adelar. The way the two boys hurried off, filled with boyish excitement to rejoin their companions, eased the last of her worries about them.

Her hand held firmly in Brian's, Arianna allowed him to lead her up the stairs as he followed two plump maids. "We didnae greet your father yet," she said.

"We can do that once we have washed away the dust of our journey," he said. "He will be waiting for us in the great hall when we go down there to eat."

She said nothing else as the maids led them into a large bedchamber. Arianna watched Brian talk to the maids and realized that this was not his bed-chamber. Either he did not live at Scarglas as she had thought or his sleeping quarters were not suit-able for sharing with a woman. Considering how many brothers and half-brothers the man had, she suspected all the unmarried men who slept within the keep shared quarters.

Hot water was brought in and Arianna turned her attention to cleaning up. She was a little uneasy about meeting Brian's father and wanted to look her best. After washing up and brushing out her hair, she was studying two of the gowns Jolene had given her and trying to decide which to wear when Brian stepped up behind her. He wrapped his arms around her and kissed the side of her neck, sending a tickle of interest winding its way through her exhausted body. She was astonished that she could feel anything aside from the urge to fill her belly and then collapse on a bed.

"Wear the brown and gold one," he said. "It will compliment your hair and eyes."

"But, I wouldnae have thought it a good color for me when I have brown hair and brown eyes."

"Ye have honey-gold hair with intriguing hints of red and soft amber eyes, nay just brown. Wear the brown and gold gown."

Arianna shrugged aside her bemusement over his description of her and donned the gown he had chosen. When she was ready she chanced a look at herself in the large looking glass over the fireplace. Surprise widened her eyes as she stared at herself in amazement. Instead of making her look like a little brown wren as she had feared, the color of the gown made her hair seem brighter, her eyes lighter and more prominent. That Brian could know what color would make her look her best gave her a dangerously warm feeling for it meant he had truly looked at her, honestly noticed what were her best features.

She was startled out of her thoughts by Brian's kiss on her cheek. He hooked his arm through hers and led her out of the bedchamber. Knowing they were headed for the great hall that would undoubtedly be full to bursting with his kinsmen had all of Arianna's nervousness returning in a rush.

"Brian, I am nay certain it is wise for us to be sharing a room here," she said.

"I am nay letting ye out of my sight," he said. "Whene'er I have, ye have gotten into trouble."

Before she could protest that, he dragged her into the great hall and through a crowd of curious MacFingals straight to the table the laird and his wife sat at. Fiona sat on Sir Ewan's right. An older man who looked a great deal like Sir Ewan sat on his left and next to him was a pretty, well-rounded woman with graying brown hair and big brown eyes. Arianna was not surprised when the older man and woman were introduced as Brian's father, Sir Fingal MacFingal, and his wife, Mab. The man had left a very strong mark on all of his sons.

Brian helped her to a seat and then placed himself between her and Fiona. Arianna looked around and found Michel and Adelar seated at a table with two maids and over a dozen young children. Fertile lot, she mused as she met Sir Fingal's narrowed gaze.

"Another lass who needs some meat on her wee bones," said Sir Fingal.

Arianna waited for the pain of those words to strike her and nothing happened. Her slenderness was one of the things Claud had always criticized, yet hearing this man speak of the same thing only amused her. Sir Fingal was one of those older men who felt free to say whatever he pleased, but actually meant no true harm. She then suspected that he always had and that age had very little to do with it. Perhaps, she thought, having a lover who seemed to be more than satisfied with the curves she had had given her some armor against such remarks.

"Lady Arianna is just fine the way she is," said Brian.

"I didnae say she wasnae fine," snapped Sir Fingal, scowling at his son. "I said she needed to eat more. And ye need to tell us why there is an army forming barely a day's ride from here."

"Oh, Brian," Arianna began, terrified that she had brought a true danger to his family.

Brian patted her hand, which was clenched into a white-knuckled fist on the table. "We kenned it might come to this, love." He looked at his father and then at Ewan. "There is an army gathering?"

"Aye. A wee group of Frenchmen are gathering a large number of hired swords," replied Sir Ewan. "I dinnae think many of the hirelings are verra skilled and probably willnae stand firm when faced with a hard fight. Have ye found out any more about the why of all this?"

As he ate, Brian told them everything he had learned. He also told them some of the questions he and Arianna still pondered and the possible answers they had come up with. As he talked it out with his brother and father, Brian could see it all more clearly. Arianna was right. There had to be more than a wee bit of land, Lucette's need to be the heir, and the DeVeaux's need for vengeance against the Murrays behind all of it.

"Aye, there is something ye dinnae ken," said Sir Fingal. "That fool Lucette sounds a mon who might do all of this just to gain an inheritance. Wheesht, a mon who would kill his own blood, or want to, and then try to beat a wee lass to death will do most anything. There isnae enough there to make that Lord Ignace act this way, though."

"Nay, there isnae," agreed Sir Ewan. "Nay sure we will e'er ken what that reason is though, for if these fools attack Scarglas, they will die. Hard to get answers from dead men."

"I still find it hard to believe that they sunk a ship just to try and kill two boys," said Fiona.

"That was terrifying," said Arianna, "and enough to get them hanged. Did Captain Tillet and his men heal?"

"Aye," replied Fiona, "and they have already sailed for home. Nay certain if anything can or will be done about what happened to his ship, though."

"I pray he is cautious for, if he points a finger at the DeVeaux with nay more proof than his word against theirs, he could find that his survival is a verra short-lived one."

"Are they all so truly evil then?"

"Weel, I doubt there are many of that family who dinnae deserve a hanging."

"Someone needs to cut away the rot like we did to the Grays," said Sir Fingal.

"Aye, someone should," Arianna agreed, "but it would take a long time and many a good mon would die in the doing of it. Right now all I care about is killing the ones who want to hurt my boys."

"They willnae get those laddies. Ye dinnae need to worry on that."

Arianna smiled at Sir Fingal. The determination weighing each word he said warmed her heart. The slow smile he gave her in return and the look in his eyes made her blush. She could easily see beyond the signs of age to the man who was able to seduce so many women. Then a scowling Mab elbowed him in the ribs and he frowned at his wife.

"Wheesht, Mab, I am truly wedded to ye but I am nay dead," he said. "E'en with all that bruising on her wee face, she is a bonnie wee lass." He winked at Arianna. "Pleased to see that my lad isnae as much like Ewan as he was pretending to be."

Brian blushed, cursed, and ignored Arianna's look of curiosity to glare at his father. "There was naught wrong with Ewan and ne'er was."

"The mon was but a vow away from being a cursed monk," snapped Sir Fingal. "It wasnae monly and ye were near as bad."

"Da!" Ewan yelled, and slapped his hand on the table, making a sound so sharp and loud it drew the attention of everyone in the great hall. "We have a battle to plan. Ye can discuss Brian's failings later."

Brian glared at Ewan. "Thank ye."

"Nay trouble. Now, Lady Arianna, we have sent word to your kinsmen. My son Ciaran and Kester, a lad from our cousin Liam's keep, were sent out the moment your lads arrived and told us what was happening. We havenae gotten a reply yet but I expect one to arrive soon. We kenned who of your clan was the closest because Fiona and Liam's wife, Keira, a cousin of yours, are forever writing to each other."

Fiona frowned at her husband. "Ye make that sound like some crime."

Ewan winked at her. "Just nay sure how ye can have so much to say to each other."

"We both have husbands and children. There is always something to say when a lass has those."

"She is telling tales about us, Ewan," said Sir Fingal. "Think ye ought to put a stop to that."

An argument started between Fiona and Sir Fingal but Arianna's unease about that rapidly turned to amusement. She could see the glint of amusement in Sir Ewan's eyes as well. It took only one look at Fiona to see that the woman was heartily enjoying herself. And so, Arianna realized, was Sir Fingal.

The argument soon veered off to one concerning what to do about the army that was being gathered by Amiel and the DeVeaux. Arianna wrestled with a crushing guilt over putting these people into the middle of her fight because she knew she would not change that even if she could. She also knew that Brian and his clan would not change it, either.

Arianna struggled to listen closely, even smiling at Sir Fingal's insistence that they just ride out and kill the whole lot before they came to Scarglas, but her thoughts began to grow cloudy with exhaustion. It had not been a very long or arduous journey from Dubheidland to Scarglas but the fact that she was still healing from the injuries Amiel had inflicted on her had made it seem so. Her body was demanding more of the rest it needed to finish healing.

Before she could quietly ask to be excused so that she could seek that needed rest, Brian was doing it for her. He then called to a maid to escort her to their bedchamber. Arianna wanted to protest Brian's arrogance, to remind him that she was a grown woman who needed no nursemaid, but the maid Joan was a big, sturdy woman who quickly, and somewhat forcefully, escorted her out of the great hall. Arianna decided she was just too tired to put up an efficient protest. She would let Brian taste her displeasure over such treatment later, after she had had enough sleep to sharpen her wits as well as her tongue.

"Ye are going to pay dearly for that," said Fiona, crossing her arms over her chest and looking at Brian as if he had just called her *wench*, a word that never failed to rouse her temper.

"She was about to fall asleep at the table," Brian said.

"Doesnae matter. Ye just had her marched out of here as if ye were afraid she would hear all our secrets and then run to our nearest enemy to tell him everything."

"I didnae."

"Aye, ye did."

"Nay, I didnae."

"Och, aye, ye most certainly did."

"Sir, is Anna nay weel?" asked Michel as he reached Brian's side and tugged on his sleeve.

Relieved to escape what had sunk into a rather childish exchange, Brian looked at Michel. "Nay, she is just verra tired."

"And hurt. I saw the bruises. Did she fall off her horse?"

"Nay, truly, she was just verra tired. 'Tis a verra long ride from Dubheidland to here."

"Did ye hit her?" demanded Adelar as he stepped

up behind Michel, his hands clenched into tight fists at his sides. "When I saw the bruises I thought it was from the injuries she got when we had to jump from the ship, but then I got to thinking and realized the bruises she has now are too fresh."

"None of my lads would e'er strike a lass," snapped Sir Fingal.

Brian held up a hand to silence his family's outrage and met Adelar's steady stare. "Nay, I would ne'er strike a lass, especially Arianna. I fear she was briefly a prisoner in your uncle's hands." He nodded when both boys winced, revealing that they had tasted some of Lord Amiel Lucette's cruelty during their short lives. "She is healing nicely but still needs a lot of rest."

"Aye, I see. Thank ye for saving her, sir."

Brian watched as Michel and Adelar returned to their table and then he looked at his family. "The reason for all of this lies in just exactly whom those two lads really are."

"Agreed," said Ewan, "but wouldnae the lass have told ye if they were more than just the sons of some bastard-born village lass and the laird?"

"They are but wee lads. They may have nay seen the importance of who fathered their mother. Aye, especially when that mother had as little to do with them as possible. They may have also heard how many scoffed at the tales of her birth."

"Anyone ask them about it?" demanded Sir Fingal, and he grunted in irritation when Brian just stared at him. "Michel and Adelar, do ye ken who your grandsire was?" he yelled at the boys.

"The lord and lady of Champier, the Lucettes," replied Adelar.

"Nay, I mean your mother's sire. Did she tell ye who sired her? Did he claim her?"

"*Maman* said it was the king's first cousin and that he may nay have openly claimed her, but there was a record of her birth and who sired her. She didnae tell us his name, though."

The great hall became so silent the boys began to grow nervous. Brian glared at everyone and gave a sharp nod toward the boys, making everyone aware of the effect the silence had on the two children. It was enough to ease some of the tense silence and he watched both boys begin to relax.

"Adelar, does Arianna ken that?" he asked the boy.

"I dinnae think so. *Maman* liked to boast that her papa had given her noble blood, but she told us we must ne'er say whose blood it was. She ne'er did. Weel, she only told Papa."

"Then we shall continue to hold it secret."

Both boys nodded and relaxed. Brian wished he could so easily shrug aside the tension gripping him. He talked to the boys while Ewan signaled the children's nursemaids that it was time for the young ones to go to bed. The moment all of the children were gone from the great hall, Brian finished off his ale and poured himself another full tankard of the strong brew. He was not surprised to look up and find everyone in the great hall now staring at him.

"Weel, I think we ken the reason for the gathering army now," said Brian.

"They dinnae mean to kill those lads," said Sir Fingal.

"Lucette does. If he kens this he cannae do anything else for there's a verra good chance the boy's grandsire will use the blood connection to grab all Claud left for his grandsons."

"Lucette will probably be killed by his own allies if he tries."

"Da, they sunk a ship the lads were on. Doesnae that prove that they want the boys dead?"

"That may have been a hasty judgment. Or, that Lucette did it whilst the others slept. Mark me, if they did try to kill them, now they want the lads for a different reason." Sir Fingal frowned as he thought it all through. "Or, there is something that noble gave his daughter, something the lads now hold, that those DeVeaux want."

"And probably havenae let Lucette ken anything about," Brian murmured, seeing the logic in that.

"It doesnae matter," said Fiona, drawing everyone's attention her way. "Two wee lads are in danger. That is all that should concern us. Let us end the threat to them first and then we can talk about what their blood kinship matters. I am nay sure it matters at all anyway."

"Nay?" Brian grimaced. "Anyone related to a royal is naught but trouble."

"Those lads are sweet, weel mannered, and show great promise. They are nay trouble."

"Fiona, I ne'er said they were nay good wee lads. I but wonder on how safe they can e'er be with a blood connection to the king of France. If that first cousin was a favorite of the king . . ."

"Oh, hell."

"Aye. The best we can hope for is that their mother was truly a bastard and nay the child of some secret marriage such as Claud had with Marie Anne, their mother."

"Oh, hell."

Brian could not help but fully agree with Fiona's concise opinion on the matter.

Chapter 17

"Those cursed Camerons are here."

Brian lifted his head from Arianna's plump breasts and glared at the door. He was pleased to see that his father had gained enough sense not to simply walk in. The man's timing was still bad, he thought as he met Arianna's sleepy but shocked gaze. Brian had anticipated waking her with his lovemaking. His father pounding on the bedchamber door and yelling at him had spoiled that.

"Good. We have need of more men," Brian said, pinning Arianna to the bed when she tried to squirm away. "I will be down to talk to them by the time they have washed and sat for something to eat."

"So ye mean to leave me to have to see to them? Just as Ewan always does?"

"Aye, just like Ewan."

He groaned and rested his head against Arianna's breasts as he listened to his father stomp off, his grumbling about ungrateful sons slowly fading away. Brian suspected Ewan had not appreciated their father banging on his bedchamber door any more than Brian had and probably for the same reason. He looked down at Arianna and kissed each blush-stained cheek.

"Should we nay go and greet them?" she asked, idly trailing her fingers up and down his spine. "They have come to help us fight our enemies, after all."

"And will be taking some time to wash the dust of travel away first. I intend to properly welcome the new day first."

"But your father will ken what we have been doing once we join the others."

"Arianna, ye do ken that ye are fretting about the sensibilities of a mon who has filled this keep near to bursting with bastards and continued to rut with every woman who didnae knock him over until he married our Mab, dinnae ye?"

She had to bite her lip to keep from laughing. Sir Fingal MacFingal was a very strange man. She would think him a bitter, heartless fool if she had not seen him with the children running all around Scarglas, did not stop to think on how he had gathered all those carelessly bred children of his close to him. From what little she had seen last night, the man was also good to Mab, his wife, in his own peculiar way. Before she could say a word, however, Brian kissed her. Arianna wrapped her body around his and let the hot desire he so easily stirred within her push all thought from her mind.

He made love to her with a fierce greed she reveled in. His every touch, every kiss, fed her need for him until she was just as greedy as he was. Arianna clung to him as he drove them both to passion's heights, her release so hot and wild, she could do no more than gasp out his name as it tore through her. The way he growled her name as he emptied himself inside her only intensified her pleasure.

Arianna was not certain how long it took her to come back to her full senses, but she did not try to pull away from Brian as she did. His weight on top of her, the warmth of his strong body, and even the lingering scent of their lovemaking filled her with contentment. At that moment she could almost believe that she could hold him this way forever. A banging at the door startled her out of her dreamy lethargy.

"Some of those Murrays are here," bellowed Sir Fingal through the door. "They want to see the lass. Want me to send them up here?"

Brian found himself abruptly shoved aside. He sat up and caught a brief, delightful, glimpse of Arianna's tempting backside as she hurried behind the privacy screen in the far corner of the room. Sighing, he climbed out of bed, slung his plaid around himself, and strode to the door, his annoyance with his father growing every step of the way. He flung open the door and glared at his father.

"That isnae amusing, Da," he snapped.

"Didnae intend it to be," drawled Sir Fingal. "Thought ye might prefer your old fither disturbing ye again rather than having her kinsmen find ye when they started searching for ye. Suspicion they will be starting to look for her soon."

Brian cursed and hurried to collect his belongings. He hated the thought of leaving Arianna's bed but he had no choice. She might enjoy some freedom as a widow, but he doubted that her kinsmen would calmly accept her openly sharing her bedchamber with her lover while they were around.

"Ye are leaving?" asked Arianna as she stepped out from behind the privacy screen still lacing up her gown.

"Ye heard my fither," he said. "Your kinsmen are here. I dinnae think ye want them to catch us together like this. I need to hie off to my old quarters."

"Ah, weel, hie away then. At least I dinnae call to have ye dragged away by some burly guard." She was pleased to see him blush and look uneasy.

The soft snickering coming from just beyond the doorway told Brian that his father was still standing there and listening to every word. "I cannae talk about that now." He kissed her. "Later, love. We will talk about it all later."

With a sigh Arianna watched him leave. She wanted to hurl herself on the bed and weep, but forced herself to calmly endure the pain twisting her heart. Brian still had not uttered one word about a possible future for them, of how he felt about her aside from lustful and protective, or even if they would find a way to be together later. This was the beginning of the end of her time with him and, if she did not know her kinsmen would soon be with her, she would be on her knees wailing out her grief. It was too soon for it to end. She had not had the time needed to make him want to keep her.

Suddenly not wanting her kinsmen to come anywhere near the bedchamber she had so briefly shared with Brian, Arianna went in search of them. She was only halfway down the stairs when she heard men arguing. Having a very good idea that her kinsmen were in the middle of that argument, she hurried down the rest of the steps. Shock brought her to a stumbling halt at the bottom of the stairs and she stared at the four men arguing with Sir Fingal.

Her cousins Harcourt and Brett had been strong warriors by the time she had left for France and they were even more so now. Brett was stunningly handsome with his black hair and green eyes, his mother always lamenting his lack of a wife at the grand age of five and thirty. Harcourt had a softer type of handsomeness, the mischief in his amber eyes and the curl in his black hair muting the harsh lines of his face. He, too, was often the subject of complaints by the matriarchs of the family for at three and thirty he was also unwed and was an unrepentant rogue.

It was the sight of the two boys she had often played with at family gatherings that truly held Arianna speechless. They had finished growing. Uven and Callum MacMillan could be twins, and were often mistaken for ones, even though Uven was a full three years younger. The last time she had seen them they had been eighteen and barely twenty, still all arms and legs and youthful bravado and eager to finish their training with the MacMillans. Now they were broad-shouldered, leanly muscled warriors. Their red hair had darkened to a coppery color and their green eyes sparkled with a mature mischief to equal the look in Harcourt's eyes.

"Weel, cousin, do ye plan to greet us properly or just gape at us?" asked Callum.

Arianna laughed and ran to hug them one after another. She was just hugging Callum, marveling at how strong he was now, when she felt him tense. Looking up at his face and idly wondering when he had gotten so tall, she frowned at the expression there. He looked as if he was readying himself for battle.

"Cousin, why is there one of those MacFingal men looking at me as if he wishes to cut my throat?" Callum asked, his voice pleasant enough except that she recognized the steel behind every word, the tone of a warrior prepared to defend her if Brian turned out to be a threat.

"That be my son Brian, *Sir* Brian," said Fingal, standing beside Harcourt, his arms crossed over his chest and a smirk on his face. "He is the one who saved your kinswoman's wee life."

There was something about the look in Brian's eye that had Arianna stepping out of Callum's arms and hurrying to Brian's side. She ignored the open curiosity in her cousins' expressions as she took Brian by the arm and led him over to them. As she introduced them to each other and they shook hands, she tried to ignore the silent contest of who could produce the strongest grip and who could withstand it without any sign of pain that all the men indulged in. Even though she thought it a strange thing for grown men to do, she could not suppress a twinge of pride when Brian obviously won.

She was just about to escort them all into the great hall when her cousins surrounded Brian. Sir Fingal responded to a hard look from Brett by grinning and pointing to a door just down the hall. A moment later her cousins and Brian were gone. Arianna started after them, a little concerned about what her cousins intended to do to Brian. They had not looked as if they intended to share tankards of ale and discuss old battles.

"Nay, lass," said Sir Fingal. "Ye were nay invited.

'Tis monly talk going on in there. Why dinnae ye go and make certain there is hot water for your kinsmen and beds for them to sleep in. With that horde of Camerons that just arrived, we might be needing a few more pallets made up."

Sending me off to do women's work so that the big, strong men can plot how to take care of the poor helpless woman's trouble and enemies, she thought crossly. "I could be of some help in answering what questions my cousins might have." Arianna started toward the door again.

"Do ye really wish to hear it all explained again? Hear about what Lucette did to ye, how your mon in France lied to ye and mistreated ye? I would have thought ye fair sick of it by now."

Arianna turned to look at Sir Fingal. His words had been spoken in his usual grouchy tone but there was sympathy in his eyes. She thought over what he had said and sighed. The very last thing she wanted to do was talk about Claud, the Lucettes, or the De-Veaux again. She did not want to be facing her cousins when they heard all about how Claud had deceived her, either. Arianna had not yet recovered from the humiliation of it all.

"Fine then, I will tend to the beds and baths like a good wee lass," she said, and ignored the way his lips twitched in an almost smile at her cross words. "If they have anything to ask me they can come and find me."

"I will be sure to tell them to do just that. Let the lassies in the kitchens know that we will be needing a lot more food."

By the time Arianna reached the kitchens her annoyance over being excluded from the talks between her cousins and Brian had receded. She knew her cousins were not going to take the news Brian had to tell them very well and she would rather not spend time in a small room with four angry kinsmen and Brian. Arianna just hoped that Brian had the time to tell her what was said before she met with her cousins again. As her father was fond of saying, kenning the facts can keep ye from doing or saying something witless.

Brian moved away from Arianna's four large kinsmen and poured each of them a drink of ale. The barely contained anger of the men made the ledger room feel even smaller than it was. Their impatience to know exactly what danger their kinswoman was in and their suspicions about him were clear to see on their faces.

All their very handsome faces, he thought, with a tug of jealous anger as he served them each a drink. The jealousy he had felt when he had seen Arianna being hugged by young Callum had thoroughly surprised him. He had wanted to tear Callum's arms off.

"What has happened to Arianna?" demanded Callum as he sat on the edge of Ewan's large worktable. "The message we got didnae give us many details."

"Did any of ye ken that her husband had a mistress?" Brian asked instead of answering Callum. "That the two wee lads we need to help are his sons by that woman? Or that he ne'er once turned away from that woman?" He nodded in full agreement with the fury that darkened all their faces.

"She ne'er told anyone in the family," said Brett. "Such news would have spread swiftly and Claud would have found himself facing some verra angry Murrays."

"Weel, those Murrays would have been even angrier when they kenned the whole truth," said Brian, and proceeded to tell them about the false marriage and the way Claud, as well as the rest of his family and retainers, had treated Arianna.

"She should have told us all this!"

"She did, but those letters never left France."

Callum cursed long and viciously with a style that Brian had to admire. "So Arianna believes that we just didnae care how she was treated, doesnae she?"

"Nay," replied Brian, and then he shrugged. "Weel, mayhaps she did, now and then. I think she was more puzzled o'er it all than anything else. Then, when we realized that her letters had all been read and the ones the Lucettes thought too damning tossed into the fire, she did feel guilty about her moments of doubt. Howbeit, Claud is dead now, murdered by his own brother."

"Tell us who threatens her now. We saw what looks to be an army forming but a day's ride from here. Were those the men doing the hunting that ye mentioned?"

"Aye. Lord Amiel Lucette and Lord Ignace De-Veau. Lord of what, I dinnae ken and dinnae care. There is even a question about which Lord Ignace we have chasing us but I dinnae care about that, either. They want those lads and your cousin." He told them everything that had happened to Arianna since she had left France, all that they knew about Lucette's plans, and all that they had surmised. Then he told them what had been discovered about Michel and Adelar, something he had not yet told Arianna.

"Jesu!" Harcourt dragged a hand through his long black hair. "We should have brought more men with us. None of these Frenchmen can leave here alive. What they ken about Arianna and those wee lads has to die with them."

"Agreed," said Brian, "although I would like to ken who else might have learned the truth about the lads. I suspicion the king and his first cousin ken the truth, but who else? DeVeau would have that answer. S'truth, I doubt he has told Lucette for that mon was still speaking of killing the laddies."

"We can decide on that when they come to the gates—and they looked verra ready to do that as we slipped round them to get here. That is, if they dinnae all die in battle."

For almost two hours they drank ale and talked on Arianna's troubles. There was some talk about the battle to come but they all knew no final plans could be made until there were Camerons and more MacFingals involved. Brian was just beginning to believe he would escape any questions concerning him and Arianna when the men decided to go and wash before joining everyone in the great hall, only to watch Callum shut the door on the other three. The younger man then turned around, crossed his arms over his chest, and gave Brian a look that was both surprisingly mature and a bit threatening.

"I dinnae believe there is anything more that I can tell ye," Brian said.

"Nay?" Callum smiled but it was not a particularly friendly expression. "Ye have spent many a night alone with my wee cousin."

"We were fleeing her enemies and hoping to draw at least some away from those boys."

"All day and all night?"

"Fleeing an enemy is an exhausting business and your cousin is a fine, weel-bred lady unused to such things."

"Yet she found the time and strength to tell ye all about Claud and his unkindnesses, her sad life with the Lucettes, and, I think, her fears. Or did ye just discover them bit by bit as ye drew closer?"

"I am nay certain what ye are implying."

"Och, aye, ye are. A mon who does naught but help a lass run and hide or turn a kind ear to her woes doesnae look ready to gut some mon just because he is holding that lady in his arms."

Brian hid a wince, heartily cursing the man's keen eye. "Lady Arianna is a grown woman and a widow. If ye have any questions about what did or didnae occur between us mayhap ye should talk to her."

"I will and she will eventually tell me everything. The lass cannae lie to save her life. What I wish to ken is what ye mean to do about what did or didnae occur between the two of ye."

"Lady Arianna returned to Scotland to rejoin her family. She is a bonnie, weel-bred, highborn young woman who will undoubtedly make a verra good marriage with a mon of equal standing."

"Ah."

"What do ye mean by *ah*?"

"Just that ye are an idiot." Callum opened the door and then looked over his shoulder at Brian. "Ye may wish to ponder on the fact that the lass already walked the path of making a good marriage with a mon of equal standing and it led her straight to misery, didnae it?"

Brian glared at the door after Callum shut it behind him and resisted the urge to throw something at it. He had thought a lot on how Arianna had once done as society and her family had expected and how he could give her so much more than that thrice-cursed Claud. It did not matter. If he convinced her to stay with him, marry him, everyone would think he had done the very thing he had sworn he would never do—marry for land and money.

He winced. That concern carried the strong taint of wounded pride. Brian did not like to think that he was so deeply concerned with how others would see him. If Arianna ever thought he had wed her for whatever dowry she would have, for what he could gain, bitterness would settle into her heart. He had seen it happen, watched what everyone had thought such a perfect match turn sour, man and wife no more than cold, bitter strangers. Brian was certain it would hurt less if he let Arianna walk into the arms of another man rather than marry her and watch the warmth they shared fade away.

Shaking his head, he refilled his tankard. There was very little time left for him and Arianna to be together. Tonight would be his last chance to savor the passion they shared for the battle would come tomorrow and, when it was done, she would leave. He sat down, put his feet up on Ewan's worktable, and began to plot a way to spend at least part of the night with her without risking a long, painful death at the hands of her cousins.

* * *

The door to Arianna's bedchamber began to ease open and she tensed. She could not believe any of the men in Scarglas would attempt to force their way into her bed. In fact, she had looked around the great hall earlier and thought there was probably not another keep in the entire world so fully packed with big, strong, handsome men. Not one of those men would need to try and steal a woman's favors.

"Arianna?"

"Brian! Ye frightened me," she complained as she sat up and watched his shadowy form approach the bed. "What are ye doing here?" She thought that low chuckle he made one of the most seductive sounds she had ever heard.

"Why do ye think I am here, love?"

"But what if my kinsmen catch ye in here?"

"They are all abed and I will be out of here ere they open their eyes in the morning."

"And ye dinnae fear that one of the men ye are sharing quarters with will say something?"

"Nay, as I am sharing quarters with three of my brothers," he replied as he shed his clothes.

He was pleased that, despite her questions and concerns, she readily curled into his arms when he slipped beneath the bedcovers and reached for her. Brian quickly removed her shift and tossed it aside, his whole body growing taut with need as her warm, soft flesh touched his. He had found his empty bed unbearable. It galled him to have to creep into her bed as if they were doing something shameful, but, as he kissed her, he knew he would do it again. He would do almost anything to hold her in his arms.

"Ye go into battle soon, dinnae ye?" she said.

"Aye," he replied with reluctance as he pushed her onto her back, for he wished to keep all talk of the battle to come out of the bedchamber tonight. "The enemy has been slipping inside the berm since the sun set. At sunrise they will be outside the gates."

"They are already attacking?"

"Nay, just gathering for the attack on the morrow and nay too wisely. They are putting themselves between a berm with only one pass through it and a keep with high, weel-monned walls. Nay a good strategy." He kissed the hollow at the base of her throat. "But I am nay here because I face a battle on the morrow."

"Nay?" Arianna sighed with pleasure when he kissed her between her breasts and she ran her feet up and down his calves, enjoying the hair-roughened strength beneath her soles.

"Nay. I would be here nay matter what I was facing on the morrow, e'en if it was just mucking out the stables." He grinned against her skin when she laughed.

"Good. And it will be e'en better if ye make verra certain that ye dinnae fall asleep and sleep beyond the sun's rising." She sighed and stroked his arms with her hands. "'Twould be e'en better if we didnae have to worry about that at all."

"Aye, but I dinnae think ye want me and your kinsmen to be at odds with each other."

"Nay, I dinnae." She wrapped her arms and legs around him. "So best ye get right to work, my fine knight."

"Your wish is my command, m'lady."

How she wished that were true. If it was, her one

and only command would be for him to love her as she loved him, for him to keep her close by his side forever. Arianna pushed away such thoughts, for they brought only sadness, and kissed Brian. Knowing it would be the last time she held him added an urgency to her lovemaking, but she did not care. She could be facing a lifetime aching for what only Brian could make her feel and she intended to fully indulge her greed until she was glutted with it.

"That was some verra poorly done sneaking about for a MacFingal," said Sigimor as he shut the door he had been peeking out of and looked at the four other men in the room. "Going to drag him out of there?"

"Nay," said Brett as he sprawled on the narrow bed he had been given. "She is a widow of three and twenty, nay some innocent maid."

"True, but I am surprised that ye are being so reasonable. Nay sure I believe that is the only reason ye are nay all trying to rush out and beat my poor cousin into the floor. Unless, 'tis a wise fear that I will attempt to protect the fool with my deadly fists and lethal skill with a sword." He grinned when all four men glared at him.

"He makes her happy," said Callum. "I think she hasnae been happy for a verra long time and I will-nae take that from her. 'Tis just a shame he is such an idiot. Ye would think such a weel-bred, highborn lass would have chosen more wisely."

Sigimor shook his head. "Aye, he is an idiot."

"Weel, we will allow him to remain one unless it begins to cause our wee cousin pain."

"And then what will ye do?"

"Drag him outside and pound him into the mud until that idiocy is pummeled right out of his thick skull."

"Fair enough."

Chapter 18

"Send out the boys and the woman and we will ride away!"

"What boys and woman are ye talking about? We have a lot of them!"

Despite the thick walls and how high up the Mac-Fingals stood on those walls, Arianna could hear everything from where she sat on the wide stone steps leading into the keep, and she winced at the mockery in Sir Fingal's voice. That was not going to calm the belligerence of the men gathered before the gates of Scarglas. The laughter of the men on the walls was undoubtedly salt in the wound to the overweening pride of Lord Ignace and Amiel.

"I dinnae understand why they didnae just attack them by that berm," muttered Fiona as she paced back and forth before the steps of the keep.

"They have a plan," Arianna said.

Fiona snorted, stopped pacing, and placed her hands on her hips. "I ken it. I just wanted this done with quickly. They obviously wanted to play with the Frenchmen first. Men. They are all idiots."

"It does appear so at times." She and Fiona both grinned briefly, and then Arianna sighed. "I still have nay thought of a real good reason for all of this. Weel, aside from the fact that Amiel has obviously lost his mind."

"Didnae Brian tell ye what the laddies said?" Fiona asked as she sat on the steps beside Arianna. "The lads told us something the night ye and Brian arrived that might explain it all."

"Nay, he didnae tell me that he may have finally discovered the why for all of this. He had to know I would have liked the answers to all the questions I have had ever since this began."

And Arianna was furious about that. Did Brian think her too weak to hear the truth? That thought infuriated her. It was a moment before she calmed down enough to look at Brian's apparent secrecy with some clarity. Whatever the boys had told him, they had done so only two nights ago. Neither she nor Brian had talked that night, falling asleep the moment they were in bed. The next morning her kin had arrived and the keep had begun readying itself for an attack. He could have said something when he slipped into her bedchamber last night but she could not complain about how they had spent the time together before he had had to creep away. Looking at it all very carefully and calmly, she could see no true crime or affront, just a little negligence.

"What did Michel and Adelar tell him?" she finally asked Fiona.

"All done being angry?"

"Aye. I dinnae think he planned to keep any secrets from me and it was the thought that he had that made me angry."

"Nay, he was just being a mon." She grinned when Arianna laughed. "It seems your wee laddies may be kin to the king of France."

"Why would Michel and Adelar think that?"

"Their mother told them. She said their father was the first cousin to the king."

A chill of fear for her boys turned Arianna's insides to ice. "Nay. Marie Anne always boasted that she was sired by a high noble but she ne'er once claimed kinship with the king himself. She could ne'er have kept such a thing a secret. She was the sort of woman who would have heralded that from the highest hill if she had kenned that it was true."

"Nay if it would cost her in some way, as I suspect it would. Mayhap her mother was given money or this Marie Anne was. Enough coin a year, as a living, to be worth the keeping of such a secret. A good hard threat would be enough to silence her as weel. And we both ken that few nobles support their bastards, let alone one born of some poor village lass."

"True, curse them." Arianna thought it over for a moment. "I dinnae think Amiel kens it. Marie Anne must have told Claud, though."

"If she told him, he would understand the need to keep it secret as weel."

"I have to wonder now if Amiel does ken it."

"If he does ken it, he would also ken that the power that noble could wield could prove enough to stop the Lucettes from annulling Claud's marriage to Marie Anne and making his grandchildren bastards. S'truth, the noble might see all manner of advantages to ensuring that his grandchildren profit weel from it."

"Jesu, ye are right. I can see it now. Aye, Amiel

does ken it. There were a lot of small wounds upon Claud's body and I thought whoever had killed him had tried to gain more coin than Claud had with him. But it seems Amiel had his own brother tortured, whether for the pleasure of it or to find out something, who can say. But once he kenned that there could be strong opposition to the annulment, he became set upon killing the boys. If Lord Ignace also kens who sired Marie Anne, though, he will nay want the boys dead. He will have some plan to make use of them."

"In other words, there is a verra good chance that DeVeau has planned to betray Lucette from the verra beginning."

"I wouldnae be surprised. DeVeau doesnae need the lads dead; he can just force their guardian to sell his family back the land they want for a pittance."

"That guardian being you."

"Aye, and trying to capture me to get that makes far more sense than them trying to get me to extract some vengeance upon my family for what happened long ago."

"DeVeau gets his hands on ye and he could achieve both those things. But, that is nay longer a concern. He will nay leave Scarglas."

"Killing Lord Ignace could make the DeVeaux seek vengeance against ye and yours."

Fiona shrugged. "If they do, we will deal with them."

"They can be a vicious, tenacious enemy."

"Who live in France. And, e'en if they send someone to take revenge, we can deal with them. I am certain Brian told ye some of his clan's history, if only to explain this place." Arianna nodded and Fiona continued, "Weel, my clan the MacEnroys didnae have any better a life. It was one of three clans that fought until little was left but ruins and graves, and all the remnants of the clans who were struggling to rebuild were nearly destroyed by treachery. My own uncle tried to stir up the killing again and had actually had a part in what had nearly killed us all before. So, treachery, enemies determined to kill us, plots, and lies?" Fiona shrugged. "Naught a thing that we have nay faced before and survived."

"I had heard that my cousin Gillyanne had wed a mon with a dark past. But . . ."

"Nay. The men out there wish to drag three innocents into their plots, think naught of killing two wee lads just to gain more coin, more land, or more power. Any right-thinking mon would fight against that."

There was no arguing that. Arianna had clung to the hope that there would be no battle, that at some point her pursuers would decide they were simply wasting their time and retreat. She knew that, from the beginning, she had ignored that little voice in her head warning her that it was all so much more complicated than just Amiel wanting to be the heir. She looked up at the men lining the walls of Scarglas who still taunted Amiel and Lord Ignace.

"I just wish they didnae act as if they enjoyed the thought of battle so much," Arianna murmured.

"Ach, weel, they actually do at the start. They are men and men are a strange lot."

"True. Verra true." She laughed along with Fiona.

* * *

"Why havenae Fiona and Arianna gone inside?" Brian asked Ewan.

"They are safe enough where they are," replied Ewan, his gaze fixed upon the men confronting them.

"Nay if someone begins to shoot arrows o'er the wall."

"I see no archers, Brian."

"They had a couple at Dubheidland."

"Ye and Sigimor must have killed them."

"They would still be safer inside instead of right down there where they can hear and smell the battle."

Ewan looked at his brother, leaving the verbal harassment of the enemy to his father and other brothers. "I believe my wife is weel acquainted with the sight and sound of battle. Now, Arianna may nay carry knives all o'er as my loving wife does, but I suspicion she is also acquainted with the scent and sound of battle."

"They may be acquainted with it but that doesnae mean they have to face it when they could go inside the keep."

"Dinnae worry. Fiona will go in soon and take your lass with her. She will be safe." He looked down at the men gathered before the walls of Scarglas. "They are so busy making demands they havenae noticed our men at all."

Deciding he would get no help in making Arianna go inside, Brian also turned his attention to Lucette, DeVeau, and their hirelings. He could see at least two score men who were undoubtedly well-trained men-at-arms. The rest were just men with swords who thought joining this fight was worth the few coins they got. Even the trained men did not notice that they were now surrounded, but then the MacFingals and their cousins were also well trained.

"I would think it time to start this rout," Brian said.

"A few more minutes. Our fither is having fun."

"My lord," said DeVeau.

"Och, I am nay the laird," said Sir Fingal. "He is." He pointed at Ewan.

The look on DeVeau's face told Brian that the man would probably give his soul to be able to get his hands on old Fingal. It was an expression all Fingal's sons, and many another who met their father, had worn at some time or another. The man's skill at keeping someone intent on winning an argument with him was just the skill they had needed, however. While Lucette and DeVeau had tried to talk reason to Fingal, Scarglas men and their allies had slipped out, using the berm as shelter as they had slowly encircled DeVeau and his men.

DeVeau turned his attention to Ewan. "You should have spoken up."

"Why? Ye were nay saying anything I was interested in."

"Enough of this!" Lucette yelled. "Those boys are my nephews. They are French and we intend to take them back to their home. You have no right to them."

"Nor do ye. They are where they belong. With their guardian."

"My brother was mad. No one appoints a woman

to be a guardian. The courts will end that insane arrangement."

"Then bring me the court's demand and I might think on it." Ewan glanced at Brian and said quietly, "Time to go down to the gates. Sigimor is waiting for my signal. I will give it as soon as ye and the others are in place. Wish I could join ye in killing these arrogant fools, but if I leave they may pause to finally look around."

Brian hurried down to the bailey. Once Ewan gave the signal everything would happen fast for Sigimor would give that fierce battle cry of his and all the men hiding behind the berm would be over it. It was Brian's intention to be the first one to get to Lucette. The man needed to pay for what he had done to Arianna.

The thought of Arianna had him looking toward the steps to the keep. He was pleased to see that she and Fiona had gone back inside. Once the gates were opened to let him and his men out, it would no longer be safe for the women to be outside the keep.

Brian mounted one of the waiting horses and looked at Callum as the man moved up beside him. "Thought ye would be with Sigimor and the others," he said.

"Changed my mind." Callum smiled but there was a coldness to it that told Brian this man would be a real threat to anyone who got in his way. "Much prefer being mounted to start the fight." He patted his horse's neck.

"Lucette is mine."

Callum just smiled again but before Brian could demand the man give his word not to go after

Lucette, Sigimor's battle cry rent the air. The gates were swung open and Brian had a brief glimpse of the horrified looks on the faces of the Frenchmen before he fixed his gaze on Lucette and charged.

It did not surprise Brian when Lucette attempted to turn and flee. Any man who beat a woman usually proved himself a coward when faced with a man. He rode in front of the man, cutting off his retreat. Lucette quickly proved himself a poor rider as well, yanking on his mount's reins until the horse reared and tumbled Lucette into the dirt. Brian was down and facing him by the time Lucette scrambled to his feet.

"I surrender!" cried Lucette, and fumbled to pull his sword out of its sheath.

Brian was briefly tempted to just kill the fool and turn away to help the others. He watched Lucette carefully, however, for the man could be acting inept in order to lull him into a dangerous sense of ease. Although it was hard to believe anyone could act that well.

"There is nay surrender for ye, Lucette," Brian said. "Ye die here."

"Ye can keep the boys and that bitch."

"I intend to. But, I am thinking ye ken too much to be allowed to go back home. And ye dug your own grave the first time ye struck Arianna."

Lucette drew his sword and the way the man did it, his eyes narrowing, told Brian he had been right to be cautious. He had no doubt he would defeat the man but was pleased to see that it might well be a fight instead of an easy kill. Brian wanted Lucette to sweat before he died.

When Lucette attacked, Brian was ready for him. He was a little surprised at the skill the man revealed but then fixed his mind on ending Lucette's life. Lucette proved nimble and it was not long before they were both bleeding from several small injuries. But Lucette was already weakening, sweat stinging his eyes and his chest heaving with the effort to breathe.

"You do not even understand the worth of what you fight for," Lucette said as he and Brian circled each other. "Those whelps are related to the king of France. They need to go back to claim their heritage."

"All ye want to give them is death, Lucette." This time when their swords clashed, only Lucette bled.

"You could make a fortune off them, fool."

"Mayhap, but I still want ye dead."

"For the sake of that stupid bitch? My brother did not even linger in her bed the few times he did what he had to to please our parents. He found the attentions of a coarse village whore more entertaining than Lady Arianna. Or do you think to get the dowry that she had? Too late. It is gone."

"I will leave the settling of that to the Murrays. All I want is to kill the coward that beats women half his size."

Lucette bellowed out his fury and frustration and charged. It was not hard to use that blind anger against the man. After a furious clash of swords, Brian quickly cut the man down. He was standing there, panting a little, and staring down at Lucette's body when a warning cry drew his attention. He started to turn toward it and the man attacking him from behind caught him in the side instead of through the back. The cold fire of steel in his side nearly brought Brian to his knees, but he held firm and easily cut the other man down.

Chaos ruled all around him. Breathing slowly and deeply, Brian fought the pain as he studied the battle. Some of the Scots were slipping away, retreating as fast as they could. He could see that Sigimor and his men merely kept an eye on any of the hired swords who looked to be escaping the trap, but held all the Frenchmen firmly within the berm.

Determined to hold fast until it was over, Brian began to make his way to where Sigimor, Callum, and Harcourt were cutting down the French guard around DeVeau. DeVeau showed far more skill than Lucette but he was clearly tiring. By the time Brian was close enough to hear what little was being said, DeVeau stood with only two men and was trying to bargain for his life.

"Wait," Brian said as he moved to stand next to Sigimor.

"Thought ye wanted all the Frenchmen dead," said Sigimor.

"I certainly have nay trouble ending the life of a DeVeau," said Harcourt.

"I ken it, but why add to the feud when ye may nay have to? It is a feud that has grown cold. Killing another DeVeau could change that," said Brian. "Ye ken why we want ye all dead?" he said to DeVeau.

"So that the children remain lost," said Lord Ignace.

"Aye, so that this threat to them ends here. Now, which Lord Ignace are ye? The winemaker or the torturer?"

"Ah, the winemaker. The name is a curse but

fortunately I travel to few of the places where my notorious cousin has been."

Brian believed him. "Then 'tis up to ye whether it ends with ye walking away or being buried."

"Naturally, I would prefer to walk away."

The man was a lot younger than Brian had thought, even though he now knew him to be the winemaker. He doubted Lord Ignace was much older than Ned. If the DeVeaux knew of the value of the boys, surely they would have sent someone older and more experienced, he thought. One who would not have ended up in what, to an experienced warrior, was an obvious trap.

"How many of your people ken the truth?"

"Three. Me, my uncle, and my mother. When Lucette came to us, he spoke mostly with my mother so I am not exactly certain how much my uncle knows. My mother does not like or trust my uncle. My uncle, he prefers to work with the grapes."

"Jesu," muttered Sigimor. "Beginning to think some of these French have families a lot worse than ours."

Brian ignored the chuckles of the men who had gathered around them. "Your mother sent ye to get the boys?"

A faint smile touched the young man's bruised mouth. "You have not met my mother. She saw this as a way to make our part of the family more powerful. She believes we are scorned and treated ill by the rest of our family. She wishes to be the one who does the scorning and the ill treating, *oui*? She believes the children will help her get that power for they are protected. Only some, not much, but . . ." He shrugged.

"Did ye ken that Lucette planned to slowly kill off many of the landed and titled people of his clan? That he claimed he had the DeVeaux as allies?" Brian saw his answer in the widening eyes of the young French lord.

"I only knew that I would have to kill him for he intended to kill the children. As for having my family as his allies? I fear I am all he had and I was reluctant. The rest of my family knows nothing about all this or Amiel."

"What about the land?"

Lord Ignace shrugged again. "It is strategically important but we have lived without it for years. I considered getting that a good thing but not necessary. The woman, the guardian, might have been persuaded to sell it. Mayhap to come home here with the children or to live quietly somewhere with them. That was a thought."

"And what did ye want from all this?"

"What I wanted matters little. My mother and uncle hold the money until I am thirty or wed. I did suggest to her that sending me here might be the death of me but she was not troubled by that."

Brian looked at Sigimor, who sheathed his sword, crossed his arms over his chest, and nodded. It was all the agreement he needed. They did not have one of the worst of the DeVeaux here, just a young man with little choice. He doubted anyone would cry for revenge over the loss of some men-at-arms, but killing a young lordling of the clan, even one they did not favor, could renew the feud between the Lucettes and DeVeaux, and the Murrays, with a vengeance. He also thought that sending someone back to tell some truths and a few lies would help keep the boys safe.

"Tell me, if ye had a choice, what would ye have done? What do ye want to do?" he asked DeVeau.

"Go home alive. I would not have done this. What my mother wants does not matter. I think it would just get us killed. I like being of so little importance to the rest of my family that they barely acknowledge me." The two men with him grunted in agreement. "Why do you think Lucette approached us and no other? Because we are no real threat to any Lucette. We have a small vineyard far away from most of the others and they only notice us when they need a place to rest on some journey. They come, eat our food, drink far too much of our wine, and then forget us as soon as they ride away. I would like it to stay that way."

"And the sinking of the ship?"

"Stupid," he spat out, anger bringing a light flush to his cheeks. "Unnecessary. I was asleep and did not know what Lucette was doing. I would never have agreed, which I think is why I was not awakened and told about it. My father was a sailor, *oui*? What he did for France and the king is why we have our vineyard and the title."

"Then ye will go home, alive, with your two men. But ye will tell your mother that the boys died, that ye were attacked as ye tried to bring them back to France."

DeVeau frowned. "That may cause trouble with the grandfather. They are bastards but the grandfather, he is a man who believes in caring for any with the family blood in their veins."

"Ye will find a way to go and tell him, secretly,

that the boys live. They are ours now. Lady Arianna got them a piece of land here from the Lucettes and here they will stay. And, as ye can see, they will be weel protected. That grandfather can deal with the Murrays or us if he e'er has need to speak to the lads."

"She got the Lucettes to give the lads their Scottish lands?" DeVeau asked in surprise. "Mayhap she was not a madmon's choice for guardian, eh? Do you think she will be wanting to be rid of their French lands?"

"If and when she and the lads want to, ye will be the first they offer them to. If ye do as I say."

"And if ye dinnae," said Sigimor, "then ne'er close your eyes, lad."

The way DeVeau stared up at Sigimor, slowly blinking and paling a little, revealed his youth as nothing else had. Brian winced and knew he had to end this soon. His wounds had cost him a lot of blood and he was growing light-headed.

"I swear upon my father's honor that I will do all you have asked," DeVeau said.

"Go home, DeVeau," said Brian. "If ye keep your vow, then it all ends here."

"What of Lucette's body?"

"We will see that he gets back to his family with a warning," said Harcourt.

"Oh, and if ye truly were appalled by the sinking of the ship, ye may wish to speak to a Captain Tillet." Brian gave the man Tillet's direction. "It would serve ye weel to do so as I dinnae think ye want your name tied to that sinking, nor have it brought to the attention of the rest of your kin."

DeVeau nodded. He and his men sheathed their

swords and moved to gather their horses. Brian knew that would be all they would leave with for his kinsmen were already busy gathering up anything of value left on the battlefield. He frowned when he saw Callum fall into step beside DeVeau for he did not believe the young man would go back on his word.

"Callum?" he called.

Callum looked at him and grinned. "Naught to worry about, Brian. Just talking about wine and ships."

Brian shook his head and then stumbled. Sigimor moved to steady him. He looked at his cousin and knew he was not going to be able to stay conscious much longer.

"Jesu, Brian," muttered Sigimor. "Ye are bleeding like a stuck pig."

"Just how does a stuck pig bleed?" asked Brian.

"And now ye are talking like a fevered mon. We need to get back to the keep and see to those wounds."

Brian looked toward the keep. It appeared to be miles away and surrounded by a thick haze. He looked back at his cousin.

"Sigimor?"

"Aye?"

"Catch me."

Sigimor caught Brian before he hit the ground. He picked his cousin up in his arms and, cursing softly, started toward the keep. "Arianna is nay going to be happy about this."

No one disagreed.

Chapter 19

Arianna wrung out the rag she had just dipped in a bowl of cool water and bathed the sweat from Brian's face. The terror that had gripped her when he had shown signs of fever had eased now. It had been two days and his fever had not risen very high. His wounds were healing nicely as well, with no signs of infection.

She shivered with dread as she remembered her first sight of him after the battle. To see him bloodied and carried in Sigimor's arms had nearly brought her to her knees. If Brian had not groaned softly at that moment she would have started wailing like a banshee. The mere thought of him dying had torn the heart right out of her. She had actually been relieved to hear that he was only wounded, until she had seen the wounds. It had taken Mab and Fiona a few moments to assure her that none of the wounds were mortal.

Fiona and Mab had done wonderful work. Arianna was ashamed about how little she knew despite all the teachings of her family. She had been too young to understand the importance of such teachings. Her love had been the garden and still was. In her youthful arrogance she had thought the ability to grow all the plants the healers needed was enough. In France she had been better than the healer they had used but, next to Fiona and Mab, she was a fumbling novice.

"I just assumed that everyone had skilled healers," she told a sleeping Brian as she bathed his arms. "That was verra foolish of me. Just because I grew up surrounded by women who had great skill didnae mean there were a lot of skilled healers outside the lands of my kinsmen. If I had taken a moment to consider the matter, I would have recalled how often one of my kinswomen was called away because of her skills. Then I would have kenned the idiocy of my belief. The fact that I was just a child doesnae excuse me, either."

"Why not? Many of us dinnae think much on the future when we are children," said Fiona as she closed the door behind her and moved to the side of Brian's bed. "He looks better."

"His wounds are still clean and already show signs of healing," Arianna said.

"Good. I have come to sit with him for a while and Mab will follow me. Ye go and visit with your lads, get some rest, or go and enjoy this rare sunny day in the gardens."

Arianna forced down the reluctance she felt, the need to stay at Brian's side. Fiona was right. She did need to get some rest, to leave the room and breathe some fresh air. She would do Brian no good if she exhausted herself. With a nod to Fiona, Arianna stood up and walked out of the room, intending to find Michel and Adelar.

Two hours later, Arianna sat down on a stone bench in Fiona's garden. She knew she would have to seek her bed soon. The visit with the boys had quickly revealed to her just how tired she was. But, the sun was shining, the gardens were full of the signs of new growth, and she needed to savor that for a while. She leaned back against the tree behind the bench and let the sun warm her.

"Ye would probably be more comfortable sleeping in a bed."

Blinking rapidly, Arianna sat upright and looked at Callum as he sat down next to her. A glance up at the sun told her that she had fallen asleep for a while, but her body was demanding a much longer rest. She was a little surprised that her cousins were still at Scarglas.

"I had thought ye and the others would have left by now," she said, a little embarrassed that she had paid so little attention to where her cousins were after they had come to help her.

"We are waiting on ye," Callum said.

"Ah, weel, I cannae say when Brian will be fully recovered."

"Actually, we are waiting to see what ye wish to do when he is. Stay or leave. I can see by your face that he has ne'er given ye a hint of what will happen about that. So, ye and the rest of us will wait until he does."

Callum was too astute, she decided. He always had been. Arianna suspected the horrors of his childhood had something to do with how easily he could see into a person's heart. Orphaned and abused, he

had known the worst of humanity until her cousin
Payton and his wife, Kirstie, had saved him. He had
gained a true skill at judging what a person was or
what they wanted from those dark days. Now accepted by his paternal family, the cherished grand-
son of a powerful MacMillan, he had fulfilled his
boyish pledge to grow strong and learn to fight so
that he could protect the innocent. She did not believe she needed his protection, however.

"There has been little time to think about the
future," she said, and was not surprised by the way
he just cocked a brow at her for the thin excuse was
worthy of derision.

"Nay? He found time to be your lover."

She could feel the heat of a blush stinging her
cheeks but ignored it. "That is none of your concern."

"Ah, but it is. Arianna, we failed ye."

"Nay!"

"Aye, we did. All of us. We didnae stand by ye as
we should have as a family. Ye were in France for
five years, lass, and not one of us came to visit."

That still stung but she told herself not to be a
child about it. "Ye didnae ken that I wanted ye to.
The Lucettes didnae let ye see the letters that might
have made ye want to come to see how I was faring.
They didnae let me see any letters from my family
that might have spoken about visiting, either, so ye
couldnae have kenned that I wished to visit home
or have ye visit me. As far as all of ye kenned, I was
content."

He moved closer and put his arm around her
shoulders. "E'en if ye were truly content, someone
from the clan, from your family, should have gone to

visit you. The verra fact that ye ne'er asked us to visit
or asked if ye could come home for a visit should have
made us wonder why. We definitely should have had
some suspicions roused by the occasional missive
from your husband or his family telling us that ye were
far too busy to visit with us."

They should have and Arianna suspected the fact
that they had not would hurt for a while. She knew
how the days could pass, how long a journey it was,
and how many obligations her family had. Soon
that would be enough to soothe the sting. They had
written so they had not forgotten her. And with the
Lucettes watching all letters coming or going, her
family must have begun to wonder if she cared
about any of them anymore. The wound she had
suffered had mostly been inflicted by the Lucettes
and it would heal.

"I didnae ken that the Lucettes wrote to any
of ye."

"Only now and then. I believe it was at those
times when they saw something in our letters to you
that told them we were becoming unsettled by the
lack of any invitation to come to France or your un-
willingness to visit with us here. They kenned verra
weel that we wouldnae have tolerated the way ye
were being treated. That doesnae excuse us, though.
Someone should have traveled there to see how ye
fared, nay just taken the Lucettes' word for it."

"The Lucettes, aside from Claud's family, are good
allies and good people. There was nay any reason to
be suspicious of them. Of course, I was ne'er allowed
to see any of the other Lucettes, either. I fear I
thought they ne'er wished my company, but now

I ken that the Lucettes or Claud made sure none of them came to visit, either."

"'Tis the way of such people. They cannae have the ones who care for ye come anywhere near. Claud certainly couldnae allow it or all of his lies would have been revealed and one of us would have freed ye of the trap he had put ye in."

She sighed. "Brian told ye everything, didnae he?" She had the feeling that Brian had done so because he was angry at what he saw as their neglect.

"About how Claud abused ye? Aye."

"He ne'er hit me, Callum."

"What he did was still abuse."

"I ken it now. Brian made me see that, although it did take a while for it to become clear to me."

"I will confess that it took me a while to ken how ye didnae see what he was doing from the verra start. Then I understood that what he did was feed ye a slow poison."

"That is exactly what Brian calls it. Insidious is what it was. Rather like that wee drop of water that slowly wears a hollow in a rock. When I became aware of what he had done to me, I was ashamed. Why had I allowed it? I have thought about it a lot and have decided that I wasnae as certain of myself as I had thought I was. A part of me accepted the implication that I needed a great deal of improvement. I also come from a clan with a lot of strong, good marriages. I wanted that for myself and I think I was willing to believe Claud wanted that, too. Many of his criticisms were weel disguised as advice." She shrugged. "It doesnae matter. I am recovering. I dinnae e'en hear his voice in my head as often as I did before."

"I think ye are still wounded enough that ye now hesitate to reach for what ye want."

"Both people must want it, Callum," she said quietly, knowing that he spoke of Brian.

"Aye, but that doesnae mean one cannae at least try to convince the other that they both want the same thing."

She laughed with him and promised him she would think about it. There was some wisdom in his jesting words, however, she thought as she finally left the garden to seek her bed. One could not force love from a person, but that did not mean one had to just sit and wait, hoping it would grow. She could, at the very least, try to show Brian that there was love just waiting for him if he wanted it.

What she knew she could not do was openly declare her love and hope for the best. If Brian could not have his mind changed about sending her home, she did not want to leave knowing she had handed him her heart only to have it tossed aside. Arianna decided that what she needed to do was show him in every way she could that she cared for him. If he wanted her as some thought he did, he would see how she cared and ask her to stay.

Brian woke to the soft sound of Arianna's voice. He had heard it often during his recovery. The way she had cared for him as he had healed made him think she had some deep feelings for him. He tried not to let that tempt him into reaching for what he knew he could not have. He saw no harm in basking in her warmth for a little while longer, though.

"Ah, ye are awake," she said, and hurried back to the side of his bed to kiss his cheek. "Hungry?"

"Och, aye," he said as he sat up and rested against the pillows she stacked behind his back. "I will be glad to get out of this bed, too. A fortnight abed is too long."

"I ne'er liked being bedridden, either. I once thought that the sun only came out when I was too ill to enjoy it."

He laughed and then murmured his pleasure when she set a tray of hearty meat, bread, and cheese before him. Another sure sign that he was healed for Fiona was very strict about what an injured or ill person could eat. This food was only for the healthy.

Arianna kept him entertained with tales of what everyone was doing while he ate. It was evident that she had settled in nicely at Scarglas. He knew she and Fiona had become very close. He prayed Arianna would not be too hurt when he sent her home.

Brian then wondered if she was reluctant to leave because she still thought her family had deserted her. That wound had been deep and he doubted it was fully healed yet. Arianna had the sense to know it was not her family's fault, not entirely, but that did not mean she was eager to face them all.

"So, your cousins are still lurking about?" he asked as he picked up his tankard and then inhaled the scent of good strong ale, another thing Fiona had denied him while he healed.

"Just Callum and Uven," she replied. "Brett and Harcourt had to leave as they had places they had promised to be." She frowned. "I have the feeling there is something troubling Brett but he didnae tell me what. I think he got tired of me asking him if everything was fine." She smiled. "Might be why he left."

"Could have given him a nudge but I suspicion it was more about some place they had said they would be, some promise they had made. And, at times, a mon doesnae want to talk about what troubles him, nay if it is personal."

She nodded. "I had to wonder if it was a woman."

"And that would most assuredly nay be something he would want to speak to ye about."

Before Arianna could reply, Callum strode into the room. She resisted the urge to kick him as she walked by him to leave. He and Brian probably had some business to discuss, she decided as she made her way to the gardens. It delighted her to find Michel and Adelar there helping Fiona weed the herb beds, and she quickly joined in.

"How is your campaign to win that fool's heart coming along?" asked Fiona when the boys moved away.

"I think it goes weel but I cannae be certain," Arianna said.

"He hasnae told ye to go home yet."

"True. Of course, he has only just finished his healing. He may have waited because he likes to be coddled."

Fiona laughed. "Oh, aye, they do. Ye have certainly made my life easier by taking o'er his care. He has healed enough now that he can begin to move around and regain all his strength and I havenae had to suffer through any monly tantrums."

"A true blessing."

Fiona glanced at the boys to make sure they were

still at the other end of the garden and then asked, "He hasnae asked ye to stay yet, has he?"

Arianna sighed. "Nay. And, although he hasnae yet asked me to leave, he sometimes speaks as if I am soon to go. I begin to fear entering the room as I expect to hear the words I dread each time I do now."

Fiona hugged her. "I shall pray that ye get what ye want."

"I think a few prayers may be needed as naught I have done has seemed to make him see that I care for him, that I have no trouble with his life as it is. I shall just have to wait and see what happens when he is back on his feet and fit again."

Brian stood up and stretched, enjoying the feel of just moving around without pain or weakness. He looked at Callum and sighed. They worked well together and the younger man had a good eye to making a profit in trade. Brian hoped that would not change when Arianna left.

His heart clenched with pain at the mere thought of her riding away from him but he fought to ignore that. Now that he was healed, there was no more reason for her to linger at Scarglas. If he was honest with himself, there had been no need for her to stay and help him heal as Fiona and Mab were very skilled healers. He had allowed himself the time with her, enjoying her caring for him, out of pure selfish need. It was time to stop being selfish and send her back to the life she deserved.

"Ye have a look on your face that isnae making me feel verra kindly toward ye," said Callum.

"What look?"

"The one that says that now that ye are healed enough to stretch and prance about, ye will do what ye think is the honorable thing and send my cousin away." Callum held up a hand to stop Brian from speaking. "Please, dinnae lash me with the talk of how she is so high ye cannae touch her. I just ask that ye make the cut ye are about to give her quick and clean. Once ye do this, dinnae change your mind and come looking for her as I willnae allow it."

Brian was tempted to respond to that threat with a bit of belligerence of his own, but bit back the words. They had one more item to discuss as far as their business dealings went and then the man could leave. He just hoped that Callum did not carry grudges. The trade deals they had made together could prove to be very rich ones and he liked the man.

"We have received word from Lord Ignace that Captain Tillet has a fine new ship. Our first shipment of wine will be headed this way in about a month."

"Good. Does he say anything about the lads?"

"Aye, their maternal grandfather agrees that they are safer here, that it is safer that the world thinks them dead as weel. The blame for that was put on Lucette. The man will be sending some boon for the lads soon. It appears that his son has died and the mon bred only lassies on his legal wife." Brian frowned. "I hope he doesnae think he can make them his heirs for then the world will ken that they are nay dead and they are legitimate. It will also mean that Paul Lucette cannae be the heir to the Lucette land."

"Leave it to them to sort out. The lads are safe here. What happens when they are grown will be their business to deal with. I doubt the old mon will be making his wishes clear for a long time. Arianna says Paul is a verra good mon, studious and kind. For all we ken, he and the old mon are working together in secret. And, we cannae work against those boys getting a fortune in lands and titles when they are older just because we fear for their safety. We will just make certain they are always protected and trained weel in how to protect themselves."

"Agreed. Lord Ignace also says that his mother has retired to a convent. Seems his uncle suggested it. Says the mon wasnae happy about her plans to stand up against the rest of the DeVeaux or her lack of regard for her only child, his heir. He felt we would be pleased to ken that she willnae be sending him on any more journeys to add to her power and prestige."

Callum chuckled. "And I suspect he and his uncle are still rejoicing. Obviously the uncle had some power of his own to get that woman out of the house and tucked away in a convent where she can do no more harm."

"It does seem as if we have found that rarest of creatures, a likeable, honest DeVeau."

"Aye, so let us hope the rest of his family continues to ignore him. I think 'tis the fact that Lord Ignace is the son of a sailor that has saved him from the others. He may be a DeVeau but he is still tainted by the common branch of the family tree."

"From what I have heard of the DeVeaux and having met this lad, I think they would do weel to get a little more of the common blood into their family."

"Aye." Callum stood up. "I will be off soon I am thinking, but let us nay shake hands right now as I am sore tempted to strike ye down for what I ken ye are about to do." He nodded at Brian in farewell and walked out of the room.

Brian stared at the door Callum shut behind him and sighed. He supposed he would feel the same if it was one of his cousins. Callum and Arianna had also been close when they were children. Even he had seen what good friends they were once he had gotten past his jealousy.

He sat down at his worktable and dragged his hands through his hair. This was going to be hard but he had to do it. He was healed enough now, after three long weeks, that he was finding it very difficult not to drag Arianna into his bed and make love to her until they were both too weak to even twitch a finger. If she did not leave Scarglas soon he would be doing just that and that would be wrong. A man did not make love to a woman and then turn around and tell her to leave. The trouble was that the need for her was growing so strong he just might sink that low.

He was searching his mind for the right words to say, ones that would carry no taint of rejection, when she stepped into the room and smiled at him. Brian wondered how such a sweet smile could make him feel so wretched. He knew she cared for him but wondered how much of that was because he had been so much kinder to her than any of the Lucettes and had helped her save the boys. A part of him wanted to hear her tell him how she felt about him but he knew that would be cruel because he would still have to let her go.

It did not surprise him when her smile began to fade and her steps slowed as she approached him. Callum had guessed what he was going to do today and she was nearly as astute. It puzzled him that doing the right thing, the honorable thing, should be making him feel like the worst of heartless bastards.

"Arianna, I have been meaning to talk to ye," he said.

Arianna stopped a foot away from his desk and clasped her hands in front of her skirts. There was a look in his fine eyes that was easy to read. He was going to send her home, just as he had always said he would. The fact that he looked sad about that did not ease the pain of it at all. She kept her hands clasped tightly so that she did not give in to the urge to either cling to him or grab something heavy and beat him over the head with it.

"About what?" she asked.

"Weel, first, let me tell ye what Lord Ignace wrote. I received his missive just today." He proceeded to tell her nearly everything the man had said even as a voice in his head scoffed at him for this pathetic attempt to delay doing what he had to do.

The news concerning the boys both pleased and worried her. They were safe for now but the future could bring problems. Arianna wondered why he was bothering telling her this because he must have just told Callum, who would be sure to tell her. He did not need to waste time before breaking her heart. Now that she knew what he was about to do, she really just wanted him to get it over and done with.

"Weel, that is good news. For now. There may be trouble later, however," she said.

"Callum and I are aware of that, and everyone will be alert. I believe Lord Ignace will be sure to send us word, too, especially if he gains from the wine trade with us."

"Of course. So, is that all?" She desperately wanted this over with as she was nearly shaking with pain and anger.

Brian cleared his throat and clasped his hands together on the top of his worktable. He wished she were not looking at him as if he was about to draw his sword and lop off her head. She had to know that this was best for her.

"I want to thank ye for all the care ye took of me while I was healing from my wounds."

"Ye got those wounds fighting for my laddies."

"Ah, weel, aye. And ye. But, I am healed now and your family is eager to see ye. So, I have arranged for an escort for ye and the boys for the ride to your family. Callum and Uven are preparing to leave with ye, too. It was my greatest honor to have been of help to ye in your time of need. If ye e'er need help again . . ."

"I will ask it of my family. Now, if ye will kindly excuse me, it appears I have packing to do and fare-weels to give."

He watched her walk out of the office and had to bite his lip to keep from calling her back. Brian did not think he would ever be able to forget her expression as he had so politely thanked her and wished her well. She had looked both devastated and furious.

For a moment he had almost leapt up to take her

in his arms and try to soothe the pain he sensed he had inflicted. That would have been the greatest folly and he knew it. Once he had her in his arms he would not have been able to let her go. It was one reason he had not made love to her despite having been able to and wanting to for at least a sennight.

"I did the right thing," he said aloud.

He poured himself a tankard of ale and wondered if he had enough so that he could just hide in this room and get stinking drunk until she was long gone. It could be the only way he stopped himself from running after her. Considering the way she had looked at him, if he did run after her, he would probably also have to get down on his knees and beg her forgiveness. Getting drunk was less painful.

Chapter 20

"What are ye doing?"

"Packing," replied Arianna without looking at Fiona. "I am nearly done and then I will go and help my boys pack all their things."

"May I ask why?" Fiona sat on the bed and watched Arianna fold a gown with far too much care.

"'Tis time to leave, or so I was told. Time to return to my family and the life that I deserve because I was born to it. Somehow my birth demands that I marry only certain men and live only in a type of untold luxury that my parents have ne'er enjoyed and . . ."

Arianna grabbed the gown she had just packed and threw it across the room. That felt so good that she rapidly did the same with everything she had packed until all her clothing was scattered from one end of the room to the other. Cursing softly, she sat down on the bed and glared at the floor.

"Feel better?" Fiona asked as she pushed the saddle packs aside and moved closer to Arianna.

"Nay, not much, and now I shall have to do my packing all over again."

"Brian told ye to leave, did he?"

Just hearing Fiona say it sent pain slicing through her heart, but Arianna nodded. "Aye. He thanked me kindly for how I cared for him but he is healed now and my family is anxious to see me. Told me how honored he was to help me and even said I could call for him again if I was in trouble. I told him I would just ask my family and left, saying something about needing to pack. Those things I was just saying are what I ken he was thinking, what he has said to a lot of people."

"And do ye always do what he says?"

She looked at Fiona. "What choice do I have? He wants me gone, Fiona."

"Nay, he doesnae. He is just doing what he thinks is right. Brian is far too aware of the fact that he is a younger son without land or much coin, a mon of one and thirty who has earned his knighthood yet still lives in his father's house. Ye, Lady Arianna, are a verra high reach for such a mon."

"So his pride will send me home? His pride will bar us from even trying to reach for more than an adventure and a few nights of passion? Why doesnae his pride tell him that he is good enough for me? What good is pride when ye are all alone?"

"None, but I think there is a wee bit more than that to it all. Ewan says Brian has seen a lot of sour marriages, ones made for land, title, or money, and has always said he would never marry for that. Mayhap he fears that is what everyone would think he was doing if he wed you. Worse, he might fear that even ye would begin to think so."

"Why would he think I am so unable to ken what I want or what I can be content with? Aye, the way I let Claud and his kin treat me may have made me look weak, but I have certainly shown him o'er the last few weeks that I have a mind of my own and can make decisions. If he cannae see that after all the time we have spent together and all we have gone through, then how can I e'er make him see it?"

"Look at me. I am called Fiona of the ten knives and pulled a sword on my husband the first time I met him, yet he still tries now and then to make decisions for me. Men cannae help themselves. They often think they ken what is best for us without even asking. That is why we must occasionally let them ken, in the strongest way possible, that we have minds of our own and can make our own decisions about what is best for us."

"I would have thought ye had all the MacFingals fully aware of that by now," she said, and managed to share a brief smile with Fiona.

"I also think that, if ye just walk away now, ye will regret it for the rest of your life."

"And he willnae?"

"Oh, aye, he will, but he will still think he has done the right thing and that will comfort him. Probably thinking this was the honorable thing to do will make him accept it all as something he had to do, too." She nodded when Arianna snorted softly with scorn. "He truly believes ye are too high a reach for him and he wouldnae be doing the right thing if he tried to make ye stay."

Arianna put her elbows on her knees and bent to rest her face in her hands. "It may be for the best anyway. It may be that I can convince him that I want to stay with him, dinnae care about blood-lines, finery, or the like, but there is something I cannae give him nay matter how much I love him."

Fiona frowned. "And what would that be?"

"Children." She told Fiona about thinking she was barren and all that Jolene had said about the possibility that she was not. "I had thought to talk to ye about it but with everything that has happened, I forgot. Then my bleeding time came last week and all I could think about was that Brian hadnae been able to seed me, either."

"Ah, weel, I dinnae think ye are barren. Ye were nay with Brian long enough for that to let ye judge the way of it. I am thinking Jolene has the right of it. But, there isnae any way to be certain the problem was with Claud and nay you. There is a hint or two that it was. I also dinnae think that Brian would care."

"Nay? Men want children. Wheesht, *I* want children. The fact that I actually wanted Claud's children should be enough to tell ye that."

Fiona smiled, but then said, "I wager Callum could find ye a few in need of a home and family."

"I did think on that but they wouldnae be of Brian's blood. That might trouble him."

Fiona shook her head. "I doubt it, truly I do. As for ones of his blood? This keep fair bursts at the seams with them. The MacFingals have more than they need. Ye have seen that. We have a whole army of MacFingals and, being the rutting goats that they are, they are still making more." Fiona stood up. "There is only one way to find out if ye are barren or nay, isnae there? And ye just told me that ye dinnae have that as proof yet."

Arianna shook her head, the pain she had suffered

when she had bled last week still fresh. She had not realized she had hoped for Brian's child until that hope had been crushed. Her mind knew that the fact that Brian had not seeded her in the few times they had made love meant nothing, but her heart did not. The fear that she was barren had returned in full strength.

"Weel, all I can say is that I wouldnae let it stand," said Fiona. "I would go right back to the fool and tell him what an idiot he is. There is a chance that, if ye make your own feelings on the matter verra clear, he will change his mind. He could be thinking he can send ye away now because it will nay hurt ye much. Ye need to convince him that he is wrong."

"Why must it always be the woman who needs to take that first step?"

"Because men are idiots. And as I told ye, they are also verra fond of making decisions for us without discussing it all with us first. So, rouse that anger I saw when I first came in here and then hunt the mon down. Aye, there may be a chance, a verra small one as I see it, that he will still send ye home. But, when ye go, ye will do so kenning that ye had done all ye could to make him ask ye to stay, aye?"

"So then all the blame will then rest on his shoulders?"

"Exactly. Right where it belongs."

Arianna remained seated on the bed for a while after Fiona left, staring at the mess she had made. It was going to take a lot of courage to go and confront Brian, to lay herself bare in the hope that he would want to keep her. It was also going to be a hard fight to get him to see that she did not need all those things he thought she did, that she did not care if he had land, a castle, or a purse bulging with coin. She had had that for five years in France and had been utterly miserable. Claud had been one of those high-born, landed, and titled men Brian thought she should find and marry, yet the man had been a cruel bastard with no care for her at all.

She tensed. Her fury over being sent home like some wayward child was returning. Arianna smiled. She might be a little lacking in courage but, when she was furious, she tended to forget that.

"So ye dinnae plan to come out of your room and wave us all on our way?"

Brian scowled at Callum. "Strange. I didnae hear ye knock."

Callum sat in the chair across the worktable from Brian and helped himself to a drink of ale. "Might be because I didnae." He took a drink, sighed with pleasure, and then fixed a cold, green gaze on Brian. "As her dearest cousin, I should have beaten ye soundly for taking her to your bed, but she was happy. Now I think I shall beat ye soundly for kicking her out of your bed. Ye have made her verra unhappy."

"Ye kenned I was going to do it when ye were in here earlier."

"Aye, but I saw her face when she left."

"She was angry."

"Och, aye, that she was, but she was also hurt."

"And I am sorry for that but this is for her own good." He glared when Callum made a harsh sound of derision. "'Tis. I am but a knight and that honor was given to me by my own cousin. If I wasnae here, I would have to be selling my sword to some laird.

Now that I am healed I will be back to sharing a room with three of my brothers. I have no land. I dinnae e'en have a wee cottage to put her and the lads in. Aye, I have a wee bit of coin but nay enough to keep a lady like her."

"But ye will."

"What?"

"The trade ye started. It has served ye and Scarglas verra weel. I was shown some of the improvements that trade has brought ye, as weel as some comforts and luxuries."

"It isnae a particularly safe business. Ships sink and take all the coin ye spent or would have gained down with them. And, aye, this wine trade with Ignace may prove profitable but 'tis too early to tell. I havenae built the trade up beyond the one ship, either."

"I can provide ye with the names of a few of my kinsmen who can help with that."

"But only if I wed your cousin."

"Nay, I wouldnae do that to my cousin. Wouldnae do that to the mon I will be in trade with, either. If naught else, it would constantly put me in the middle and that is nay a place I want to be."

The door to the room slammed open startling both men. Brian gaped at Arianna. Her gown was wrinkled, her hair was half down and half pinned up, and if she had a sword in her hand he would have been considering making a run for it. He did not think he had ever seen a woman so furious.

"Callum," she said, and Brian was surprised that such a dainty, bonnie lass could sound like she was growling.

"Aye, cousin?"

"Leave."

"Going."

Brian thought that wide grin on Callum's face was unnecessary. He also thought, that as a fellow man, Callum should have made some attempt to protect him. If nothing else, the man should have shown some concern about the fact that his cousin looked ready to murder his new trading partner. He could not stop himself from jumping slightly when she slammed the door behind her rapidly retreating cousin.

"Arianna," he began, trying to use the most soothing voice he could.

"Ye are an idiot," she snapped. "Who do ye think ye are to make my decisions for me as if I am some child? Did ye ask me if I wanted to leave? Nay. Ye decided it was best for me."

Brian wondered how she could make that sound like some perversion.

"Weel, I will have my say now and I will tell ye what I think and ye will listen."

Since she was silent and glaring at him, Brian decided she was waiting for some response. He nodded.

"I allowed ye to make love to me. Do ye think I do that with just anyone? I didnae e'en do it much with the mon I thought was my husband."

"Aye, but the passion . . ."

"Shut up. I am talking. I ken that I was weak, allowing Claud to make me think less of myself, but am I nay recovering from that weakness? Aye, I am, but 'tis clear ye still think me some weak child or ye wouldnae have been deciding things for me. And ye think I care about silks, jewels, fine homes, and all? What have I done to make ye think that, I ask?

Naught. I ate thrice-cursed rabbit for days and ne'er once complained, did I?"

"Nay?" Brian was not sure what eating rabbit had to do with anything but he was beginning to think he would be the idiot she claimed he was if he interrupted her now.

"Nay, I didnae. I didnae complain about the dirt, sweaty horses, cold beds on the ground, or the lack of clean, silken gowns. I cannae understand why ye think I am such a delicate, particular lass. As for all this weel-born nonsense? I was born in a bed just as ye were. My parents have coin, aye, and enough to make sure all their daughters have dowries and their sons some sort of inheritance that will allow them to wed where they please, but they are nay wealthy and they are nay particular about who their children wed. My sister married a blacksmith. My mother was the bastard daughter of some rutting goat of a laird and the village alewife. Ye, sir, are the only one who seems to fret o'er such things."

"But . . ."

"Shut up. I thought this all out and I have to say it. If ye interrupt, I willnae get it all out. I am going to tell ye what *I* want. I want a mon who can make my eyes cross when he makes love to me. I want a roof o'er my head and I dinnae much care if the roof is only thatch. I want enough food to keep us from starving and enough coin to buy something pretty when I have to go to some special celebration. I want bairns. I may nay be able to bear any of my own but there are many, many poor wee bairns who need a home and I will be looking for some. And . . ."

Arianna suddenly realized that Brian was sitting

up straight in his seat staring at her in a way that made her a little nervous. It was such an intense look that she found it difficult to recall the rest of what she had planned to say. Her fury was also fading and suddenly so was her courage.

"And . . ." Brian demanded.

"And I want ye to give them to me. I want to be with ye, in your bed, in whate'er home ye make for us, and I want ye to try and love me as I love ye. And if ye try to send me away again, I will come right back."

"Ye are nay going anywhere."

He moved so fast she had no chance to elude him even if she wanted to. Arianna was astonished at how quickly he got her down on the floor. She was swiftly drowning in the heat of his kiss when she heard a slight tearing noise.

"My gown," she began.

"I will get ye another."

Brian did not think he had ever undressed her so fast or shed his own clothing with such speed. He needed to be skin to skin with her so badly he did not care about what ripped or where their clothes landed when he tossed them aside. If he did not have the proof of her kisses and the touch of her hands to tell him that passion had gripped her as tightly as it had him, he would be worried about how rough he was. Instead, he thought only of burying himself deep inside her.

Arianna cried out with joy when Brian joined their bodies with one hard thrust. She wrapped her arms and legs around him, reveling in the ferocity of his passion. Her own desire rose up hot and wild, her need for him a greed she doubted would ever wane. When her release crashed over her, she was faintly aware of shouting out her pleasure and her love. Then she was lost in the pleasure that swept all thought from her head as he joined her in that blissful fall, saying her name against her neck as his body shuddered from the strength of his release.

"So, ye are staying then," he said once he regained the power of speech.

"Only if ye truly want me to," she said, praying that she had not mistaken what had just happened, that what they had just shared meant he loved her, too, or was at least very close to loving her.

"I ne'er really wanted ye to leave." He kissed the hollow at the base of her neck. "I just thought that it was what I should do."

"But do I stay as just your lover or am I to be more?"

He lifted his head and kissed the tip of her nose. "Ye have always been more, Arianna. Always. If ye stay, it will be as my wife. 'Tis one reason I was insistent on making ye leave. I kenned that, if I kept ye close any longer, I would ne'er have the strength to let ye go. I thought that was wrong, even selfish, when ye could find a mon who could give ye so much more that I can."

"Ye give me what I need, Brian. That is all that matters. I wish I could give ye a child," she whispered.

"If ye dinnae, then ye dinnae. I shall nay be upset. I have so many kin I cannae recall half their names anyway." He returned her quick grin. "And I like your thought of finding some wee ones who desperately need a home. I think we shall do that e'en if we are granted one of our own."

He eased free of her body and picked her up in his arms. "And I shouldnae have my soon to be wife lying on the hard floor." He settled her down on a small bed tucked against the wall and quickly joined her there.

"Ye have a bed in your ledger room?"

"We have wee beds where'er we can fit them and this isnae really my ledger room, but the room where anyone who has some work to do can come and do it." He frowned as he stroked her hip. "I fear that will be the way of it for a while, Arianna. I have no home save this one."

"This is a fine home. All we need is a bedchamber that doesnae have a few of your brothers in it." She smiled when he laughed. "Or, if ye want, we could go and live in a wee cottage on the land the boys hold."

"Where is that?"

"About a half day's ride from here in the same direction as Dubheidland."

"Jesu, that close?" He shook his head. "Weel, we can talk on all that later. I want to enjoy the first day of ye becoming part of Scarglas."

She sighed with pleasure when he licked the hard tips of her breasts, fondling them in an almost idle manner that had her blood heating in a deliciously slow way. There was only one small shadow on her happiness. Brian had not told her he loved her. Arianna thought she could sense it in the way he made love to her, in the way he looked at her, but found that was not enough. She wanted to hear the words.

"Brian, I said I loved ye," she began with a hesitancy she hated but could not shake free of.

"I ken it. I dinnae think I have e'er heard anything so beautiful."

She looked down at the top of his head, enjoying

the way he was kissing and licking her breasts but needing to look him in the eye as they spoke of such serious matters. Just as she reached to turn his face up to hers, however, he slid his hand between her thighs and began to caress her in a way that made thinking of serious matters almost impossible. Arianna gritted her teeth and forced her mind back to the problem of finding out whether or not the man she loved and would soon marry actually loved her.

"Brian, I love ye."

"Aye, and I will ne'er tire of hearing ye say it."

She frowned. There was a teasing note in his voice. The man was teasing her about something so very important to her? She rapped her knuckles on top of his head and scowled when he lifted his head and grinned at her.

"Ye can tease me about it all ye like later. Right now I am feeling as if I am at a disadvantage here," she said, not surprised that her voice did not hold the tone of prim reprimand she wanted for he was still stroking her, sliding his fingers in and out of her in a way that had her beginning to pant.

Brian kept his hand busy right where it was but slid up her body far enough to brush a kiss over her mouth. "I love ye, Arianna. I have for a long time but I kenned it for certain when Amiel took ye from me. I loved ye enough to let ye go because I thought it was what ye needed."

Arianna rapidly blinked, not wanting to cry when she was actually so happy she felt choked with it. She wrapped her arms around his neck and kissed him, trying to imbue the kiss with all the love that filled her. When he slowly entered her, she sighed with pleasure, stroking his back as he stroked her with his body. Release came slowly to them both, whispered words of love adding to its beauty. Arianna knew she was crying while she held him close as they both trembled from the force of their release.

"I dinnae ken how ye would have e'er thought of being without this," she whispered against his cheek.

"Weel, mayhap ye were right to call me an idiot." He lifted his head and grinned at her when she laughed. "Ah, lass, I still think ye are too good for me but ye are stuck with me now."

"Good. 'Tis the only place I wish to be."

"We should get off this wee bed and get dressed before someone tries to get in. I dinnae want any of my kin seeing all this bonnie flesh. 'Tis mine and mine alone."

"Are ye mine and mine alone, too?"

"Aye, lass. I should have said so. I ken my family isnae one to inspire belief in the faithfulness of a MacFingal but—"

She stopped his words with a brief kiss. "Your word is enough. Now, let us get dressed before—"

"Am I to unpack or pack the horses?" yelled Callum from outside the closed door.

Brian had to bite back a grin at how deeply Arianna blushed and how swiftly she leapt from the bed to start getting dressed. He sprawled on his back and watched her, enjoying the way she moved. She loved him. He felt like a king and could not seem to stop grinning.

"Weel? Have ye gone deaf in there or has my wee cousin killed ye and she is now weeping o'er your rotting corpse?"

"'Tis too soon for my corpse to be rotting," Brian

yelled back as he got up and began to dress, biting back a grin when he saw a flustered Arianna struggling to disguise the tear in her gown.

"So are we staying? Am I invited to a wedding?"

"Callum, go away!" yelled Arianna.

"That was what I was going to do but since ye two have been in there together for so long and I didnae hear any screams of pain, I thought there might have been a change of plans."

Brian was glad he knew how to dress quickly for Arianna rushed to the door, flung it open, and glared at her cousin. "Have ye been out there the whole time?"

"Weel, nay the whole time," Callum said, and then winked. "Just long enough to ken that we probably willnae be leaving."

Brian caught up to Arianna just in time to catch her little fist as it swung toward Callum's nose. "Tell my fither that we need a feast so that I can announce that I am about to get married."

Arianna heard a round of cheers and finally looked beyond Callum. There had to be two dozen MacFingals standing around in the hall outside the door of the little ledger room. Right outside the door of the room where she had been yelling at Brian and then yelling in pleasure. She groaned, turned around, and hid her face against his chest.

"Tell them to go away before I die of embarrassment," she told Brian.

Callum patted her on the back. "Congratulations, cousin. Best ye find time soon to write to your family. Come on," he said to the gathered MacFingals. "We need to prepare for a celebration. Your brother is nay longer an idiot."

Brian put his fingers under Arianna's chin and tilted her face up to his. "Welcome to the MacFingal family, my love."

"I think I need to warn ye about my family now."

"Nay, I have a good idea of what faces me after meeting your cousins."

"Callum," she snapped, and glared in the direction her cousin had gone, "needs to have a care. I think he insulted me. Ye had best go and avenge me now."

"Och, aye, I love avenging ye." He picked her up in his arms and started up the stairs.

"Callum went the other way," she said between giggles.

"I'll see to him after I do some avenging."

She was still laughing about that when he dropped her on the bed they had shared once. She held out her arms and welcomed him into them when he joined her on the bed. This was what she had been searching for. Laughter, love, family, and passion. For the first time in five long years Arianna knew she was home.

Epilogue

One year later

"What is taking so long?" Brian shouted at the ceiling.

The sudden silence in the previously noisy great hall of Scarglas caught Brian's attention and he looked around at all the MacFingals, Camerons, and Murrays gathered there. They were all staring at him as if they feared he was going to need to be chained down. Brian feared they might have to soon as this waiting was driving him mad.

Sigimor was the first to make a sound. The man started laughing so hard he was in danger of falling out of his chair. A moment later, just as Brian decided he needed to go over and kick his cousin, all the rest of the crowd started to laugh as well.

"Och, weel, 'tis verra glad I am that I can provide ye all with such amusement," he grumbled, and flung himself into a seat next to Harcourt. "I doubt any of ye who have been through this were verra calm and sensible."

Harcourt grinned. "None in my clan."

"Sigimor wasnae, either," said Fergus, earning a slap on the back of his head from his laird and brother.

"Ye have been through this often enough," said his father. "Dinnae ken what ye are fretting about."

"It was ne'er *my* wife or *my* child," snapped Brian, and he quickly poured himself a tankard of ale, hoping the drink would ease the knot of fear in his chest.

"Wheesht, if ye had just told me that the fool lass thought she was barren, I could have settled her mind about it."

"What do ye mean?"

"I could have told her she wasnae."

"And just how would ye have kenned whether she was or wasnae?"

"Nay sure how I ken it, I just do. Always did. Ken when a lass is a fertile wee thing and when she isnae. My Mab can tell when a lass has quickened. We make a fine pair."

"If ye can tell when a lass is fertile or nay, then why did ye keep breeding them?"

"Weel, didnae seem to trouble me much when the fire was burning, did it?"

Brian was not surprised when Sigimor started laughing again. He was torn between joining his cousin and knocking his father right out of his chair. The fact that the man could tell if a woman was fertile was not nearly as startling as the fact that he had gleefully bedded them anyway. After the first half-dozen bastard children he had, one would have thought the man would have taken more care.

Before he could give his opinion on that idiocy, a scream from up the stairs cut through the air. Brian leapt to his feet only to have his father and Harcourt yank him back down. Despite all his efforts and several minutes of wrestling in a vain attempt to break free of their hold, they held him in his seat. He knew that he would not get free unless he wanted to get into a brawl. He glared at both men. It would not be easy to knock them both down but he was in the mood to try, especially when another scream rent the air.

"I need to go up there," he snapped. "Arianna just screamed. Twice. She screamed twice."

"Suspicion ye would scream, too, if ye were pushing one of those out of your body," Odo said, and then stuffed an oatcake into his mouth, shrugging when everyone stared at him.

Ewan cleared his throat. "Verra true but, mayhap, nay something one should say, young Odo. Weel, at least nay without making verra sure there are no ladies or bairns about." Ewan nodded toward Adelar and Michel, who stared at Odo with wide eyes and worried frowns.

Adelar looked at Brian. "Anna will be fine, will she nay?"

"Aye, she will be," Brian said, and then slouched in his chair to drink his ale, wishing he were as confident of that as he sounded.

The others worked to reassure Adelar and Michel while Brian returned to staring up at the ceiling. He had spent the last few months, from the moment winter eased enough to allow travel, making sure that the house he and Arianna would share was readied for their family and the land Claud had left his sons prepared for planting. He had done the same with the property Arianna had brought to their marriage.

He had also done a great deal of strutting about as if he had accomplished some rare and wondrous deed by putting a bairn into his wife's belly. The larger she had grown, the more he had coddled her, and the more he had strutted. He did not feel much like strutting now. Somehow he had blissfully forgotten all the danger and pain of childbed right up until Arianna had been taken to hers.

Once Arianna no longer feared miscarrying their child, her happiness had helped to blind him to those dangers. Even when ill every morning or suffering an aching back as her belly grew rounder, she had been happy. It was not until a fortnight ago when Jolene had arrived to help with the birth—followed quickly by Arianna's cousins, Fiona's sister-in-law Gillyanne, and Liam's wife, Keira—that a hint of fear occasionally shadowed her eyes. Brian knew it was not caused by the possible dangers to herself that came with childbirth or the pain, however. Arianna worried about the health of the child she carried. Nothing he had said had fully banished the fear that, even though she had carried their child to full term, she might still lose it.

All Brian could do was pray that Arianna would soon hold a living child in her arms. He would grieve if they lost the child, but his deepest fears concerned what such a loss would do to Arianna.

The prayers he constantly whispered in his mind were mostly for the life of the child. He prayed for Arianna, too, but he was doing his best not to allow his thoughts to linger too long on all the dangers a woman faced when bearing a child. That way led to bone-chilling terror.

"Brian?"

He blinked and looked to find Fiona standing by his chair. "Is Arianna weel?"

"Arianna is just fine. The bairns are fine, too. Ye can go up and see her now."

Brian was just stepping through the door when what Fiona had said finally settled into his mind. He slowly turned around to see her sitting on Ewan's lap and grinning at him. Everyone else watched him, too, every last one of them grinning at him.

"Did ye say *bairns*? As in more than one?" he asked.

"Aye, I did," she replied. "Ye have two bairns, Brian. One lass. One lad."

His legs were suddenly too weak to hold him upright and Brian braced himself against the door. He refused to swoon like some terrified maiden in front of all these grinning fools. Two bairns. Arianna had given him twins.

"Both bairns are weel?" he asked, pleased to hear how calm he sounded.

"Aye. A goodly size, hearty cries, have all the right parts. Go and see for yourself."

Steadying himself, Brian started to do just that. As he strode through the door, he heard Odo say, "Wheesht! She was carrying two bairns in that belly? They must have been fair crowded in there."

That boy was going to be trouble, Brian thought

as, once out of sight of the great hall, he started running. He did not slow down until he reached the door to their bedchamber. Brian paused to take a few deep breaths to calm himself down and then entered the room. Mab rose from her seat by the bed and walked over to him. He briefly hugged her when she stood on tiptoe to kiss his cheek.

"She is just fine, lad," Mab said. "The lass can toss aside all her fears. She was made for this, for giving ye lots of plump, healthy bairns."

"I heard her scream," he whispered, his fears for Arianna not easily assuaged. "Twice."

"Ye would scream too if ye were pushing that out of your body. Twice."

He frowned at Mab. "Have ye been talking to Odo?"

Mab just laughed as she left, quietly shutting the door behind her. Brian moved to where his children were settled in the huge cradle his father had made. Swaddled and asleep, it was impossible to tell which was which. One had a surprisingly thick head of black hair and the other had bright red spikes of hair.

"The one with the black hair is the lass. The one with the red is the laddie."

Brian hurried over to the bed to find Arianna smiling at him. She had obviously been thoroughly cleaned up after the birth and only looked very tired. He sat down on the edge of the bed and gently kissed her.

"Thank ye, my love," he whispered. "Ye are weel?"

"Verra weel. And thank ye, Sir Brian. Ye have given me such a wondrous gift. Two of them."

He cleared his throat in a vain attempt to hide the emotion choking him, and said, "Weel, I had planned on only giving ye the one."

"We shouldnae be surprised that there are two." She winked at him. "Ye are a true MacFingal, after all. Verra potent."

He laughed as he settled himself on the bed beside her, one arm around her shoulders to hold her close to him. "Did ye finally decide on a name? Ye need two now."

"She will be called Reine and he will be called Crispin, if that pleases ye."

"I like both the names, love. Are ye certain ye are weel?"

Arianna smiled at him. This man loved her, accepted Michel and Adelar without hesitation, and had given her two beautiful bairns. She doubted he would ever fully understand just how much he meant to her, how deep and fierce her love for him was. Then again, it never hurt to keep a man guessing just a little, she thought, grinning.

"I am verra weel indeed, husband. 'Tis hard to believe any woman could be better than I at this moment. I have my bairns, my laddies with me, a home, a family, and ye to love."

Brian held her close and rubbed his cheek against her hair and recalled the advice Sigimor had given him not long ago. "Always."

She closed her eyes and sighed with complete satisfaction. "Always."

Sigimor was right again, curse his eyes, Brian thought as he held his wife close and gazed at his children. *Always* was a very good word indeed.

More by Bestselling Author
Hannah Howell

Books by Bestselling Author
Fern Michaels

___The Jury	0-8217-7878-1	$6.99US/$9.99CAN
___Sweet Revenge	0-8217-7879-X	$6.99US/$9.99CAN
___Lethal Justice	0-8217-7880-3	$6.99US/$9.99CAN
___Free Fall	0-8217-7881-1	$6.99US/$9.99CAN
___Fool Me Once	0-8217-8071-9	$7.99US/$10.99CAN
___Vegas Rich	0-8217-8112-X	$7.99US/$10.99CAN
___Hide and Seek	1-4201-0184-6	$6.99US/$9.99CAN
___Hokus Pokus	1-4201-0185-4	$6.99US/$9.99CAN
___Fast Track	1-4201-0186-2	$6.99US/$9.99CAN
___Collateral Damage	1-4201-0187-0	$6.99US/$9.99CAN
___Final Justice	1-4201-0188-9	$6.99US/$9.99CAN
___Up Close and Personal	0-8217-7956-7	$7.99US/$9.99CAN
___Under the Radar	1-4201-0683-X	$6.99US/$9.99CAN
___Razor Sharp	1-4201-0684-8	$7.99US/$10.99CAN
___Yesterday	1-4201-1494-8	$5.99US/$6.99CAN
___Vanishing Act	1-4201-0685-6	$7.99US/$10.99CAN
___Sara's Song	1-4201-1493-X	$5.99US/$6.99CAN
___Deadly Deals	1-4201-0686-4	$7.99US/$10.99CAN
___Game Over	1-4201-0687-2	$7.99US/$10.99CAN
___Sins of Omission	1-4201-1153-1	$7.99US/$10.99CAN
___Sins of the Flesh	1-4201-1154-X	$7.99US/$10.99CAN
___Cross Roads	1-4201-1192-2	$7.99US/$10.99CAN

Available Wherever Books Are Sold!
Check out our website at www.kensingtonbooks.com

Romantic Suspense from
Lisa Jackson

See How She Dies	0-8217-7605-3	$6.99US/$9.99CAN
Final Scream	0-8217-7712-2	$7.99US/$10.99CAN
Wishes	0-8217-6309-1	$5.99US/$7.99CAN
Whispers	0-8217-7603-7	$6.99US/$9.99CAN
Twice Kissed	0-8217-6038-6	$5.99US/$7.99CAN
Unspoken	0-8217-6402-0	$6.50US/$8.50CAN
If She Only Knew	0-8217-6708-9	$6.50US/$8.50CAN
Hot Blooded	0-8217-6841-7	$6.99US/$9.99CAN
Cold Blooded	0-8217-6934-0	$6.99US/$9.99CAN
The Night Before	0-8217-6936-7	$6.99US/$9.99CAN
The Morning After	0-8217-7295-3	$6.99US/$9.99CAN
Deep Freeze	0-8217-7296-1	$7.99US/$10.99CAN
Fatal Burn	0-8217-7577-4	$7.99US/$10.99CAN
Shiver	0-8217-7578-2	$7.99US/$10.99CAN
Most Likely to Die	0-8217-7576-6	$7.99US/$10.99CAN
Absolute Fear	0-8217-7936-2	$7.99US/$9.49CAN
Almost Dead	0-8217-7579-0	$7.99US/$10.99CAN
Lost Souls	0-8217-7938-9	$7.99US/$10.99CAN
Left to Die	1-4201-0276-1	$7.99US/$10.99CAN
Wicked Game	1-4201-0338-5	$7.99US/$9.99CAN
Malice	0-8217-7940-0	$7.99US/$9.49CAN

Available Wherever Books Are Sold!
Visit our website at **www.kensingtonbooks.com**

More from Bestselling Author
JANET DAILEY

Available Wherever Books Are Sold!

Check out our website at www.kensingtonbooks.com.